Angel Falling

An Azshael Story

A.D. Landor

Copyright © A. D. Landor 2022

All rights reserved.

All characters in this publication are fictitious and any resemblance to real persons, living or dead, is purely coincidental.

This book is sold subject to the condition that it shall not, by way of trade or otherwise, be hired out, lent or resold, or otherwise circulated without the author's/publisher's prior consent in any form of binding or cover other than that in which it is published and without a similar condition including this condition being imposed on the subsequent publisher.

The moral rights of the author have been asserted.

Dedication

For my parents Neil and Diane and my sister Roz and her daughters Arielle and Sophia - all the love xxx

Acknowledgements

Working in the word mines can be a long and gruelling business so it's most helpful to have some fellow canaries and donkeys to help along the way. Big thanks for the help of the following - Moreno Airoldi my first reader, Miss Snark and Anne Mini for sharing their industry wisdom and Johan Bert for being the founder of the feast.

Self-publishing guru: Michelle Emerson
(michelleemerson.co.uk)
Proofing guru: Carol Sissons
Art guru: K. D. Ritchie of Story Wrappers (storywrappers.com)

Sanity savers: Adrian Joseph, Adrian Lulham, Greg Baker, Ian Hogston, Jon Higgins, Jono Tooth, Kirsten Bayes, Larry Noyes, Mikko Lahti, Neil Randerson, Peter Bailey, Peter Hart, Rob Hrabi, Tish Sheridan, Trevor Duguid Farrant

Life savers: Katherine Young, Kate Davis, Stu Hollister, Saffery and Rhianna Durrant

Web site: www.7th-flight.com created by Jo Hewson

Oh and Azshael for sharing his stories with me...

Prologue

I remember the first time I saw Cerule. Like all worlds seen from the Horta Magna it looked peaceful and calm, unaware of the Angels above preparing to descend and deliver the final Judgement of Excelsis. The Powers sealed the surrounding space so that no soul could escape us as we shaped the Great Garden that we call home.

We are the Seventh Flight, led by the Archangel, Prince Anael. We have judged the living and the dead of countless planets, and no false idol, race or power ever stood in our way. That was until the inhabitants of this world, a race of immortal vampires, chose to resist. The terrible struggle that followed is known by many names—the Forever War, the Cursed War— and in whispered tones away from scheming Heralds, the Fool's Errand. Our archivists named it simply the Succae War in respect of the race we came to judge.

At one point in their long history, the Succae worshipped vile deities and rapaciously conquered other worlds, draining them of their life energy to feed the Necrene Well, the primal source of power that sustains them and their wraith like spirits. Yet, somewhere in an antique age before our arrival, the Succae found enlightenment and left their old ways and older gods behind. They developed a strict honour-bound society where lives of service won the right of rebirth and a better new existence.

They fought us in a bitter war of attrition that endured for just over a hundred years, with the Succae able to replenish their ranks with freshly possessed bodies and powerful creations of flesh that could stand against our mightiest Throne powers. As our numbers dwindled, we set about destroying the planet that was their lifeblood and they retreated to a satellite moon where eventually, some twenty years ago, a truce was signed.

In the uneasy peace that followed I became an ambassador and fell in love with my former enemy, a Succae diplomat. Her name was Ischae, and she is dead now, murdered in the bed we once shared. I lost my love, lost my way—and that is how all this began.

Part One

more than a grimace and gurgle, spittle flying from my mouth to briefly spot the Sunpup's soft, lucent skin. In response, the creature gave me a sour glance, shuddered, and white heat cascaded over my hands, burning urine dripping through pale fingers to spatter on the slick stones below. I gave up on providing cold comfort and pushed on, up a steep cobbled path that led towards the grand arch and the brilliant white light of the Tether that separated my world from the dark Succae labyrinth into which I had come.

A sharp keening cry cut through the narcotic haze, and I felt my hearts quicken with vivid memories of war. Chaotic landings lit by brilliant swords of light, and Nimrod, my sacred spear, shrouded in fire, shining talismans against a foe that coveted the shadows. Those same chilling screeches rising around us as enemies erupted from ashen remains with claws to shred and teeth to tear. Wave after wave would grasp at us, a snarling, roiling mass of rotting flesh, propelled by necrotic energy.

That pulse-quickening sound of the dead gave me new momentum, its echo reverberating around the hewn walls of the dark tunnels through which I now ran, feet slipping and sliding on slick cobbles. I risked a look behind me only to stumble again as the path rose steeper. I looked ahead and came to a jarring halt, my worst fears realised. They emerged from the black yawning maw of the archway; four nightmares vomited from the darkness. They were living weapons made for battle, and I hadn't seen their like since the war. The first two were hunched and simian with gangling arms that ended in sharp bone. They scrabbled forward on all fours, bearing sharp teeth in a deadly grin. Behind them came a pair of massive hulks, advancing in slow, solemn purpose. They were barely sentient, just a tall shambling mass of bludgeoning flesh with rudimentary form

Chapter One

"What is the definition of regret? Flying naked in a lightning storm carrying nothing but your lance." That's an old saying in the Flight, and it's a ready reminder that sometimes, you can be your own worst enemy. That's how it was for me at the start of all this. Yes, I was flying headlong into that proverbial maelstrom with little care for the consequences.

In the eyes of many in the Flight, I was disgraced or perhaps deranged. Many probably thought of me as both. I was a fallen soldier with no war to fight except the one that raged within. In my hands, I held a struggling infant in stolen swaddling that I had 'borrowed' as a flimsy excuse to venture down the Tether into the dark tunnels that ran under the city of Scarpe on the Succae moon. There, as I indulged my addiction to a Succae drug called Rain, my charge had managed to wander off and it had taken me a day to notice that fact and another one to find it again.

The abductee poked its canine snout up above the blanket in which it was wrapped and sniffed the air. Not liking whatever it scented, it whined and squirmed, rolls of white wrinkled flesh struggling and straining against my grip. In my less than lucid state, I bumped into walls and shared its growing sense of panic, afraid of the cyclopean darkness where both our lights could slowly dwindle and die.

Rain had me in its grip, affecting the functions of speech, and my intended words of reassurance came out as little and features, outsized hammer appendages ideal for beating things to a pulp. It was shaping up to be a bad day.

I put the Sunpup down and rose to my full height as the four walking weapons scrabbled to a stop within a few feet of me. I made my wings visible, and light spilled from my corona. Words swirled in my mind, trying to find a way to be fashioned in my mouth, but all that came was laughter. I reached for powers within, seeking to reduce my enemies to so much dust and be the Azshael I once was before everything had changed. I called on the power of Angelfire to flow from me, but nothing happened. The hulks rained down powerful blows that sent me crashing to the slick stones of the tunnel floor, my own surprised laughter an incongruous echo in the all engulfing darkness.

I awoke, naked and chained, on a slab in a cold chamber. The Sunpup whimpered behind me, and I turned my body enough to see its now much diminished glow.

"What are you complaining about?" I asked, probably a little unkindly. "You're not the one in chains! And by the way, this is what happens when you don't sit and stay."

The creature had no reply and snorted unhappily before barking so fiercely that its layers of fat shook with the effort. I gave it a withering glare and tested my bindings, but I was held fast. The effects of Rain were slowly receding, and I shuddered as its layer of cosseting warmth gradually slipped away from the core of my being. I feared the sharpness of pain, but I had obviously slept longer than I thought, for nothing came. Whatever harm had been done to me, there had been adequate time for my body to heal and only its memory remained.

My eyes slowly grew accustomed to the dim surroundings and my preternatural senses filled in the things I could not see. I felt pain and sorrow seeping from the walls, felt the fear and terror this place had borne witness to. I was not the first of my kind to be here, and now I knew none of those that had been here before me had left alive, their souls beating against the cold stone. It was a place of special misery, and it made we wonder whether a few hours of escape from my grief and sadness had ended up costing me everything. I laid back and closed my eyes, trying to picture Ischae's face, something my drug of choice was capable of conjuring in brilliant detail, but it was too late. I was on the down, and my confused mind could not bring her to life. All I could see was her corpse, that exquisite porcelain skin torn open, strands of ancient blood dripping down precious alabaster skin. Her face was a mask of terror, mouth open in a silent scream. I descended into feverish dementia as the walls closed in.

I was still raving when the door opened hours later, and the room filled with blurred shapes and cacophonous noise. The Rain's continuing symptoms of withdrawal played malevolent tricks on me as it twisted any power of understanding inside out. I was aware of something cold and wet being slapped on my naked chest, followed by a curious, almost gentle caress as the shapes moved around me. Then as suddenly as they had come, they went and I was alone again in the dark, completely this time, for the Sunpup was gone. I groaned as my senses began to sharpen, and I could imagine Sariel's cherubic face fall downcast. After the war had ended, we all needed something to calm the fears and for her, the Sunpup had served that purpose, a charge to care for, shepherdess to a flock of one. I didn't want to dwell on my part in the sorry creature's disappearance. Just another dumb decision I would be held responsible for.

The door opened again, and this time light shone from beyond as several more squat and bulbous flesh constructs shuffled in. Flames danced in silver dishes that had been placed upon their flattened heads. Jasniz entered the chamber with two others in tow. He was a Succae fixer whom I had known for many years but had previously dismissed as being in any way dangerous. He was tall and broad, his bald head covered with intricate tattoos. Ischae had taught me to read some of this ornate language, but I could hardly claim to be fluent. What I could decipher told me he had been a faithful servant of several high caste masters, all of whom he had fought for with distinction. He had the right of Freeman, a position of equal opportunity and risk in Succae society. He had bought himself free and could serve any and all, yet without the shelter of a higher master he walked a precarious line, for no-one was obliged to reach out to catch him should he fall. In that regard at least, we were two of a kind.

The people behind him phased in and out of my blurred vision. One was a slender, hooded figure whose pale face was just visible. The other wore a Succae war mask, face etched in a permanent snarl. Even in my addled state, I registered a familiarity within. We had surely met before. Jasniz smiled at me as my face registered dumb comprehension. It was a feral smile with a mouth full of sharp white teeth.

"How the mighty have fallen my dear Azshael. One night, walker of worlds, respected and feared. The next, meat on a slab, ready for carving. It is lucky you have two hearts, for that will just about pay what you and your dearly departed owe me." In sudden, terrified realisation, I looked down at my chest and understood Jasniz's purpose. Blazons of dark ink had been painted directly over where my hearts had started to beat faster. Jasniz grinned as I strained at the shackles, and his Succae companion took down his hood to reveal a red swirl of markings that, in the flickering light, seemed to have a life of their own. I felt the world slow as he walked forward and turned the wheel that tightened the chains that bound me. I was held fast against the stone, shackles biting into flesh. With an audible grunt, he climbed onto the stone block and straddled me, his eyes rheumy red pits in a sunken, sallow face. It was his almost bored stare, devoid of any recognisable emotion, that frightened me the most.

Long sinewy arms came free from within the folds of his robes. They were withered, yet out of proportion to his body, tapering to slender fingers with pointed nails blackened by age or design. I waited, breath held, eyes wide open. He traced a lazy pattern around my left heart, and I felt my skin yield as razor sharp nails parted flesh. Warm blood ran down my chest in dark rivulets. There was a sudden wrench as he casually reached in and pulled the organ free of my body, its glistening golden core held aloft in his twisted claw of a hand. My mind screamed at the violation, but I felt no actual pain. My body shuddered and I lost the sight in my left eye as physiological defences sprang into life. Already, my body was mending, healing, seeking to bypass the damage and keep me going. I was, after all, a creation designed to take and mete out vast destruction, even with half of my body effectively shut down.

The surgeon handed my left heart to Jasniz, who dropped it into a lacquered wooden box. They exchanged brief words in a Succae dialect I had never heard before and the vile creature smiled at me. Then Jasniz turned his attention back to me, his masked companion waiting at the door.

"Farewell, Azshael," he said, "and thank you for your kind donation." I wanted to hurt him, burn all of them to ashes, but only a whimper escaped my lips. Jasniz left with the masked figure, his laughter echoing down the hall.

The creature turned his attention to my right heart and once again, I heard skin separate under his scalpel nail. I wanted to close my working eye, let Ischae be the last sight I saw, but dread fascination and the realisation of mortality had me in its grip. I stared at the new open wound, waiting for the end, when a sudden blur behind its head caught my eye.

The blade scythed down in a slanted arc designed to strike through the neck and shoulder, before cutting through the upper body and the heart, effectively slicing my assailant in two. The blade was bone white and got as far as the upper sternum before my would-be murderer leapt away from my body and twisted free of the sword's bite. My saviour was Succae, and she pressed her advantage, weaving deadly cuts that my would-be murderer ducked and weaved away from with deliberate and unbelievable precision. He held his arm and shoulder together as he did so, no sign of blood, his left hand occasionally jabbing back at her face, its knifepoint easily capable of lancing her through. She paused a moment and drew a second, shorter blade from a sheath on her back. They exchanged quiet words in a dialect of Succae I had never heard before and then the contest stepped up a notch.

She moved like a dancer in a series of fluid leaps and strikes that used time and space to the best possible advantage. To my surprise, her opponent stayed with her, impossibly predicting every twist and turn so that her blades missed him by a hair's breadth. It was dazzling and beautiful to watch, the sheer athleticism and form so mesmerizing, it was easy to forget I was watching a fight to the death. The pace suddenly increased, the dance changing into a blur of attacks and evasions so complex that with only one eye on the combat, I was sure I was missing moves as they whirled around the chamber like a small tornado. Then a hand went flying, followed by a foot and an arm, and she came to a stop as his body literally fell apart, the top of his head a dull red mass of bone and brain, the last piece to fall. Air rushed through the chamber as if the lid of a tomb long sealed had just been opened and I fancied I heard hideous laughter. The entrance to my prison slammed open and I heard further doors rattle and shake as it howled and shrieked through distant halls. My saviour seemed to stay in her stance for a moment, her lips mouthing words unheard. Then with practised reverence for her art, she slowly, respectfully flicked brain matter from her blades, sheathed her weapons and turned to look at me for the first time.

It would be a while before I learned my rescuer's name, but I already knew what she was; a Serrate, sacred protector to the Succae Lords Ancestral. I had never seen one of her kind close up. In fact, I had not seen one at all, not since the signing of the Accord some twenty years earlier. It was said that they were ancient spirits of war, eternal warriors bound to vessels of flesh and, just like our Archangels who ruled the Spheres and led the Flights, few in number.

I studied her carefully as she led me silently through the barren halls of my prison, soft boots silent on worn stone floors. She was tall, slender, and shrouded in the colour of night, her pallid face angular and gaunt, black hair laced in a tight braid. It did not look as if she had ever smiled, as if the porcelain mask of her face would crack if it were to do so. Her stare was discomforting, unblinking violet irises that cut straight into the soul. She caught me staring, fixed me with that alien gaze and waited until I looked away.

I had no idea where I was. This was clearly not Jasniz's Den, but rather some ancient refuge, now deserted and empty but clearly not completely abandoned. I thought again about the remnants of my kind who had clearly met terrible ends in this place, and Jasniz's role in their demise. Perhaps it should have surprised me that he had been responsible for their deaths, but in truth I was not that taken aback. There had always been an edge to his feigned deference, his face and mouth saying one thing, while his eyes said another. It was much clearer in hindsight than it had been at the time, but of course, such truths always are.

Soon, we climbed spiral stairs that led out into an open courtyard where more diminutive flesh creations stood in sightless, motionless vigil, the dull red embers of fire rocks glowing crowns atop flattened heads. I looked around and noted the broken statue of Yggael the Serpent, one of the Succae's long discarded goddesses. Ischae had told me they once followed a rapacious pantheon that had led them to conquer other worlds and enslave their peoples until an Age of Disenchantment had seen the old ways collapse and give way to an altogether more learned and peaceful era. Until we had arrived, the agents of judgement come to hold their ways to account.

My rescuer pointed to a well that lay beyond the base of the shattered statue and indicated that I should pull on the leaden chain that spiralled away into the impenetrable darkness below. Before long, a thin glow cut through the gloom, and I recognised Sariel's pup sitting in a lead bucket atop my armour and clothes. I felt her eyes on my scarred body as I dressed as fast as I could while the pup snuffled and whimpered a greeting. It was so close to death that it could barely lift its head and I turned to the Serrate, only to see her unblinking gaze seemingly fix me with grim purpose. I wondered for a moment if I had completely misunderstood the situation. Perhaps her strict honour code required me to be at least armoured before she cut me down. Words of gratitude caught in my throat as she strode towards me, but that unflinching stare drifted past, and I felt the tension in my body fade with relief. She walked up to the upper half of the broken statue where it lay on the ground, the fallen goddess's face set in a permanent gape-mouthed, fanged grimace. She knelt, reached into the stone maw and withdrew a coin. It seemed to fascinate her as she turned the tarnished metal over and over in her hand. Then the Sunpup shuddered, and I cleared my throat.

"I need to get this creature to safety," I said, and she turned her head sharply at the interruption.

"You or it?" she asked, and all I could do was shrug. The longer I stayed in this forlorn charnel house, the more edgy I had become, aware for the first time of only one heart beating, an unwelcome reminder of how close to mortality I had come.

She pulled a small bone whistle from her necklace and blew softly. I heard the beating of wings, and something shifted in the darkness above, displacing the air around me before the dust in the ancient courtyard swirled and leaped under the impact of a great weight coming into land. At first glance it had a draconic shape, yet fine feathers could occasionally be glimpsed at the tips of the wings. She beckoned me to follow her as she climbed aboard the beast and told me where to sit. It was broad-backed, and I sat upon its frame cross-legged, Sariel's pup held close to my chest. It was a soft and downy seat, like sitting on a feather bed, and I secured myself with my free hand before my pilot called a hushed command and then we were suddenly racing upwards, the ground beneath us disappearing at surprising speed.

On through the black night we flew, over The Twisted Wood and back within the inner rim of the mountains until the perennially dark city of Scarpe, centre of Succae existence, came into sight. I concentrated on the thin beam of light to the north of the city. There was the Tether, my path home, and as we drew nearer, the creature balked and roared and I saw more of its form, long serpentine neck, membranous wings, and a talon as large as a sword blade and just as deadly. The Serrate landed us at the edge of the shadow and watched silently as I climbed down and walked towards the light. I felt power surge through me again as I touched the brilliant strand and turned to look at my saviour.

'Don't thank me,' she said, tossing a blackened coin, not dissimilar to the one I had seen her dwell on in the ruins. It was a mark of indenture, so worn that only the vaguest of traces as to whom it belonged remained. My debt had simply passed from one to another. By the time I looked up again, she was gone.

Chapter Two

Travelling back from darkness into light, I felt the usual sense of well-being that comes with returning through the Throne shell to the Horta Magna. This construct simulates one of the great Angelic spheres that we once called home. It is a world built to order and within the sub spheres, a thousand microclimates and environments that blend seamlessly one into another. Primeval forests, cool deserts, rugged mountains, arctic ice wastes, verdant steppes and wild oceans await. Of course, the real array of worlds that we once inhabited are long gone, fractured and destroyed in our own vicious tribal wars. All that remains are the memories made real by the Shaper and Maker Powers.

Long gone was a state I was soon to fervently wish for, as I was unfortunate enough to arrive at the glowing gates of the Horta Magna when Captain Varael was commanding the watch. We had history, none of which was good, and as he looked down from the white battlements of Vigil Keep to where I stood, tattered, torn and tired in the half light of their glow, I could tell I was in for another round of our ongoing conflict.

"Well, well. If it isn't our very own Azshael" he said, golden eyes glittering with malice. "Finally remembered which side of the Tether you call home, have you? Or maybe that shadow witch of yours has finally thrown you back into the gutter where you belong?"

I felt a familiar rage building inside, vision narrowing as an all too familiar darkness rose from within. I knew where it was headed and that it would generally make things worse but there was nothing I could do to stop it. I'd like to say it gave me no satisfaction to scream abuse at the Commander of Vigil Keep but the truth is it did.

"At least I did not betray my own brothers, Varael. I never set Angel against Angel or spied on those I swore to fight and die with. That takes a certain kind of bastard doesn't it, Varael? Well? Doesn't it?"

He was tall and slender, with ash blond hair that was far too long but it made for visible statements of anger as he threw his head back, whipping the air with his white locks. I saw his hands clasp the crenellations of the gatehouse, eyes locked in a bitter staring match with me until the moment passed and he laughed as uncertain garrison soldiers gazed uncomfortably at the both of us.

"You're drunk, Azshael," he said calmly, "so you'd best stay down there until you're fit to walk among us more civil folk. From where I am standing, that could be a long, long time." He turned smartly and left me alone, giving orders to the gate guards in strident tones. I felt the bravado drain from me as quickly as it had arrived. I had walked right into his trap, dooming myself to more hours in the semi-darkness. I knew any entreaties to the guards would be met with polite but firm rebuttals. It had been that way when I ran the keep myself, overseeing the first uneasy years of the Accord. Pale faces crowned with golden locks looked back at me from behind the portcullis bars as the Sunpup growled in disappointment. I sat down by the Tether, making sure the poor creature was bathed in its radiant glow, and felt a steady gloom descend over me. I had always had a talent for expression that bordered on the insolent and in better times it had even been considered amusing. These weren't better times, though, and I heard that voice that called me to abuse make its nagging tone ever more audible. I thought about Rain and my tongue felt dry and my eyes twitched. How quick and easy a way to eradicate the pain. I was on the verge of standing up and heading back the way I had come in search of my special medicine, when Cam emerged from the darkness and saved me from myself.

Camael, Throne power and the best wingman I ever had the grace to know, padded into the outer glow of the Tether. He had shifted into one of the many forms his powers allowed him to adopt—a great leopard, spotted and grinning. The Sunpup snarled and barked until Cam snarled back and it recoiled, relieving itself all over me for the second time in one day, scrabbling back to cower in my shadow. Cam transformed instantly into his more usual massive Angelic frame and laughed so hard that the earth vibrated with the resonance. The Thrones were forces of nature in general but with Cam they really needed to redefine the category.

"You know, Azshael, that walking a dog usually requires some form of forward motion?" he said stroking his bushy copper beard.

"Would that I had that option," I replied, and Cam's eyes narrowed.

"Varael again?"

I didn't reply except to shrug and shake my head at my own foolishness. Cam looked up at the gates and sighed.

"You should have had it out with him a long time ago, Azshael, when no-one would have cared except the Eyes themselves."

Very occasionally, Cam was right about things. Varael had fallen from grace in spectacular fashion, thanks mostly to his over-reaching ambition and my overprotective nature.

Yet, in twenty years of peace, I had tried to leave the worst of myself behind, bury bitterness and bile in a deep tomb that would be forever sealed. Somehow, Varael had a way of breaking the seals on that vault. Yes, there was a time when I could have hurt him badly, but I had turned the other cheek and opted to humiliate him instead. Now that time was gone and he rather than I stood in charge of Vigil Keep. It was just something we would all have to get used to.

"I still don't understand how he managed to get back in Anael's good books," Cam grumbled loudly enough for the warriors on the walls above us to hear.

"Archangels move in mysterious ways," I replied, and Cam laughed at the old truism every Angel that ever flew in the Host had uttered at some time or another.

We passed hours lost in the chat of old friends and it took my mind off recent events. In the lull of our conversations, however, I would hear that mono beat in my chest, a stark reminder that I had been foolish enough to fall into a trap and violation beyond any measure I had previously known. As the sky beyond the gates shimmered in a reddish golden haze, the gates opened, and I heard my name being called.

"Azsh! Azsh!" came the cry, and Sariel literally flew into my arms, her small childlike body crushed against mine.

"There you are!" she exclaimed gathering the Sunpup up against her chest.

"You found him! I knew you would. I said so, didn't I Cam? Azsh would find him, I said, and I was totally right, as usual."

There was nothing to do but laugh. Sariel had that effect on everyone she ever met. I felt the black gloom lift until my finger touched the blackened coin in my pocket, and I knew it would not be long before events would carry me back into the darkness from which I had come.

Chapter Three

The call came a few days later. In the intervening time, I was happily lost in my Sphere, a refuge of first resort where the passage of time is uncertain and unwatched. In that dreaming, a world of living memories, imagined space and illusion, I slept on scented silk aboard a simple boat adrift on a sparkling night sea. The gentle lull of the waves and the creaking of the wood were as calming as a lullaby whispered to a sleepy child. Somewhere in that endless night, Ischae's shade slipped into my arms, and we embraced, securely entwined, my great wings sheltering us both in feathery down. Streaks of light across the deep blue night heralded the dawn and her spectre faded as fast as I awoke, a brief parting kiss still lingering on my skin.

As I returned to shore, I saw a familiar figure standing on the beach. He was tall, his body wrapped in a toga made of fine silk that was edged with the purple lines that spoke of his seniority as an Elder of the Flight. Warm, wise eyes sparkled, and a smile beamed from his chiselled, handsome face. His commanding presence seemed to grow as time went on and it was clear he had lost none of that stature in the years it had been since we had last met. His name was Benazzarr, one of the few Heralds I had ever trusted and a long-time mentor and friend.

I called his name as my vessel hit the sandy bottom with a gentle thud and he waded into the water to help me drag the boat ashore. We embraced and I thanked him for coming to see me.

"You may want to save your thanks for later, Azsh," he said as we both sat down on the sandy strand. "I come from the Trinity with a summons from Archangel Anael."

"The Prince? What does he want with me?" I said, suddenly wary. Had Varael reported me and if so, on what basis? Benazzarr must have noticed the dark look on my face as he smiled gently and placed a hand on my shoulder.

"Worry not, Azshael. If I am being completely honest, it is not Anael that asks for you. It is the Succae Vod." I thought about the black coin that the Serrate had given me. It hadn't taken long for that debt to be called in. I nodded, my mind full of questions.

"The Prince did ask me if you were...," Benazzarr paused to pick his words carefully "...willing to work with the Succae once again. They seem to be in quite an uproar." I understood what he meant. "Willing" really meant "able"; anyone other than Benazzarr saying that would have got my back up. I forced a smile back at him. "Of course. Whatever the Prince needs of me. I am at his service." Inside, I felt my stomach churn and my remaining heart quicken ever so slightly.

I prepared to leave for the Prince's palace as fast as I could. After Ben had left, I hastily dressed in the Flight's ambassadorial tunic and white sash although I was uncertain that I had any current right to do so. It was the closest I came to having a 'dress' uniform short of wearing full battle armour, and all things considered, I had a feeling that was probably inappropriate.

Trinity Palace nestled in its own park surrounded by beautiful gardens and was an historic monument as well as a functioning hub of Flight organisation. The Palace's three halls represented the achievements of the Flight's previous leaders, and when Anael finally abdicated the throne, the Trinity would become a Quad.

As soon as I came into land outside the central Hall, also

known as the Day Palace, I felt tension in the air, like static before a thunderstorm. Angels armoured in gilded chainmail guarded the entrance and stood aside as I made my way into the ornate lobby. The ceiling of the Hall was decorated with images of Heaven that could bring any Angel to tears if they were to study it long enough. Here, I could feel the Prince of the Seventh Flight's presence calling me, his vibrant power coursing through marble, granite, and stone. Without knowing it, my voice whispered in response, every fibre of my being bent to serve the Archangel's purpose. I didn't just serve Anael, I desired his adoration, longed to bask in the warmth of his affection and approval just as much as I longed for the home behind the Eternal gates that I had once known.

The scene that greeted me in the monochromatic marbled Chamber of Open Hands almost made my remaining heart skip a beat. All heads turned my direction as I presented myself before the court and out of courtesy for the wingless Succae, concealed my wings. I heard murmurs of disapproval ripple through the gathered Heralds except for the group that stood closest to Anael's throne led by Benazzarr, who signalled his support with a barely perceptible nod of encouragement. Prince Anael looked up whilst his opposite, the Succae Vod stared through me. I had only seen him once before, at the cessation of hostilities between our peoples. His name was Karsz, and he was an imposing presence, his rank and position earned through secret rites of challenge. He was the Succae Warlord incarnate and all around him light diminished as inevitably as the dusk devours the day.

"Perhaps. now that Ambassador Azshael has arrived," Anael said in a mellifluous but nonetheless pointed tone, "you can explain what brings you here, Vod Karsz, Leader of the Succae."

Ambassador? It was a name I had not been called in over a decade, and even though I was dressed for the part, it surprised me to hear it again now. Had he not heard of my fall from grace? I did my best not to show any sign of confusion as Karsz stood and looked up at where Anael sat upon his tall silver throne.

The Vod could only be described as small if your comparative reference point was a mountain. His pale ebon hulk blocked hallways and without fail, he loomed over almost everything and everyone. He was dressed in a high-collared martial brocade coat that had been dyed a deep blue with the familiar swirling patterns of the Succae woven in. Belted at his waist was a wide-bladed sword with a gold hilt and ivory grip that was crowned by a large oval piece of jet mounted in the pommel. He also carried the mark of his office, a flanged war mace set with precious stones that glittered in the bright rays of light that filtered through the Hall.

By comparison, the Seventh's Prince had chosen a bright white gown lined with ermine, silver and gold that enhanced his inner luminance. Between that and the throne itself, he sat in a corona of dazzling light, and I fancied I could see the dark edge of Karsz's shadow burr against its edges.

"One of my most valued concubines has disappeared," Karsz said, his voice like low rumbling thunder. "I have searched our lands for her to no avail. I want her returned, and quickly." Anael considered the Vod's terse words in a long silence that bordered on being rude.

"What makes you think she is among us?" he said finally, and Karsz turned to his hooded entourage and beckoned one of them forward. From within the folds of a cloak, a small doll was passed to him. He took it and tossed it to me.

"Explain, Ambassador," he commanded, and Anael's eyes narrowed, the only outward sign of irritation at the Succae leader's tactless manner in giving orders to one of his Angels in front of him.

I turned the rudimentary lump of cold flesh over in my hand

before addressing Anael directly. "It is a homunculus, my Prince, designed to protect oath blood. The Succae swear pacts to their Lords and their oath is magically sealed within. A Succae's blood will always seek its host."

"So, this flesh enchantment has led you here?" Anael asked.

"It led me to the Tether, where the trail ended. It would be a breach of our agreements for me to activate our magic on your land without permission," Karsz said in a surprisingly measured tone, his eyes fixed on me as he spoke.

"I thank you for your wise judgement," Anael said, "and you can be assured that we will make every effort to find your missing child."

Karsz turned his gaze away from me and back to Anael.

"Your words are welcome Prince Anael, yet I would discuss this matter further with you. Alone."

"Clear the court," Anael said, and I fancied the Vod's gaze followed me as I left.

I walked the halls outside the Chamber, ignoring the whispers of the Heralds that gathered in their hushed and disapproving cliques. It was obvious that my sudden reappearance was unwelcome. I looked for Ben but there was no sign of him, although I did find Karsz's Succae escorts waiting in quiet contemplation, flanked by sentinel Angels radiating menace.

For most of the Host, the Succae remained an enigma and a menace, an unvanquished foe with whom a reckoning was still to come. As I passed by the group for the umpteenth time, one of the Succae swiftly rose and walked in step with me in a move so graceful and deft that they were past the sentinels before there was any time to protest. We walked on together in silence until I realised, they were waiting for me to speak first.

"May I be of service?" I asked softly.

"Not to me," came the whispered response and I recognised

the voice of my Serrate saviour. I stopped and turned to face her. She was slightly shorter than me, which made her tall for females of her kind. She was clad in a black martial *jhat*, a thick velvet jacket that cinched at the waist. She wore a pair of matching quilted *zho*, trousers that matched her slim contours but gave good freedom of movement in combat. On her feet were a pair of soft leather boots that were laced up to her knees. It was a martial outfit offset by the sword scabbarded on her back and a pair of shorter ceremonial long knives that sat at her waist. She had little other ornamentation except for a topaz set in silver that she wore around her neck. I guessed this was a token of her host's choosing rather than her own. The Succae are not much for ostentatious frippery.

"I want nothing of you, but my Master does," she said finally. "He asks your Prince for your service in the matter of the missing concubine, and that I be allowed to witness your efforts in this regard. He may have other wishes direct of you regarding your debt, but that would be between you and him."

"Why are you telling me this?" I asked, slightly taken aback by the frankness of her words.

She looked at me briefly in what looked like surprise but said nothing, stepping back into place among the rest of the waiting Succae as nimbly as she had left it. As we were called back inside the Hall, it turned out neither Vod nor Prince had any special words for me, but Anael's command soon confirmed it was as the Serrate had said.

The Pact Doll sat on the table in front of me, dull and lifeless, ugly black stitches around its neck, legs, and arms where it joined the torso that was marked by a livid purple scar. So far, my Serrate had been good to her word as far as being an observer was concerned. She had quietly watched over several hours of travel and preparation for our search without saying a single word, except for her name—Lytta.

"Are you always this noisy?" I said in a clumsy attempt at levity, only to see her eyes narrow in genuine confusion. Irony has never been big in Succae culture.

"I'm sorry," I said hastily, "it's just you are so quiet I almost thought you were…" I paused as I realised what I was about to say and how stupid it would sound, but she got there ahead of me.

"Dead?"

All I could do was nod my head and try my best dazzling smile, but her attention was on the doll.

"I do not see the value of empty chatter designed to fill space," she said quietly. "If the words are worth nothing then the void remains, rendering the whole exercise pointless."

"I think I preferred it when you were silent," I said, turning my attention to the lump of inanimate flesh on the table.

"You want to tell me how this works?"

Lytta lent over my shoulder and peered at the doll, her right hand resting on my shoulder. Carefully, she placed my hand on the homunculus and lent in close to my ear. I felt the brush of her hair and smelt a musk that reminded me of dried rose petals.

"It needs animating," she whispered, deftly running a sharp fingernail along the side of my right index finger. Blood oozed lazily from the graze, and she held my hand still as it trickled down on to the still flesh. For a moment nothing happened, and I wondered whether I was being played with, but then the doll's body went into spasm, rudimentary arms and legs flailing around. The thrashing ceased abruptly, and it used its stump of an arm to help it stand up on rough-hewn legs. It took a few faltering steps and then fell headlong from the table to the ground where it lay still. Lytta put it back on its feet and suddenly it was off again. It strode out of the door, its magic internal compass leading us to a hideous discovery that would change both of our lives forever.

Chapter Four

Our pursuit of the Pact Doll took us back into the grand Gardens and beyond its gates, into the verdant vale below Anael's Trinity known as the Princelands. It headed directly for the House of Memory where our lost and fallen of the Flight are remembered in stone statuary and mausoleums.

Sangael, the House's red-shrouded Seraph guardian, blazed into existence above us as the doll breached the outer wards and Angel-fire danced over its skin, blackening and popping its flesh. Acrid smoke rose from blisters in the corrupted skin. With effortless grace, the Seraph's six wings beat as one, buffeting the construct backwards. Lytta caught the doll in her right hand, literally snapping it out of the air. It writhed in her grip, clearly still driven to finish its task.

"What is this?" Sangael said, his voice a soft crackling whisper.

"Anael's bidding," I replied, and the Seraph fell silent for a moment. As close cohorts of the Ophanim, Varael's old order, I did not know how his fellow Angels would treat me, but no member of the Host would stand in the way of a Prince's warrant. Sangael doused the flames and appeared in his most personable guise, perfect high boned features framed by auburn locks that glinted with gold. He wore a reddish bronze breastplate, so highly burnished that we could see our faces reflected in it. He leant against his long spear, its blackened tip still flickering with flame.

"Your presence here I can understand, Azshael. Yet it is against our Laws for one of the Enemy to defile our sacred sites, even if we are not presently at war with them." Sangael nodded his head in Lytta's direction as if I had forgotten who I was with. I smiled, hopefully disarmingly. "This is a Succae Ambassador under the Prince's protection. Where I go, she goes. It's as simple as that."

The Seraph's perfect features contorted into an ugly scowl, but I was only confirming what he already knew.

"It should interest you to know though" I said, "that by your definition, this sacred place is already defiled."

"Impossible!"

I turned to Lytta and pointed at the Pact Doll, still writhing in her hand.

"This magical enchantment says otherwise. Its purpose is to find the Succae whose blood is held within, and it has brought us here."

Sangael frowned, aquiline nose wrinkling in disgust at the charred lump of flesh.

"Go then," he said, standing aside. "But I can assure you, there is nothing to be found. I searched the Hall this very morning and saw nothing untoward."

Frustratingly, Sangael's words were proved correct. Lytta and I stalked along row upon row of statues erected to the memories of Angels of the Seventh felled in battle without finding any sign of trespass. Noble faces looked down upon us, eyes forever open, faces serene and occasionally pitying. Sangael walked in our wake, silent in his discontent and unspoken condemnation. Every soft step that Lytta and I took upon his hallowed ground seemed to wound him, as if we were violating everything that he held sacred. The more I thought about that, the more my own temper began to fray. I was back to being judged by those who I felt had no right to do so. I was about to open my mouth when Lytta laid a gentle hand upon my arm and relaxed her grip upon the doll. It lay still in her hand, and I looked around, realizing we had found the end of the trail.

We had almost returned to the entrance to the Halls, which was dominated by one stone Guardian, the statue of Chorael the Herald. In a bitter twist of ironic fate, Chorael was the first of our kind to die in the war with the Succae, even though as a Herald he was exempt from fighting. His role in the Seventh Flight was to act as a liaison between the judges and the judged. When only his head was returned it was clear the Succae weren't interested in playing by our rules or likely to surrender to Judgement lightly. His was the first of many sad sacrifices in the long conflict that followed.

Sangael and I exchanged horrified glances, albeit for different reasons, as Lytta suddenly drew a thin serrated blade from the top of her boot and filleted the doll in a swift cut. Dark blood spilled from the cavity in the enchantment's chest to spatter at the bottom of Chorael's plinth, little drops of red rain, the prelude to a potential downpour. The Seraph's horror was rooted in what he saw as sacrilege, and he wielded his fiery spear in an impressive whirlwind of martial ability. My horror lay more in the prospect of explaining to Anael how another favoured member of the Seventh Flight came to be a permanent addition to the Halls of Memory rather than just its guardian.

As it turned out though, the blood distracted us all. For a moment it pooled where it had fallen before snaking up the bleached white marble of the plinth like a red serpent in search of prey. Across carved sandaled feet and folds of cloak it continued to climb the Herald's statue, and we stood transfixed in fascination as it inched closer to Chorael's chiselled face, eyes open, forever vigilant. Lytta looked at me and raised an inquisitive eyebrow as I realized exactly what it was trying to tell us. Across Chorael's face the blood slithered and rolled, seeking openings that were not there. It was seeking the Herald's inner self and I turned to ask Sangael a question.

"Is Chorael's Sphere intact?"

I might as well have slapped him, such was the look on the Seraph's face, but he recovered quickly and nodded.

"It is held in the catacombs with the others that could be retrieved. Follow me, I'll take you to it." For the first time since our arrival, Sangael seemed genuinely intrigued and it was our turn to follow in his wake as he led us down wide stone steps, deep below ground.

Chorael's Sphere shimmered dimly in the dark catacomb. Into the distance, the coronae of many others lit the subterranean vault with an eerie blue haze, living memorials to the vast ranks of the silent dead. Sangael looked at me expectantly and I shrugged uncertainly. "I don't know what the protocol is on this, Seraph," I said and Sangael nodded as if my ignorance was a foregone conclusion. "There is no precedent," he said haughtily, "except for those nominated by the departed. They may spend as much time within as a Prince deems appropriate. In your case, I believe you have free rein."

"And you?"

"It would not be appropriate. I am a Guardian, nothing more. I will stand watch here until you and the Succae Ambassador return. The act will be recorded in our rolls and sent to the Prince with our usual reports."

"I am surprised that with such vigilance, anyone managed to get past in the first place," I said with a casual sarcasm that narrowed Sangael's eyes and wiped that condescending look from his face. Lytta raised an inquisitive eyebrow, as if asking why I was baiting one of my own. Why? History. Well, mostly history and the fact that I found it inordinately funny shoving sticks up tight asses. Gripping the hilt of my sword, I entered the world of Chorael's memory.

Chapter Five

I had never known Chorael in life and it was with reverent hesitation that I entered what memorial he had left behind. I say reverent not because it had been earned but rather that reverence itself is naturally presumed of us all and is ingrained in our society.

Heralds were deliberately distant, second only to the Princes themselves, and as such, out of my orbit in my time as a soldier. As an Ambassador, I had come to know most of those that remained, with a few notable exceptions, as having disdain for those beneath them. They suffered the lower ranks as one would a passing storm—something that could not be avoided and must therefore be tolerated as it would soon pass and be gone. They passed their days plotting and squabbling among themselves, only using those of lower ranks as pawns in their plots when it suited them. As I had been a victim and unwitting catspaw in more than a few of these endless feuds, I now had little time for them but like a mountain on your flightpath, you couldn't ignore the fact that they were there.

Lytta, of course, had no such reserve and quickly marched ahead of me into the twilight, deep, lush, knee-high grass parting under her feet. The air smelled sweet with the scent of wildflowers in full bloom, an intoxicating bouquet that instantly rewarded the senses. I paused for a moment to appreciate the ambience, wondering what Chorael would have thought of this first impression of his legacy. To immediately smile at the memory of someone is of course desirable, but I had lived among our kind too long to know manipulation when I saw it. I realised Chorael had left nothing for posterity. This was just a construct that those left behind had built in his memory. I had been naïve to ever think otherwise. Why would someone as arrogant as a Herald ever think they would die?

I followed Lytta up a hill that was crowned by a set of stark white ruins. Fireflies flitted through skeletal arches, their glow reflecting from the white columns to bathe the structures in a warm haze. I walked past wide stone tables strewn with gauze and silk that fluttered slightly in the gentle breeze. Towards the centre of the ruins, a giant statue of Chorael stood on eternal watch. It was imposing, dominant, his wings spread wide, banner of the Flight in one hand, scroll in the other. The sculptor had imbued grace and wisdom into his depiction and while the look on the Herald's face was serious, noble brow creased in intent, the slight smile on his stone lips spoke of warmth and open familiarity. I realised I was scowling, irritated at the sense of being manipulated again until Lytta pulled me from my moment of discontent.

"Look," she said, thrusting a smooth wooden drinking cup into my hand. I peered inside to see a small amount of red wine left at the bottom.

"It's a little early don't you think?" I said with a smile, and it was her turn to grimace. I inhaled the bouquet, but I was not enough of a connoisseur to identify the type and vintage. I could, however, immediately sense that it had been laced with Rain as my mouth went bone dry and a deep yearning for the high began to race through my veins. I forced myself to focus and poured the remains into one of the small copper flasks I kept in my satchel.

"There are twelve others," Lytta said as I put the stopper on the flask, "many of them half empty. Clearly, they were disturbed by something."

"Or the wine really wasn't that good," I said with a grin that was pointedly ignored.

Lytta showed me where cups lay strewn around. It did indeed look as if the uninvited guests who had chosen Chorael's memorial as a place for merry making had left in a hurry. There were no tracks left to speak of as grass that might have been crushed under feet in flight had long retaken the original shape of its design, but the spilled wine and general disarray told its own story.

"How far does this extend?" Lytta asked as she looked away over rolling countryside that covered the land in a green quilt for as far as the eye could see.

"There's no telling unless you explore it, but my sense of it says that were you to crest the ridge in the far distance, you'd actually be back here. This is not a real sphere of his making. Rather something created by those who wished to honour his memory."

She looked sideways at me and I felt that silent judgement that made me feel foolish.

"I didn't say it had to make sense," I said defensively, "just that it is what it is."

No reply. I had succeeded in annoying and answering myself.

"No sign of your missing friend," I said as she continued to stare silently at the horizon.

"She's not my friend," came the enigmatic reply, "and I smell blood." Her face turned feral, skin stretched tight against bone so that a profile that could have been described as having an equine grace became something more sinister and predatory. She inhaled the cool night air and then sprinted away uphill at an incredible pace. I spread my wings and flew up into the dark velvet sky, the land unfolding quickly below me, and soared in a wide circle around her. She ran to the peak of the hill above the ruins before launching herself from the promontory and for a moment we were both united in the freedom of flight, before she tumbled expertly down a long escarpment, each impact with the ground a springboard to the next, at one with the momentum until she came to a standing stop far below. With purpose she began to walk back up the path she had so swiftly descended, and I made haste upon the wind to join her. As I flew around the hill, a recess became visible beneath the peak and light flickered from within. I came in to land on the edge and peered into the earthen hollow, its entrance marked by two great temple candles whose flames twisted and guttered in a sea of wax yet somehow managed to remain alight.

Tentatively I walked forward into the hollow itself until I caught sight of a pale body draped across a stone tomb. For a moment, my mind froze, and I felt the blood in my face drain away. My head attempted reason, to tell me that I was not, could not, be seeing what I was seeing. Yet there it was. The same fragile elegance arched in frozen horror. The same blood scattered and sprayed everywhere. The same eyes wide in terror. It was Ischae all over again and I fell to my knees, suddenly breathless.

"Her name was Naschinne," Lytta said softly, and I turned from where I sat on the lip of the recess to look at her.

"You knew her?" she said.

"No. Did you?"

"I told you I did not."

"No. You told me she wasn't your friend. That is different from just knowing someone."

Lytta's eyes flashed. The Succae are precise, meticulous—and they don't like being caught out. It was the one giveaway that even she had been disturbed by what she had seen and had I not been so caught up in my own melancholy, that might have given me pause for thought.

"I did not know her," she said finally, eyes firmly fixed on my own. For a moment we just stared at each other until the light of comprehension showed in her eyes.

"This is not the first body you have seen this way," she said. "It happened to someone else. Someone you cared about." Her tone was not accusatory, just a flat statement of presumed fact and my silence seemed to condemn me.

"This is the work of your kind," she said.

"My kind?" I said, shaking my head in disbelief at the suggestion. I stood up and marched back in to the hollow.

"Let me tell you something Serrate. We don't do that!" I pointed to the dark crimson gore that covered the walls. It was as if all the blood within had exploded from her body.

"This is your work—you're masters of flesh and blood!"

Lytta stared at me as if I was mad.

"I do not believe so," she replied, her demeanour calm and reasonable in the face of my heated accusations. It took the wind from my sails and at that moment, I believed that at least she believed she was telling the truth.

I turned my attention back to Naschinne's body and prepared to bear Witness, a process long ingrained from my days as a hunter. I closed my eyes to centre myself when Lytta spoke.

"Tell me of the one that went before," she asked gently. I didn't need much pushing.

I told her the story of Ischae and myself. How her

position as a cultural advisor for the Succae and mine as Anael's Ambassador had brought us together. How friendship had developed into something more and how that something more had grown into the strongest emotional attachment I had ever known. Lytta listened carefully without interrupting me, even when I faltered, describing my lover's broken body that I had discovered in the tower down in Scarpe that we had once shared, eyes forever open, staring in startled betrayal. It had always felt as if that look had been left for me deliberately. That I had betrayed her by being absent the one time it mattered. For me it was catharsis, but Lytta's face betrayed nothing more than concentration on my words. Maybe it was her intense detachment, but I found myself growing angry again.

"Don't pretend this is the first you know of this. I find it hard to believe that you and Ischae would never have met. If this is your master's idea of getting back at me, then you can both go to Hell."

It was then she said something that surprised me and made me realise how much Ischae had kept from me.

"I have just come from there," she said, earnestly "and I am not keen to go back."

Chapter Six

"That is the reason why I do not know this servant," she said, gesturing towards Naschinne's body, "or this Ischae of which you speak. I have only recently been called back into flesh to serve the Vod."

"So, you didn't fight in the war between us?"

"No. Of course, I know about it through the memories of she that serves."

"She that serves?"

"Yes. The flesh that I occupy was once a loyal Ashai Prime in the Vod's guard. She has given me her body to wear and her spirit has returned to the Well for now. She is a sacred vessel and I bear a debt of honour to keep her body intact. Her spirit is gone but her memories remain. We are two parts of the one whole."

Lytta paused for a moment of silent reflection and I wondered how many of these sacred vessels she had occupied over the centuries and what their fates had been.

"I was told," she continued, "that it was the Vod's command that any assistance provided to you should be unfettered by prejudice."

Big of him, I thought sarcastically, but on second thought, in the honour-bound ways of the Succae, perhaps it was. That Ischae and I had lived a life without criticism was of course a fantasy. I had long believed that it was one of Ischae's own kind who had murdered her for taking up with me, but the truth was that many of my kind also objected to any liaisons, beyond the functional, between the races. There were suspects on both ends of the Tether, so sending someone from a time before such things mattered was a gesture of neutrality. Or at least that's how it might be seen. I was surprised Karsz had not made more of it but perhaps he had, alone with Anael.

"How long since you were in flesh?"

Lytta hesitated before answering. "Four thousand years. I served Vod Dursc in the last days of the Serpent Wars."

I cast my mind back to what Succae history I knew and recalled Dursc as the leader of an enlightenment movement that shrugged off the shackles of a voracious pagan pantheon at the cost of a bloody civil war.

"Looks like we're both a little rusty then," I said with a half-smile, but she didn't return it, her attention elsewhere again.

"I'll bear Witness on the body," I said, after it was clear she had nothing to add. "It might be best if you look around here and see what you can find."

She nodded then paused, looking me directly in the eye.

"Witness? What is this?"

"It's a process. An ability if you like. It should help tell us something of the way Naschinne died."

"You will touch her?"

"No, that is not necessary. It is more about feelings, emotions. The soul leaves much of itself behind in violent deaths like this. That is what I am seeking."

Lytta nodded and receded into the shadows as I breathed deeply and felt all sense of time and place slip away.

The Witness I had conducted over Ischae's body had produced almost nothing. At the time, wracked with grief, I had put it down to my own inability to become still enough to sense the tiny vibrations and sensory clues that could help recreate the last seconds of a conscious self. It had also been the first time in a long time that I had tried, as bodies found on battlefields needed little investigation. Indeed, it was not a skill I had used since I was a youth in the early days of Duma Fallenstar's rebellion, where prominent victims fell to his assassins' blades. Now, however, I wondered if I had judged myself too harshly, for once again, that same sense of emptiness prevailed over all, like a deafening silence. I gave more of myself, trying to go deeper, peel back the layers and pierce what I felt was a masking veil. It worked, and a sudden flood of information overwhelmed my senses.

Initially it was joy, edged with anxiety, the un-confessed fears of a child who knows they are doing wrong. Then I tasted wine, warm, and fiery spilling down my throat, intoxicating, exhilarating. From deeper within, a hidden rush, a spike of hysteria that surged within like a great wave crashing over a rocky shore. I could feel resistance, the fear of surrender but the wave was far too strong and gained momentum with every second, bubbling, rushing on, an inexorable tide. I knew what it was, for I had experienced the same feelings myself. Initially, Naschinne had been scared but Rain dulls all the senses, and I knew her fears had ebbed away as the drug cocooned her in its grip. Was this when her killer had guided her away from the others and committed a ghastly murder in this hidden place, out of sight?

From emotions, I moved to the more mundane staring into her glass eyes that had widened in the moment of death. Again, I pushed beyond the mirror surface seeking any trapped facet of light that might reveal her last sights to me. Finally, I found it. A stretched and warped reflection that Naschinne had perhaps only glimpsed at the last and out of the corner of her eye. The shock of it pulled me from the process of Witness and left me heaving, my heart pounding in my chest. There, in the shadow, a tall, hooded figure, face concealed behind the rictus grin of a

Succae war mask, wings visible. Surely an Angel had killed Naschinne.

Lytta and I parted company at the Tether as the bells of Vigil Keep sounded the end of the Day Watch. A solemn parade of Succae women cast ashes before the bearers of Naschinne's now wrapped and bound body. A curious collection of my own kind thronged along the walls, watching in silent respect as the small, sad entourage disappeared one by one.

"It must remind you of your lost love," Lytta said quietly as Naschinne and her bearers disappeared, the trail of grey ash all that remained.

"Not really. I never saw her being committed, as you call it."

"You didn't?"

"No. It was just too painful. I prefer my last memories of her to be living ones."

Lytta nodded and looked away. I could see that we were still both enigmas to each other. In the Succae culture of death and life, such observance was the least the honoured dead could expect. You never knew when that spirit would be returned to flesh and what power they might have over you in their next life to come. Personally, I thought Ischae would understand. Then, something occurred to me.

"It's a lot of effort for a concubine, isn't it?" I said and she thought for a moment before replying.

"Not just any concubine. The consort to a Prince in your language."

"So even prostitutes count as the honoured dead now?" I said softly with a grim smile.

"One person's prostitute is another's spy," Lytta said, the ghost of a smile playing across her own face.

"What does that mean?" I asked as she marched swiftly to the Tether, one hand holding her scabbard close to her leg.

"It means I agree with you," she said before disappearing

down the transport to her own world, leaving me confused and alone.

Chapter Seven

I knew enough about the final death rites of the Succae to be certain it would be some time before Lytta could return. The Succae's ceremonies and observances could run for days and that was time I was intent on putting to good use. I found a renewed sense of purpose coursing through me at the prospect of shining light on Ischae's death. It wasn't that Naschinne's death didn't matter to me, far from it. However, when I closed my eyes to relive the Witness, it was Ischae's face I saw. There were many questions and for the first time since her death, I had hope that answers could be found, and justice done on her behalf.

The place and manner of Naschinne's death became my focus and I began my search for answers with a visit to Asuriel's Landing, which lay several Spheres north of the Princelands. The town had been built and populated by the Bonded. It was the Archangel's reward to those of the many worlds and races the Flight had judged who had been spared for various reasons. It had grown much in size during our hundred years of war and subsequent twenty years of peace with the Succae. A refuge from carnage and horror, the Landing had eventually gained Sphere status in its own right. The Flight hierarchy left the Bonded on the ground level of the Lower Landing pretty much to themselves. They had moved to the White Acropolis, the upper city, which circled slowly in the clouds above, each full rotation being counted as a day in our calendar.

I had enquiries to make in both halves of the city, but it was the Lower Landing where I began. I flew across the great stone walls, over teeming market squares and alleyways until I saw a red roofed building nestled against the great North wall. This quarter of the city was sparsely populated due to the preponderance of fallen powers that chose to make it their home. Living next door to an ex-god is not easy unless you are one yourself.

A peal of bells from the Acropolis chimed sonorously in the distance, making it late in the morning when I came to land outside the simply named Red Roof Inn. Outside, Mama Feast and Papa Famine, Hyena-faced gods who had once been worshipped by millions were busy at work.

"Nothing you do is done well," Mama complained to her diminutive husband, as poorly cut chunks of meat and vegetables fell into a large iron pot brimming with churning water.

"I don't hear the customers complaining," Papa replied with a twitch of his ears, followed by a precautionary submissive whine, something he had once told me he was trying to eradicate in this new existence.

"It's not the customers you want to be worrying about," Mama snapped back with a snicker that chilled the blood. Papa's ears flattened and he continued his work in silence.

A natural lull in their eternal bickering, they looked up at me for the first time.

"Hello Azshael," Papa said amiably while Mama stared at me for a moment with her large yellow eyes.

"I hear we should call you Ambassador," she said, in a manner that sounded slightly derisory.

"I think we've known each other long enough to dispense with formality Mama Feast," I said. "So Azshael is just fine. I suppose Cam told you?"

"That boy would tell me anything for a portion of ribs covered in sauce."

"Just the one portion? His standards are slipping."

Mama and Papa descended into hoots of laughter, and I couldn't help but join them. It certainly sounded like Camael, who wouldn't know privileged information if it got up and bit him.

"Is he inside?" I asked as the pair's laughter began to subside.

"He's in with her Ladyship," Mama said with a twinkle in her eye.

"That's why we here outside," Papa added with a snort. "All that moaning and screaming going on."

"She's a lucky woman alright," Mama said. "I don't even remember them days wi't you."

"That's because it was me doing all the moaning and screaming," Papa said.

I stifled a laugh and walked inside as Mama growled.

Inside, the Inn was warm and welcoming. Fresh cut flowers graced the few tables that there were, the rest of the floorspace given over to small arrangements of deep plush armchairs. It was a place to tarry a while with a decent bottle of wine, have a really long conversation with close friends or while away the hours with a good book. The scent in the air varied from freshly baked bread to verdant loam, at once both enticing and reassuring.

"Care for a song Azsh?"

I looked up and saw the beauteous ethereal form of Ysabeau. She stood next to her grand harp on the small, raised stage that stood almost at the centre of the Inn, eyes covered in white lace, red lips, perfectly painted. She was slender, her elegant body clad in creamy silk, long red hair in ringlets that cascaded over naked shoulders down her back. In another time that hair had been brighter red, kept so by being soaked in the blood of those that strayed from a forest path to better see her beauty and hear her song. Nowadays her voice was just as beautiful but far less deadly, so I agreed and closed my eyes, allowing a painful ballad of murder and loss to move through me as the best music does until a string broke and spoiled the moment.

"Mother!" Ysabeau yelled, her soft voice gone, replaced by a harsh shrill. She stamped on the stage three times and a bright giant emerald spider scuttled out from below. It paused a moment and turned a mass of eyes that sparkled like diamonds in charcoal my direction before scaling the stage and spinning a new string to replace the old one. In bygone days, these had been the souls of those who, beguiled by her daughter's beauty, had begged for their lives, and on some occasions, been sent off to lure more victims her way. Now, it was just spider silk. Ysabeau tutted as she went about replacing her broken string, just as a red-faced Cam and the Mistress of the Red Roof Inn came downstairs.

Sylvenell grinned at me, pushing ash blond hair back into a ponytail tied with a green ribbon. Her skin was smooth and pale as milk, wide dark green eyes smiling. She wore a moss green velvet dress that clung to her bounteous curves in ways that left little to the imagination. It was no wonder that Cam could not pull himself away from her. He sat down next to me with a growl and a hefty slap on my back.

"You need me Az?"

"Actually, I need your good lady here," I said with a wink in Syl's direction. Cam frowned as she swished over to where I was sitting with a jug of honey ale and three mugs.

"Don't worry Cam. I just need her nose," I said.

"My nose?"

I reached into my pack and produced the sealed bottle that contained the Rain tainted remnants Lytta and I had recovered from Chorael's sphere. Syl pulled the stopper from the bottle and inhaled the bouquet briefly before recoiling in disgust.

"Tainted!" she said as honeysuckle vines laced their way from the floor to entwine the table in their sweet, fragrant grip. Cam sneezed and looked at me in annoyance as I resealed the bottle and Syl took a moment to regain her equilibrium.

"Yes, tainted it is but I wondered if you could still recognise the wine?"

Syl thought for a moment and shook her head slowly.

"It's not a bouquet I know which means it's definitely not of a grape grown on this side of the Tether."

Sylvenell's intimate connection to the earth was beyond question and I believed her.

"You should ask Hostmann," she said with a gently teasing smile and Cam grunted.

"If you can ever catch him in a state where he makes any sense of course," he said. It was the answer I had secretly been dreading but Syl was right. If anyone in the Landing would be able to identify our mystery vintage it would be a former god of Feast and Excess, and Hostmann was the only one of those I knew. The only problem would be finding him, as he could assume any appearance he liked. It was a challenge I decided to leave for the dark hours when I hoped he would be easier to track.

Having made my excuses, I left the Inn, spread my wings, and took flight. The red roof of the Inn dwindled in size beneath me until it and the teeming streets of the Lower Landing were but distant specks and any sense of the busy hubbub below was lost. I passed through dense clouds, feeling the strange turbulence that announced the presence of the grand city in the sky. Suddenly, sheer white marble walls materialised in front of me, grand buttresses anchored in dense grey nimbus that boiled and frothed like ocean spume crashing against a rocky shore. I soared higher and higher, the great walls of Prince Anael's White

Acropolis an ever-present reminder of the power of the Seventh Flight.

I landed at the arrival dais, a wide platform separated from the gates of the city by a long marble walkway. Golden armoured Guardians, soldiers of the White Guard, nodded respectfully as I walked towards the arch of the grand gateway. In a way, I felt sorry for them. They were Anael's personal Legion, yet they had not seen their Prince in years. He had chosen the walls of Trinity Keep as his personal residence and his soldiers had been left here alone. I could see questions in their eyes. Questions that I could not answer, and they dared not ask. Well, most of them anyway.

"Ambassador Azshael! What a pleasant surprise. What brings you here this fine day?" I looked up and saw the bearded face of Captain Galaeal. It just showed how long Anael had been away, for the Prince had always made a point of soldiers in his personal retinue being as androgynous as possible. In the old days, Galaeal could have lost his rank, even for such a minor transgression.

"Hail Captain," I shouted back as he took flight from the top of the gatehouse and landed next to me. In truth I was keen to press on, but I knew Galaeal would not easily be brushed off. I had been the same when I had Vigil Keep to command and had swiftly discovered that all news and information, no matter how small or seemingly irrelevant could later prove extremely useful.

"News travels fast then?" I said, silently wishing Cam had been born mute.

"Indeed so," Galaeal chuckled. "Certain people are said to be highly displeased, but I think they are the minority. You're still a hero to most of us Azshael, even if you do have..." Galaeal paused to pick his words carefully, "...rather unorthodox tastes in certain areas." I couldn't help but smile at the implied disapproval, but Galaeal was no threat to me. In fact, he had, without being pushed, volunteered some interesting information.

"Any of this minority of the displeased have names?"

"That would not be for me to say but I heard tell of it from birds that fly near silver roofs."

Silver roofs. That meant the Heralds whose silver-roofed towers dominated the skyline of the inner Citadel. No doubt Sangael and his seraphs had been swift to send word that Chorael's sphere had been defiled.

"Well, the Heralds never liked me anyway," I said looking carefully at Galaeal for any reaction, but he just smiled politely in response.

"Traditionalists Azshael. It is easy to maintain high morals when everything is black and white. Not like the shades of grey we soldiers are accustomed to."

I wondered what he was driving at and whether he was aware he had just criticised some of the most powerful people in our society. Clearly, he was reaching out to me but that instinctively made me worried. I decided to change the subject.

"I'm here to see a friend."

"Pardon?"

"You asked what I am here for. I am here to see a friend."

Galaeal nodded slowly, his face a mask.

"Give Sariel my best then," he said, clapping me on the shoulder before wandering away and leaving me open-mouthed. I obviously needed more friends.

Chapter Eight

I found Sariel hard at work in the hushed cool recess of her cell in the Scriptorium. She was painstakingly copying a scroll that looked as if it had been written by a dyslexic spider with no sense of the concept of line discipline onto a fresh cream coloured page. I stood for several minutes, admiring her artistry in silence as she outlined a word using a stylus with a thin nib before turning to her palette of coloured inks and brushes. From here, the proper process of illumination would begin and Sariel was a mistress of that art that could and had tested the patience of saints.

I cleared my throat, but she didn't look up from what she was doing.

"Sariel? It's me. Azsh," I said, instantly filling the quiet chamber with noise that seemed to reverberate from every wall.

"Mhmm," she replied, her focus still on the written page. I could feel disapproval ripple through the building as other cherubs peered around corners, distracted from their work. Sariel moved on to the margins, swiftly sketching floral decorations along the borders. I continued to stand in silence for what seemed like an eternity until she finally sighed deeply and turned to look at me.

"Can't you see I'm busy?" she said and for a moment I thought she was serious until the corners of her eyes betrayed a smile and I grinned back. For someone that looked like a child, she had a very adult sense of humour.

"I need your help Sari," I whispered, and her small smile turned into a big grin.

"Of course you do," she whispered back nonchalantly, "and I guess it will be our Hall of Records that you want."

"How did you know that?"

"Word gets around, Azsh, you should know that by now. I heard all about the body in Chorael's sphere. The Heralds are in a big uproar about it all."

"Yes, Captain Galaeal mentioned something about that. Apparently, I'm not their favourite Ambassador anymore."

Sariel laughed briefly and looked at me seriously.

"Well, you do have a history. Darophon himself came here, demanding Chorael's records but Narinel the Wise wasn't having any of it. Told him to go and get Anael's written orders that documents should be removed from the rolls. Darophon left with a face like thunder, but no orders have come since."

"So, nothing has been taken then?"

"Not to my knowledge, but that doesn't mean that Narinel will be any more willing to let you read or remove private records either. Not without Anael issuing a written request anyway."

"That's why I'm asking you for a favour," I said, sidling closer to where Sariel perched atop her writing stool and speaking in even more hushed tones.

"You're one of the archivists here. You have completely unfettered and unmonitored access to the rolls."

Sariel shook her head emphatically.

"No Azz. I can't do that. It would be betraying my position, breaking rules I helped write. If it is that important, surely Anael would write an order for you?"

She had a point but for some reason I was nervous about

involving the Archangel. The Trinity was a place where it seemed the walls themselves spoke, and with the Heralds involved, it concerned me that too many people might end up knowing my business. I was to regret what I said next, but I only did it out of the wish to get to the truth.

"You're right of course, Sariel. I should have done the same with a certain Sunpup. Sought out a request to travel, informed Vigil Keep of my business in Succae territory, made sure the creature was quarantined upon return."

Sariel's face turned bright red.

"I didn't do that because it would have taken too long. I bent some rules because I knew they were bendable, and no-one would get hurt. I'm not telling you what to do, Sari, just asking a friend for a favour."

Sariel looked at me for a moment and the look on her face made my heart sink, but I maintained a stony exterior. She turned to her lectern and passed me a piece of parchment and an inky quill.

"Write down what you need, and I'll see what I can do," she said, quietly resigned to the task ahead.

I had hoped that Sariel would go and get what I wanted from the archives straight away, but it was no surprise that my hope was a forlorn one. She sent me on my way with barely a backwards glance, saying only that she would send word when she had what I wanted. That left me time to go looking for Hostmann—or such was my intent until I left the cool, shadowy halls and found myself in unexpected company.

They came out of the shadows in the Scriptorium's entrance hall and locked my arms to my sides. They were both tall and muscular Angels, faces concealed by silver helms with stylised facemasks. They wore the sash and tabards of the Regio, the Heralds' honour guard and private army. I immediately knew where we were going and none of us said a word as we flew towards the centre of the cluster of silver towers that dominated the White Acropolis's skyline.

We came in to land on an open platform near the top of the tallest tower. In a subtle game of one-upmanship, the Heralds tried to outdo each other by adding spires, weathervanes, and other ornate accoutrements to the top of their residences in order to be the highest but in truth, they were all competing for second place, as this central tower had been built to be taller than the rest. It was a tacit reminder of who should be considered first among equals.

My escorts pulled strong cord from their belts and bound my wings with swift efficiency. One of them lifted a heavy, plush armchair with one hand and placed it at the very edge of the platform so that I could feel the wind whip around me as the other pushed me into it. There would be no flying away from here until my host allowed me to do so and he wouldn't emerge from wherever he was watching, until these demonstrations of power were complete. It was a predictable dance, almost a necessary formality which is why I didn't resist and instead took the time to evaluate Darophon's receiving hall.

I had been in the home of the Leader of the Heralds once before, during the business with Varael. Then, it had felt cold and stark, with the ordered precision of a museum. There was a place for everything, and everything was in its place. A display of trophies that left the observer with no doubt as to the magnitude of his host's deeds. Now, those trophies were still on display but there was new warmth with the addition of inviting furniture and engaging art. The entire arched ceiling of the hall had been painted in a devotional portrayal of Darophon and his Heralds in honourable service to Anael and the Princes, who themselves looked up to Excelsis. It was a clever reminder that we all served in one way or another and I fancied I could hear the echoes of whispered exhortations to impressionable members of the Host to do whatever they were asked to do out of love and duty.

Darophon was a devious and competent manipulator and at the time of my first visit, I strongly suspected him of planting the idea of the Ophanim being used as spies on their own kind in Varael's head. Our exchanges had been hostile until I called him to testify before Anael. I think he only showed up to be intimidating but he answered every accusation with such sincerity that for a while afterwards, even I thought I had treated him unfairly. That feeling had ebbed with time and the consistent rumours that he had engineered my subsequent fall from grace. Frankly, I didn't really believe that. I had done most of the damage on that score myself, but I could quite imagine him being less than happy that I was back in any position of responsibility. Sitting, bound in a chair a few inches away from a fatal fall, I guessed that was now an understatement.

My escorts left me alone for the necessary period of reflection designed to unsettle and intimidate. I closed my eyes and let the winds sing to me until I felt Darophon's presence in the room. He called my name as he approached but I didn't respond, feigning sleep. I waited until I could hear the rustle of his robes, smell the exotic scent of the oils he bathed in. Then, I opened my eyes. If he was surprised, he didn't show it. He looked down on me in the manner of a father looking in on their sleeping child. It was not the glare of confrontation I was expecting, and I must have frowned as he smiled and stepped back.

"Azshael. How nice to see you here."

Even nicer when I'm your prisoner, I thought, but I

didn't say so.

"It's Ambassador Azshael, Herald and I hope you have a very good reason for abducting me and holding me here against my will."

Darophon smiled indulgently.

"The best of reasons and the best of intentions," he said, pausing for effect. "Your own well-being."

I nearly burst out laughing, "With due respect, I am surprised you, of all people, are worried about my health."

"As Chief Herald and steward of the White Acropolis, I am concerned for all those within these walls."

"And their business too, it would seem," I added caustically but he didn't rise to the bait.

"This is our problem Azshael, we just don't trust each other and that leaves me with only one solution, given the circumstances."

I felt my heart quicken as Darophon drew a dagger from within the folds of his robe. Its wide silver blade came to a vicious point, and it reminded me of the temple daggers that are used to slice the throats of sacrificial animals. Would he really be so bold as to murder one of Anael's appointed emissaries? Had the Archangel's power over this city really diminished to the point that Darophon felt he could get away with it? I wondered why I was asking stupid questions to which I already knew the answers when the Herald surprised me. Pulling me forward he reached behind me and cut my bonds.

"I'm not your enemy Azshael. Come and walk with me and let's talk as we should have done some time ago." I stopped holding my breath, got up and followed him.

Chapter Nine

"This business with Chorael is most unfortunate," Darophon said as we walked down the steps from the platform and into a long gallery where art and antiquities adorned the walls and our footsteps fell on plush carpet.

"Well, the Succae feel the same way and it was not Chorael who was murdered," I said, possibly a little too flippantly. Darophon stopped suddenly, turned, and looked me in the eye. I could sense the anger that rippled beneath an otherwise placid surface, and I realised I had hit a nerve.

"He was murdered, Azshael, and before any formal declaration of war had been issued or hostilities commenced. Many think of him as the first casualty of the wider conflict, but in my view and that of many others, he was really the victim of a cold-blooded killing in peacetime. If that is not murder, I don't know what is." It was a nuanced debate, semantics even, but I could tell there was passion and belief in his words.

"How upset are the Succae?" he said suddenly.

"Upset enough that Karsz himself came to the Prince to demand justice," I replied. The Herald nodded with interest and walked on.

"That must be the first time the Vod has come to this side of the Tether since the signing of the Accord."

"That I know of, yes."

"And this Succae female who accompanied you. What

of her?"

I paused for a moment, realising I was being led down a path that so many others had followed. It was Darophon's reasonable tone and sincerity that inspired confidence. It was also the mark of a very efficient interrogator and I decided to tell some half-truths.

"Just a trusted servant. One that can be relied upon to report what she has seen effectively."

"A servant with a sword? That sounds like a warrior to me."

"Most of the Succae's trusted servants are warriors," I replied, largely telling the truth.

"Including the one you found dead in Choral's sphere?"

"No. She was a concubine."

Darophon laughed gently and looked me directly in the eye.

"You don't really believe that do you?" he asked in a tone that sounded as if the entire idea was preposterous.

"It's what I've been told," I said with a frown. The truth was I hadn't really had a chance to dwell on it, although Lytta's parting words about spies had certainly planted seeds of doubt in my mind.

"Do you know something about it?" I asked.

"Only that the Vod of the Succae would not venture to this side of the Tether were it just a concubine who had died. I know enough of the character of such people. Little people don't matter to them."

He had a point—and surely Lytta's presence confirmed that. Naschinne had to have been something more than she seemed.

"Who do you think she was?" I asked as Darophon walked on, but he just shrugged.

"I don't know, but if I had to guess I would say someone

important, probably related to the Vod directly—a sister, wife or daughter perhaps?"

It was subtle but I had the impression of learned lines. Was the Herald deliberately feeding me information and if so for what purpose? I decided it was time to ask rather than answer questions.

"What were you looking to remove from the Scriptorium today?" I asked as nonchalantly as I could. He looked wounded, as if our time as friends had suddenly come to a close.

"Anything of use," he replied enigmatically.

"To help or hinder my enquiries?"

"To protect. I have a duty to my Order and those that have served it."

"So, you admit you would have kept secrets from me?"

"No, not at all. I would have correctly interpreted them for you. I know, from previous experience, how facts can be twisted to make things look other than they actually are."

"You'd go to any lengths to protect your Order wouldn't you, Darophon?"

"I don't see what is wrong with that, Ambassador, as long as it falls within our laws."

"Does the death of a Succae count as lawful in your opinion?"

"It would depend on where and when and what the circumstances were. You seem to have forgotten what we were sent here for, Azshael. Just because we're not fighting them now doesn't make them any less our enemy."

"We're not at war any longer, Herald."

"Aren't we? If you look at the Accord in detail, it is nothing more than a truce, a pause in the conflict. Just because the killing has stopped, doesn't mean the war is over."

I was reminded of Captain Galeal's words about

'Traditionalists' and decided not to bother pursuing this argument that I had heard voiced thousands of times before. It was all very well for those that didn't have to fight to have such simplistic opinions, but many of the Host didn't agree and I guessed that Anael was more on the side of peace than he was of war. Yet if he returned to Excelsis without being victorious, that would suggest fallibility and Excelsis was never wrong. It was both a philosophical and practical quandary and I didn't envy the Prince his decision. Not one little bit.

I sighed deeply and changed tack before Darophon could climb any higher on his high horse.

"Chorael did not make that sphere, did he?" I said.

"No. He never had the opportunity to do so. Anael sent him to his death as soon as the Garden was constructed and the spirit shell activated," Darophon replied, the bitterness in his tone clearly audible.

"Who built it then?"

"As Leader of the Heralds, it was my task. Normally, I would have asked others within the Order to do the actual work but on this occasion, I did it all myself."

"Why?"

"Chorael was my mentor and I felt I owed it to him."

I paused for a moment as thoughts moved in my head, presenting some form of clarity.

"Do you go there often?"

"Not now, no. Why do you ask?"

"I first thought that perhaps the choice of Chorael's Sphere was a symbolic one, a message to Anael, the Host or your Order of Heralds."

"And now?"

"Maybe this is a message meant for you, Darophon."

I felt that he was surprised at the thought, but he hid that surprise well. It went without saying that as leader of the Heralds he had many enemies but the involvement of Naschinne and the Rain drugged wine didn't appear to have any place in that theory.

"It is an interesting thought," he said finally. "I will consider it and if anything occurs to me, I will be sure to send word," Darophon said, bringing our conversations to a clear ending. He led me back up the carpeted stairs and on to the platform.

"Fly safely, Ambassador," he said and as he turned to leave, I asked my final question.

"Why the hidden fane in the hollow?"

Darophon looked at me, slightly bemused.

"What hidden fane?"

I swore profusely as I took flight.

I flew through black clouds full of rain. It was a suitably moody environment and for a short while I allowed myself to be buffeted by the winds and drenched in the downpour.

My immediate instinct was to return to Chorael's sphere where Naschinne had been found glass-eyed and empty in a place I now knew was not part of the original design. However, the House of Memory was several hours away, and I still had business to take care of in the Landing. Besides, I rationalised to myself as I swept down towards the streets of the lower citadel, Chorael's sphere wasn't going anywhere and surely now the Ophanim would be hyper vigilant. Despite my own self-assurances however, some unidentified concern insisted on making its presence felt in the back of my mind. I played mental games of hide and seek, trying to flush out whatever thought was trying to make itself known but it remained frustratingly out of reach by the time the washed cobbles of the Lower Landing materialised beneath me.

I landed just a few streets away from the Red Roof Inn and hid my wings, pulling my cloak tight around me. In doorways and from inside warm hearths, the Bonded looked out at the weather in silent appreciation, the mesmerising nature of both the sight and sound of the rain a source of never-ending interest. There were dozens of drinking houses hidden away in these streets, hundreds across the lower city and in one of them, I was certain that Hostmann would be found with a suitably drunken audience, laughing, singing, and generally not caring about the consequences. The question was which one?

Chapter Ten

As it turned out, I did not have all that far to look, partly thanks to Cam and his big mouth and my own laziness in the face of arduous tasks, which was something of a post-war trait of mine. I decided I needed fortifying before seeking my quarry and that a good helping of Mama Feast's cooking would be just right. I headed for the Red Roof only to find the place packed to the rafters and none other than Hostmann holding court.

He was a tall, bulky figure dressed in a red and green tunic that had faded over time and was clearly struggling to keep all his bulk inside. A grand bushy beard, rosy cheeks, and a laugh so warm and rich that it could reverberate through stone and put a smile on the face of all that heard it, enhanced an already enviable reputation. If Hostmann visited your watering hole, you were sure of a night to remember.

For a while I could do nothing but watch a master at work as he regaled his audience with various outrageous tales of his adventures. I was entranced, unaware of the passage of time as alcohol of one form or another flowed freely around me. It was only when Hostmann stopped talking and called Ysabeau to the Red Roof Inn stage that I felt my wits truly return. Ysabeau played her harp beautifully, a sparse yet intricate melody. Above all, Hostmann's pure baritone, deep and resonant. I did not understand all the words, but I got the general message and it was a strange way to end a night of mirth and merriment, with a lament for a home to which none can ever return.

It captivated most of the audience, however, and that was all that mattered. I felt regret hang in the air like a ghost at a feast and I knew he had touched a nerve in the hearts of the Bonded. Maybe they had surrendered themselves to the Flight in times past, but that didn't mean they had to like it every day thereafter. I felt the glares and glances but didn't react. None of us like all the paths our lives have taken us down but once travelled, there is no choice but to live with the consequences.

The Inn emptied slowly as it became clear that Hostmann was done for the night, and he came over to the corner into which I had retreated. Whether for his own amusement or as a necessary part of dissipating the crowd that would otherwise never let him leave, he had changed form and sex completely, from a rotund jolly giant into a curvaceous, busty pale skinned courtesan who looked like she had seen better days, yet still had an undeniable allure.

"I hear you're looking for me," she said, sitting at my table, smoothing her long, jet-black hair. I looked Hostmann directly in his sparkling eyes to be certain it was he—it was the one part of him that never changed.

"Yes, you heard correctly. I could use your advice." I produced the leather bottle that held the recovered wine and removed the stopper. "I am told you know every vintage just by its bouquet, so please, tell me what wine this is and where it can be found."

I passed the bottle to the former god of revelry and fertility, and she inhaled deeply, eyes widening in surprise or shock, I wasn't sure which.

"Not right," she murmured. I was about to explain the

taint of the Rain when she lent forward suddenly, ample chest straining against thin fabric.

"Why do you want to know about this?"

It was my turn to be surprised and as a result, I didn't think to lie. Instead, I told Hostmann about Naschinne's death and Anael's instructions to me to find out what had happened. She, or rather he sat back, shifting form and face like a slowly shuffled deck of cards before settling back into the full-bodied shape of the courtesan again.

"Return here tomorrow morning. I will send someone to fetch you. Then you will have an answer to your question and perhaps more," she said, standing up to leave.

"Tomorrow? Why can't you tell me now?"

"I need to be certain," Hostmann replied through clenched teeth, eyes flashing angrily. I had never seen or imagined this power like this before, so used to seeing a harmless, rotund jester. Part of me wanted to argue but the old hunter inside cautioned against such a path. I had rattled Hostmann somehow and angry people sometimes made mistakes they wouldn't make were they in a more rational state of mind. Instead, I just nodded and let her go, but not before handing over the bottle.

"For comparison," I said with a smile. She looked back uncertainly before grabbing up the wine and bustling out the Inn's door.

I sat back down and thought for a short while before racing up the stairs and up on to the wet roof, collecting my sacred weapon, Nimrod, from its resting place in the room Cam and I occasionally shared. I was a little tired of being unprepared, and Nimrod made me feel at least a little more comfortable should a simple scouting mission take an unexpected turn. I took flight and followed.

Hostmann would have been hard to track in normal times,

but I had marked the stopper of the bottle with Sariel's illumination ink and even through the heavy rain it shone like a beacon, at least to my eyes. If Hostmann was aware of it, he didn't seem to show any sign of concern and I moved in and out of dark clouds, watching as he wove his way through streets and alleyways, shifting shape every few minutes.

Close to the southern gates of the Landing, the beacon suddenly vanished, and I descended as fast as I could to the last place I had seen its glow. I pushed light away from me so that I was nothing more than a black silhouette and hovered just above the ground. Before me was a long single storey building, shuttered to the outside world and apparently deserted. I sharpened my senses seeking any sound or smell of my quarry but there was nothing to be found. I flew up above the roof, seeking any crack through which I might see inside, but every slate was intact. Frustrated but cautious, I did the only thing I could do and waited, crouched in place as the rain continued to fall.

I thought about my absent Ischae and how she had loved nights like this. We would walk together through the Garden, and she would revel in the sensation of the raindrops on her skin, face upturned to the sky, eyes closed in silent reverie. We would return to my sphere, where I would comb her hair, peel wet clothes from her body and make passionate love, her dark wet locks whipping my face at the height of ecstasy.

I was disturbed from my thoughts by the sound of movement as a lanky boy emerged from the doorway below. Closing the door firmly, he pulled a hood over his head, shouldered a knapsack, and ran back the way Hostmann had come, back into the maze of streets and alleyways towards the centre of town. I focused on the bag he carried and saw the marked bottle glow dimly through the heavy canvas. I launched back into the dark sky and followed.

The boy moved swiftly, ducking in and out of doorways, stopping occasionally to look and listen around him. They were perfunctory checks, done more out of habit than any real concern. If this was Hostmann in another guise, it was strange behaviour, but I remembered the look of anger on his face when we had met, a reaction just as surprising. Maybe I had misread him, and it was not anger at all. Maybe it was fear.

The boy was heading for the Ramp, a steep hill that led up to the Landing Keep where a small garrison of the Regio guarded the path to the Acropolis. Before him lay a narrow set of alleyways with a small market square at their centre, and I lost sight of him as he entered what the residents of that area called the Squeeze. I descended to try and get a better look and realised we weren't alone. Black shapes, hardly distinguishable even to my Angel eyes, waited atop the roofs below like a pack of wolves in an urban forest.

The boy had paused at the exit to the market square, unaware that doing so improved his ambushers' chances. I soared over them silently as they flowed over slick rooftops like a black wave. I counted four of them, but preternatural senses told me there were more hidden from sight. Alternatives raced through my mind. Help was not far away, but it was a few minutes there and the same back again. Close but too far in the circumstances. I felt a familiar surge within my body, the pulse of energy that preceded combat. It was clear I was the only help the boy could count on.

Chapter Eleven

I heard the sudden whine of arrows slice through the air as I came to land in front of the boy. I flared my wings, creating an updraft that sent the wicked shafts wide of their mark, slamming into wood or clattering off stone walls. There was a roar immediately behind me and I turned as Hostmann revealed his true self, expanding in width and height so that he occupied almost half the small square in which we stood. The enemy looked unperturbed and advanced, encircling us, long black blades raised in martial stances. I heard skittering on the roofs around us and launched myself up, catching one of the bowmen as I went by the neck. I soared upwards as he struggled beneath me and then let him go, hands clawing in space, arrows tumbling from his quiver as he fell back towards the ground, crashing off a rooftop before dropping to the cobbled street below. By the absence of tattoos on the archer's face, I knew who and what these enemies were now, and cursed as my victim got to his feet and began to frantically gather up any unbroken shafts he could find.

They were Succae. Low-Nin vampires to be precise, untried would-be warriors with no ties or obligations. Most were outcasts even in their own society, their animate flesh occupied by the lesser eternal spirits of the Well and doomed to the most menial of tasks unless they could find a way to impress a Vod or other High-Nin Master. It was good news and bad news. Good in the sense that they had never fought my kind before and would not know what to expect, bad as they had little to lose and would no doubt fight to the end.

Below, Hostmann was fighting bravely, roaring loudly, and aiming massive fists and feet at his attackers. The Low-Nin were fast and lithe, though, and so far, they had avoided his hammering blows by rolling and diving out of the way. There were two small groups of five and they raced in, slicing at the giant's fleshy legs that already wept dark tears of blood from dozens of cuts. On rooftops around the square, more archers fired barbs into Hostmann's face. It was all happening so quickly that I felt paralysed by inaction, but old reflexes and a familiar anger burned bright suddenly, and I felt Nimrod vibrate in my hands as I shot back down towards the ground.

I targeted the archers first, releasing a pulse of brilliant blue light that I hoped would not just blind them but also act as a beacon to any watch point. I heard cries of dismay and cursing in the Succae's blunt tongue as I turned my attention to the group behind Hostmann, hacking at the back of his legs, trying to sever his hamstrings. I crashed into them; a warning shouted from one of the roofs behind me heard too late.

The first two Low-Nin came at me, and Nimrod's spearhead flattened and lengthened into a wide blade that severed the heads of both attackers in one sweep, bodies running on before stumbling and collapsing behind me. The pale faces of the three others looked at me in awe, black eyes wide in terror as they cringed and retreated. I was aware that I was shouting at them, daring them to attack me, and that's when I realised one of Hostmann's greatest defences was close to being my undoing. The ground beneath me was slick with blood. Blood made of pure alcohol that was leaching into my skin and intoxicating me to a state of inebriation worse than any I could remember.

I took off, trying to reach clean air that would clear my head, but the world spun around me as I shot over the enemy and collided with a wall further down the narrow alleyway that they had retreated into. I landed in a heavy heap and heard them coming after me. I felt an odd sense of elation as Nimrod became a sword, the bright, shining blade in my hand taking on a life of its own as it weaved, sliced, and cleaved as they came within reach. Heads rolled and limbs were severed until only I was left standing.

I paused for a moment, looking at the Succae dead around me. It was a reminder of my true nature, my calling as a judge, jury, and executioner of other souls. The end of the war and my time with Ischae had allowed me to believe another destiny was possible, yet was it? I was still that engine of destruction I had always been, and just because I might occasionally hate myself for it, that didn't give me the right to think I was worthy of redemption.

Hostmann's roar drew me out of maudlin thoughts, and I felt clarity return to my vision as my system purged the poisonous alcohol. I spread my wings and flew above the square again. Hostmann had deployed a second defence, encasing himself in tangled briar bristling with red razor-sharp thorns. The remaining Low-Nin had been caught in the initial sudden growth of a thicket that would tear an ordinary man to pieces. However, the Low-Nin were far from ordinary and had torn themselves loose, leaving chunks of flesh behind. Now, they scaled the sides, thrusting themselves onto the thorns for purchase before pulling free and climbing ever higher to their goal of the old god's unprotected head. I could see he was weary, breathing heavily, a worrying whine audible as he exhaled.

His eye caught mine as I decapitated one of the climbers,

his body hanging limply in space. I looked at him questioningly and he just shook his head as a black shadow arced over me and landed on his shining scalp. I saw the flash of a blackened blade and my heart sank. It was a Lacerate, a sword only used by the Ashai, the Succae warrior class. Forged in blood and fire both the weapon and the Succae that wielded it were some of the deadliest products of their civilization. The Ashai was swift about his business and my cry of "mercy" left my mouth long after he had plunged his blade into Hostmann's right ear. There was a small delay until the old god's head burst apart, the blade having detonated upwards into hundreds of deadly shards that ripped and tore through flesh and bone. Slivers of the black blade sliced through my wings, and I tumbled to the ground covered in blood and brain matter. Hostmann's great mass slumped to one side before crashing into the market square, blood still flowing freely from his ruined head.

Concussed by the fall, I lay still for a moment and watched in disbelief as the Ashai pulled the few surviving Low-Nin free from beneath Hostmann's bulk. As soon as they were liberated, a second shorter blade whipped in a blur and their headless corpses fell to the floor, thin grey spirits momentarily visible as they left their bodies. The Ashai's own body went rigid as his own dark wraith became visible and he drew the smaller spirits to him. I could hear horns sounding in the distance as the vampiric wraith returned to its host and the Ashai walked towards me, sheathing his blade as he approached.

He was compact of build, face concealed behind an iron visor that had an incongruous, demonic smiling face etched on to it. There was something that felt innately familiar, in the same way as it had when I had been Jasniz's prisoner. His guest was masked then too, and I felt the two had to be connected, if not one and the same. He bowed once, briefly, turned his back, his hands drawing shapes in the air, and literally vanished before my eyes, pulling the spirits away with him. It was the first time I had ever seen an Ashai do that and I was still speechless when the Angels from the watch arrived.

Chapter Twelve

It stopped raining almost the same moment Benazzarr came to liberate me from the Landing's Lower Keep. Watcher Pesak, a Regio Captain, and master of the guard in the Lower Landing, was clearly unhappy to see me go, rightly certain that I had been less than forthcoming with the truth of what had happened.

I had deliberately limited my role in the events of the previous night to having been in the wrong place at the wrong time, something that had given him and the other Angels that questioned me a good laugh. Arms folded, long black hair in braids and wide handsome face, Pesak shrugged as I walked down the steps with Benazzar's reassuring presence in front of me.

"Keep your secrets Azshael. Just be sure they don't kill you," he said as we passed by. He was only doing his job, but it still made me feel that I was surrounded by people I dared not talk to. It was widely supposed that every Angel in the Landing was owned by another of a higher rank, which meant all paths led back to the Heralds and Darophon in particular. After my heart to heart with him, it was still unclear as to whether that was a good or a bad thing, but I was certain that Anael would rather his Ambassador remained as tight-lipped as possible.

That didn't stop me from bending Ben's ear of course, once we were back at the Red Roof Inn.

"He just vanished?" Ben said as he watched Cam stuff a large stack of Mama's dough cakes into his mouth. It was almost mesmerising, watching the way they rolled from one side of his big mouth to the other, only to disappear like debris carried away on the tide in a large swill of Darberry juice.

"I think he did something with his hands first," I said, recalling the moment.

"That'll be magic then," Ben said with an assured certainty.

"He makes a good point," Cam said, wiping his face with the back of his hand and settling back in his chair.

"I know magic when I feel it. We all do. No, this was something else."

"Well don't let it eat you up Azsh," Cam said standing up and winking at both Ben and me before climbing the stairs in search of Sylvenell.

Cam could make light of it, but the truth was it did gnaw away at me. Hostmann's secretive behaviour and the promise of revealing something momentous, his look of surprise at the news of Naschinne's death, and the look of weary betrayal that had been on his face immediately before he died. A mysterious Ashai using powers we had never seen before and the bizarrely grateful way in which the Low-Nin had accepted their executions. There were secrets being revealed that I couldn't understand, as I had no frame of reference.

Ben looked at me thoughtfully and gave me a reassuring pat on the shoulder. "Cam is right Azsh. Dwelling on pieces of the puzzle rather than the puzzle itself can only lead to frustration. I am certain that you will find answers very soon." His certainty made me feel momentarily confident but once he had departed, I felt the same veil of confusion descend on my clarity of vision.

I was about to leave and head for the shuttered drinking house that Hostmann had ventured into before making his final journey when Sariel sauntered into the Inn.

"I thought I'd find you here in the shadows," she said, putting a bunch of ribbon-tied scrolls on the table between us. I grimaced as she grinned and stroked my face gently.

"It's been a long night Sari," I said, ruffling her hair in return until she giggled so much, I couldn't help but smile. I expected her to ask about Hostmann, but she made no mention of it. Perhaps Pesak had yet to file his report, or, I thought darkly, someone had told him not to.

"Aren't you going to read them?" Sariel said, tapping the paper with her finger. I knew an order when I heard it and started to digest the information.

It seemed like an age had passed since I'd asked Sariel to search the Scriptorium's archives for the information contained in these carefully copied scrolls and some of what I'd suspected then could now be confirmed. A case in point was Chorael's sphere, the archived document confirming that Darophon had been its sponsor and designer.

The second set of scrolls detailed the official comings and goings at Vigil Keep for the past forty days. I had asked Sariel to copy Varael's daily reports in case Naschinne and her fellow celebrants had spent time in the Landing before somehow sneaking into the House of Memory. I eagerly scanned the lists for her or any group that she could have hidden among, but there were no apparent matches in the official reports. One name did stick out and that was Jasniz, my former supplier of Rain and presumed employer of the pagan Succae monk that had taken one of my hearts and nearly killed me. He had passed through the keep on a regular basis up until the week before Naschinne's murder and the night I nearly died. I couldn't see the connections, but I was sure that Ischae, Naschinne and I had fallen foul of the same enemy. I scoured the exit logs to see if Jasniz had left but where Varael had been meticulous in describing Succae coming into the Hortus Magna, his diligence when they departed left a lot to be desired. Taciturn entries like 'one male, one female' were as detailed as he got and were therefore of little practical use. Suspicious? Perhaps. Sloppy? A matter of opinion. It looked as if there would be no alternative but to meet Varael and question him directly. I didn't much relish that prospect.

The third scroll held the biggest surprise for me, purely in its brevity. It was about Yggael, the serpentine goddess of the Succae, whose statue I had seen in the place that had nearly become my tomb. There were three simple lines that read 'Vampire goddess. Pantheon leader. Traveller.' I looked up at Sariel.

"Is this really all there is?"

"It's all I could find Azsh," she said with a frown.

"Meaning what?"

"Meaning there should be more."

"Should be?"

"Maybe. I suppose it is true that this entity was long out of favour by the time we arrived, so perhaps there was never a reason to update the records. Yet, as pantheon leader, I would have expected more details like a list of crimes worthy of judgement. I'll bring it to Narinel's attention and see what he thinks."

"Might it have been misfiled?"

Sariel gave me a withering look and I looked away. Nothing ever went missing in the Scriptorium so the presumption that valuable information had been deliberately hidden or misplaced had disturbing implications. Had I uncovered a traitor in our midst or had the Flight really flown in to judge the Succae with little in the way of detailed knowledge of their gods? It seemed unlikely but I was a lowly soldier when we arrived and knew little of the battle plans of princes and generals. I couldn't help but recall Lytta pausing and turning that votive coin, left in the statue's stone maw, over and over in her hand. I needed to talk to her again but that would mean going back down the Tether.

I was glad I still had business in the Gardens to attend to, for the thought of getting back to where Rain could be easily acquired already had my mouth dry and my mind racing. If she was still around, could Yggael's influence stretch into our own ranks? The thought conjured images of a nightmare creature, hidden in moon shadow, waiting to re-ascend, cold scales uncoiling in the darkness.

Chapter Thirteen

"What does traveller mean?" Sariel asked as we flew towards the Landing's southern gates and the building that Hostmann had visited before his untimely demise. It was the language of the Princes and truth be told, I wasn't entirely certain of the right answer.

"I am guessing Sari, but I think it means that Yggael had powers that allowed her to exist in multiple worlds at once. Either that or she's a powerful entity we have encountered before but managed to escape. Either way, if you pardon the pun, she is a slippery character."

As a younger soldier I had presumed the process of judgement was infallible, but over time I had seen similarities in the pantheons of the gods we faced and realised that some were indeed the same entities we had already defeated. To them, judgement was just a setback. There were always other places to either escape to or exist in as long as they had worshippers willing to sacrifice for them. One face, many masks, as Cam had once wisely said. We had met similar divinities but Yggael and the Succae gods in general had an odd feel about them, as if what you saw on the surface was not really the truth of what lay beneath. In Ischae's company I had learnt more in a few weeks about the real Succae than we had learnt in a hundred years of fighting. That the same could be said of the gods they had left behind seemed a certainty.

The drinking hall was the same under the hazy blue skies of the afternoon as it had been in the rainy night. Huddled in the shadow of the walls and shuttered to the outside world, it had a hulking, brooding presence not at all in keeping with the persona that had once dwelled within. I had been careful to keep quiet about the place when Pesak and his fellow watchers questioned me so that I could search it for myself without interference.

"Not the friendliest of places," Sariel said, landing in the alleyway that led to the dead end of the city wall. I nodded and pushed against the door I had seen Hostmann emerge from the night before. It was firmly shut and did not show any sign of giving way.

"Maybe there's another way in around the back," Sari said fluttering upwards and over the roof.

"No there isn't," I grumbled, putting all my weight against the door, and giving it a good shove again, only to get the same stubborn resistance.

"Are you sure?" Sariel's voice came from nearby.

"Of course. I checked when I followed Hostmann here last night."

"Well, you might want to come and take a look at this anyway."

I sighed and flew to where Sari stood staring at a thin doorway on the other side of the building. The passage in-between this side of the drinking house and its neighbour was so narrow I had to squeeze along from the far end to get to the door but for Sariel's childlike stature it was an easy shuffle.

"Well, it was dark, and it was raining," she said with an amicable grin, making me feel more than a little foolish. I tried pushing this door and it swung open with barely a sound. It was dark inside, but my eyes immediately adjusted.

"Stay here," I said, spear in hand as I crossed the threshold.

The first thing that hit me was the smell. The place reeked of wine, a heady aroma that was all pervasive. Inside, the long hall was a scene of devastation. Long trestle tables had been overturned and arcane looking apparatus smashed and broken. Glass crunched under the heel of my boot, the remains of dozens of bottles strewn across the floor. It looked like the destruction had been methodical and deliberate, an attempt to cover up whatever Hostmann had been up to here, but it had been done in a hurry and as I studied the wreckage, a clear picture began to emerge.

Hostmann had been in the process of refining or blending a wine. At the street end of the hall, I found several baskets with the remains of grape stem trampled and crushed, the grapes themselves no doubt pressed and fermented very quickly by Hostmann's powers.

Further down, in a series of flasks and filtering equipment, a red residue of the actual wine remained. I dabbed a little on my tongue, but it tasted unremarkable to me, and I shrugged as Sariel pulled a face.

She had wandered in and was looking at the last stage of the process, where the end product had presumably been bottled. On first inspection, it looked innocuous, predictable even. It was hardly a revelation that a former god of revelry and feast should be involved in the production of wine. Yet something had clearly been going on that had given him cause for concern. I remembered his face dropping like a stone when I told him about Naschinne's death. Someone had used him, and he hadn't liked it, someone who probably lived in the White Acropolis above, for that was surely where Hostmann was headed when he was murdered.

"Look, there's a down," Sariel said, breaking me from my

thoughts. I went to where she was standing at the wall end of the hall and peered down a wide ramp with smooth stone flooring at the bottom. I dropped down as quietly as I could and looked around.

Three giant barrels set on their sides against the left-hand wall dominated the chamber below. Each had a tap and I tried them in turn, but they were all dry. At the far end of the room a few smaller barrels sat empty, the fresh wood of the interior proof that they had never been used. Although I could see well enough in the dark, it was hard to make out fine detail. I fashioned Nimrod into a sword, releasing its dark fire that lit up the blade and illuminated the area. My burning blade flickered in the reflection from clear bottles of an amber spirit that sat on the shelf on the right-hand wall, dozens of pinpricks of golden light. I knelt, studied the floor, and promptly realised what had been bothering me. A layer of dust, dirt and residue lay across the stone floor as far as the unused barrels. There, the flagstones were cleaner, unblemished by the day to day, presumably protected by more barrels that were now missing. I stood back and tried to estimate exactly how many might have filled the space, but before my mind could settle on a figure, I heard Sariel scream in terror.

I ascended as fast as I could to find her hiding in the eaves of the building.

"What is it? What's wrong?"

"Something moved," she said, her eyes wide with fear. I stared down at the rubbish strewn floor but saw nothing with my regular senses. I blinked and looked again through violet eyes that saw only where life was present. That's when I saw them and nearly got myself skewered. There were two dark green ophidian shapes, long and sinuous, slithering softly on the floor below. They passed in and out of my sight, reptilian skin concealed by the debris through which they moved with a deliberate slowness. I thought they were trying to get directly beneath us when they both suddenly coiled and launched at us. I would like to say I was ready but in truth it was a sheer instinctive reaction as my blade moved in a blur and cut the pair in two in mid-flight. The tails fell to the floor, but the heads carried on past us and bounced off the ceiling, leaving ichor that scorched the wood. My sight returned to normal as the severed halves writhed on the ground and I breathed a sigh of relief.

I turned to Sariel and was about to suggest leaving but she was not paying any attention to me. With a trembling hand she pointed past me, and I turned to see for myself. From the bloody wounds new growth emerged, restoring the creatures to life. New heads emerged covered in gore, new tails grew on severed heads and soon, where there had been two, four now moved. It took less than a minute before they were flying in our direction, and I just managed to buffet them off course with my wings as they launched again. They crashed to the floor, and I followed them down, hacking and slicing at the sliding serpents that hissed and wove around me. Again, they regenerated, this time faster than before, and I shouted at Sariel to get away as four became eight and eight quickly became sixteen. I was covered in snake blood, narrowly avoiding flat-headed strikes from sharp fangs that dripped with green venom.

Things were getting desperate quickly, and I felt the first bite sink into my flesh as I retreated up into the rafters. Sariel hid behind me as I felt poison course through my system, bringing a numbing sensation to my head as if I had suddenly been plunged into ice-cold water. Snakes shot past us, some missing, some parried, and I had no choice. I wrapped Sariel in my wings and together we plummeted down the ramp into the basement and a dead end.

I pushed Sariel on towards the end of the dark chamber and the few unused barrels. My mind was shutting down slowly, but the glint of my flaming sword in the amber bottles racked along the wall caught my eye. I could hear Sariel screaming as the serpents poured down the ramp. I could hear them, scales scraping on stone, and from my own throat an ululating war scream joined Sariel's voice, a primal howl of anger and fear. The bottles rattled as our voices combined in pitch and then they shattered, showering the entire room and everything that came towards us in glass and pure alcohol. The last thing I remember was the world exploding in fire and the hiss of serpents becoming the crackle of roasting flesh as we were all consumed in the conflagration.

Chapter Fourteen

It was dark by the time I awoke, naked between fresh sheets that had the scent of a wild hedgerow in summer. I knew I was in the Red Roof Inn; the shutters open to the starless night, and I tried to sit up, only to find my limbs stiff and painful.

"It will take some time for the Lishi venom to work its way out of your system," Lytta said, her pale face looming out of the shadows like a ghost, "and until it does, you should rest." She looked down at me, impassive mask replaced by a frown.

"Where is Sariel?" I asked.

"The child?"

"She's not a child, she's a cherub."

"She looks like a child. She is asleep in the next room."

"Asleep? Is she hurt?"

"No. The dryad made it so. Apparently your 'cherub' was hysterical when she brought you here, so she did it for her own good. How did you survive the fire?"

"We're born of fire and wield it like others breathe air. It can't harm us. I need to see Sari," I said trying to stand up, only to find my legs were frozen and I collapsed to the floor. Lytta stared down at me.

"You could have said something," I growled accusingly, pulling myself back up on to the bed. She raised an eyebrow but said nothing. I manifested wings to cover my nakedness and she walked to the window, her penetrating gaze off me at last.

"Naschinne's mourning period is over then?" I asked and she gave a barely perceptible nod in return.

"What happens when you die?" she said, and I looked at her in surprise although her back remained turned to me.

"Why do you want to know?"

"I have lived in many times, worn many faces but throughout I have always been conscious of who I am. Vessels of flesh always await me as need arises, and I honour their sacrifice and protect their bodies as well as I can, but your kind have one body to safeguard from beginning to end. Is that right?"

"Unless we are slain there is no end, but otherwise yes. Why do you ask?"

"It seems you like to place yourself in harm's way. I just wondered if you were trying to hasten to a better life beyond the flesh?"

I felt a flush of hot denial spring forward, but the words died on my lips as I remembered how and where we had first met.

"If you're asking me if I have a death wish, the answer is no."

She turned and stared at me for a moment, and I held her gaze until she turned back to look out on the street below. I had the feeling she didn't really believe me, but I knew there was no point issuing continual denials. I would have to show her my words were true, and that would only come with time, so I decided to change the subject.

"When you saved me, I saw you pick up a token from Yggael's statue. What was it?"

"It was a votive amulet, an offering to the Old Gods."

"You mean a blessing?"

"Not necessarily. Amulets are used for many reasons. Worship, appeasement, fear."

"Does she still exist? Yggael, I mean. Could she be awakened?"

"No. Yggael was destroyed in the war. I saw her die with my own eyes."

Lytta's voice tailed off at the end of her sentence and I felt there was something more, something she didn't want to say.

"But?"

"The Lishi are her children. It is unfortunate you burned them all up. I would like to have seen one of their corpses for myself."

"Isn't the state I'm in proof enough?"

"There is what is and what appears to be. Without a body, I cannot say for certain."

"You're saying that if they were really live Lishi, we should count Yggael as being back from the dead?"

"I am not saying that at all. The Lishi lived on without their mother and there were many of them even when I was last in flesh."

"It has been my experience that gods have an uncanny way of surviving against the odds," I said with a grimace as I tried to spread my wings.

"It has been my experience that whatever I slay stays slain," she said simply but the look on her face made me think she didn't entirely believe her own words.

We sat silent for a while as the feeling in my legs began to return. I have never liked silence, though, and it wasn't long before I felt the need to fill the void, so I told her all that had happened, from my initial meeting with Hostmann through to the events at his hall. I left out my discussion with Darophon mainly out of circumspection and deference.

She said nothing as I spoke, only asking questions when I had finished and then purely about the Ashai and Jasniz's regular appearances in the duty logs. I told her everything I knew and saw that look of internal doubt cross her face again as she returned to her vigil by the window.

She paused for a moment, clearly deciding whether I could be trusted with whatever it was that was troubling her.

"What you describe is familiar to me; the sudden arrival and departure of the Ashai. That is how the armies of the Old Gods attacked in the wars, with speed and surprise on their side."

"I don't know if he arrived that way but that is certainly how he left. We know Yggael as a traveller. In our language that means she may have the power to move between worlds or exist in several of them at one time. Maybe she can do the same for her followers."

Lytta didn't reply but I could tell I had her thinking.

"What about the Ashai and these Low-Nin who willingly let him murder them in cold blood?" I said. "Do you know anything about that?"

She shook her head, tight black braid bouncing over her shoulder.

"I do not. Low-Nin did not exist in the time I was last in flesh."

I remembered what Ischae had said about the lowest strata of Succae society in the time we had been together.

"Well, I think I do. The Low-Nin have no expectations for this life but if they can distinguish themselves in service to a Vod or Master, they can expect to return as a full servant in the life to come. That's why they surrendered to this Ashai without fear. It was their only chance for advancement."

Lytta looked lost and I suddenly realised what bonded us together. In many ways we were both aliens in our own societies, she an anachronism out of time and me a tolerated outcast among my own people and an unwelcome intruder among hers.

"Let's talk about Jasniz," I said, and she looked at me curiously.

"Who?"

"The man who abducted me. You saved me from his servants on the night we first met."

"I saved you from a Flensman," she said.

"Yes, but it was Jasniz that took me to him."

"I wasn't told that. Only to go to the Forest Temple and free anyone held there."

"I have heard of the Flensmen before. They are banned, aren't they?"

"Yes. It's because they are pagans, followers of the Old Gods. Karsz does not tolerate such dissent."

"Did Karsz know I was there?"

"I do not know. You would need to ask him."

It was a question I had not really considered before. Why had Karsz chosen to intervene? Maybe Jasniz was an agent of a pagan resistance and I had just been in the right place at the right time when he had chosen to break that movement up. It all seemed like too much of a coincidence, though, and just as Naschinne and Ischae's deaths now looked likely to be connected, so my own near miss was beginning to look like another part of the puzzle. Jasniz was clearly much more than he had seemed to be and held many of the puzzle's missing pieces.

"I intend to find him," I said with more confidence than I felt.

Pain shot through my body as I tried to stand again. I cried out but Lytta dignified the moment by pretending nothing had happened.

"As the water rises, the ship rises too," she said cryptically, turning her back on me to look down on the night-shrouded street below.

Chapter Fifteen

"Captain Varael apologises but he cannot see you now, Ambassador." I looked at the junior guardsman who had been sent as messenger and sighed, knowing both he and the message he carried were intended as insults.

"Very well. I'll wait until he is available," I said, clearly surprising the youth, who hadn't expected to be taking a message back to his commander. I smiled sweetly as confusion swept through him like a sudden sandstorm, obscuring clarity of vision and purpose.

"You'll wait here?" he asked, once he'd decided not to follow the orders Varael had likely given him, to watch us like a hawk.

"Of course," I lied.

I waited a few moments after he left for the Command quarters in the Keep's central tower before opening the door and easing out into the main courtyard.

"I thought you said we were going to wait here," Lytta said, looking at my smirk with some confusion.

"Quickest way to get Varael to talk to us is for us to go talk to his troops. Nothing a commander hates more."

It had been two days since Sariel had pulled me from Hostmann's blazing cellar and I was nearly fully recovered from the poison that had swollen every joint and made my every move an exercise in pain. In between, I'd had a tearful reunion with Sariel, and a stern lecture on personal safety from Benazzarr and Camael. All the while, Lytta had been my ever-watchful shadow. She had not said much since our initial discussion, but it was clear that she was thinking, her head full of thoughts that she would not or could not share. I wasn't sure how that made me feel, but I knew the reserved nature of the Succae did not allow for idle speculation, and I hoped that meant that when the occasion warranted it or evidence turned theory into fact, she would speak up. In the meantime, I was following the path I had available and that brought me to my former command, the white walls of Vigil Keep.

The main courtyard was a hive of activity with craftsmen in the process of creating great wooden structures around the site. The sound of saws and hammers busy at their tasks filled the air, whilst at the four corners of the yard, grand marquees were being erected. The ones closest to the Tether were dressed in Succae colours, whilst those at the Horta Magna end were decorated with those of Prince Anael. I could see several Heralds directing the work and ambled their direction, hooded Lytta just a few steps behind me. As I drew closer to the centre of the yard and the place where the Heralds and their attendant cherubim were hard at work, I noted a queue of Succae waiting to depart the Keep and head to the Tether.

"What's going on over there?" I said to Lytta as she drew level with me.

"I don't know, but I'll go and find out," she said, pulling her hood down and striding over to where her people waited in patient silence as Varael's guards spoke to each in turn before letting them pass out the main gates to the passage back to their home.

I climbed the steps on to the scaffold when one of the Heralds looked up and saw I was not one of Varael's soldiers.

"Can I help you?" he said, his attention diverted from what looked like an overall plan of the Keep.

"Just checking that all is in order Herald…?" I let my question hang in the air.

"Misano," he replied uncertainly.

"Herald Misano! Yes of course."

"I'm sorry but I do not know who you are," he said bluntly as I stood next to him and looked at the drawings laid out on the table in front of him. I was about to haughtily deliver my title of Ambassador to the Succae under the Prince's warrant, when a deep voice I recognised interrupted me.

"He's trouble is what he is."

"Inias!" I said, turning to greet my former Sergeant, whose cold, chiselled features and shaven head had greeted me every morning, noon, and night when the Keep had been under my command.

"Azshael," he said with a smile, "what are you doing here and does Varael know?"

I walked down from the scaffold and clasped my old adjutant on the shoulder.

"Inias, Inias. Always doing your duty. That's what I always admired about you, my friend. Your commitment and loyalty are second to none."

Inias frowned for the briefest of moments.

"If this is about the other night, I am sorry, but Varael saw you before I could intervene."

I sighed. "Think nothing of it my old friend. I was as much to blame as anyone else. Anyway, to answer your question, I am here to speak with Varael, who has been told I am here but is apparently too busy to talk to me. So, what is going on here?"

Inias looked hesitant for a moment, then shrugged.

"It is no secret, least not as I have been told. In just a few days, the twentieth anniversary of the Accord is to be celebrated here, on the site where the peace was agreed. There is to be a grand gathering of the great and the good of the Flight and the Succae as well."

I did my best not to look surprised. It was the first I had heard of such an event and I was certain it would put pressure on my inquiry to deliver answers quickly.

"The Prince has ordered the Keep to be divided into two with the Garden side for him and his guests and the Tether side for the Succae. Here in the centre, a banqueting Hall is to be built, though I know not what their kind will feast upon for I ne'er saw one of them pass food beyond their lips."

"I imagine they will drink," I replied dryly.

"Well, you know far more than I do Azsh. All I know is that the Heralds are driving Varael mad with all their demands and requirements. He's a moody one at the best of times but this has pushed him over the edge. The entire garrison is on tenterhooks."

As if on cue, Varael's angry voice echoed across the courtyard and I felt sorry for the guardsman I had misled, at least for a few seconds.

"Do you know a Succae by the name of Jasniz? He is a Free Trader, comes through the gates regularly." I produced a scroll that Sariel had drawn for me. It was a good likeness of the Succae whose face had become burned into my memory and Inias immediately recognised him.

"Yes, I know him, although I've not seen him recently. He used to pass through a few times a week, but I can't say I've seen him in several weeks now." He paused and was about to add something more when Varael shouted his name across the courtyard and Inias looked at me apologetically, taking flight to go at once to his Commander's side. Varael had just emerged from the tower where we had first been ensconced and I watched him pointing at me as Inias's scalp turned a deeper shade of red.

"They're frightened," Lytta whispered into my ear as she suddenly appeared beside me. Her soft breath on my ear made me flush inside.

"I think it looks more like anger," I said in return, before I realised she was talking about the departing Succae rather than the approaching Commander of the Keep and his followers.

"Why?"

"Rumours."

"What rumours?"

"That the Old Gods walk again and punish those that live among the enemy."

"They said that?"

"They did. They knew Naschinne's name and believe her death is a warning to all Succae."

"I wonder who started that story going round. Whoever it was, we should find them."

Lytta didn't say anything more as Varael marched up to me, his face an ill-concealed mask of contempt.

"Ah Commander Varael," I said with a smile, taking some of the wind out of his sails.

"What do you want here Azshael? You have no right to question my people without referring to me first."

I looked him straight in the eye and our gazes locked, neither of us turning away for what seemed like an age.

"You're right of course," I said with a sigh, and I felt Lytta stiffen beside me.

"Please accept my apologies as a friend and brother." I extended my hand in the Angel warrior clasp and Varael looked at it as if it was a rotten piece of meat. He turned and dismissed his troops, except for Inias who fell in alongside Lytta as he walked away from the scaffold and the eyes and ears of the Heralds.

"Just get on with it," he said gruffly as soon as we were what he judged to be far enough away.

"Thank you, Varael. The Prince appreciates your co-operation and so do I."

He looked at me warily as I showed him the scroll I had already shown to Inias.

"You recognise this Succae?"

Varael gave the drawing a cursory glance and studied Lytta before answering.

"Yes. His name is Jasniz."

I glanced at Inias who looked away as soon as my eyes met his.

"Then you know he is a regular visitor to the Keep. I just wondered if you'd ever seen him leave. The duty logs of departures aren't all that detailed."

Varael shrugged, "I don't remember. Unless an individual is brought to my attention, I don't generally notice. One Succae looks much like another to me."

"So Jasniz never came to your attention, yet you know his name?"

Caught in contradiction, Varael folded his arms and looked at the ground before admitting what I already knew.

"Inias told me his name."

"So before today, you would never have known Jasniz's name, correct?"

"Yes. What's all this about Azshael?"

"He's a suspect in the death of at least two high caste Succae. If he passes through again, you are to hold him and send word to me at once. Now you both know who he is, I'll hold both of you responsible. Understand?" I said with a touch more venom than I intended, and I saw Inias blanch at the rebuke whilst Varael remained stony-faced.

"I'll add it to the duty orders," Varael said, clearly unimpressed with my implied threat. "Now if that's all, there are important matters to attend to," he said, staring at me before turning and marching off leaving us alone with Inias.

"Nothing changes I see," I said softly, and Inias grinned briefly.

"One thing, Inias. How did you know Jasniz's name?"

"We spoke a few times on his way through."

"About what?"

"The Flight, the Landing. All sorts of things really."

"You ever see him head back down the Tether?"

Inias paused and shook his head before Varael yelled his name.

"Now you come to mention it, I can't say that I did. See you around Azsh."

I patted my old adjutant on the shoulder as he flew back to Varael's side.

Lytta studied my face.

"They're lying," she said.

"About what?"

"Everything."

"How do you know?"

"Their blood runs faster."

Chapter Sixteen

"I don't know what to say," Sangael said, auburn locks framing a sad-looking face. We were standing in Chorael's sphere, or rather a version of it, for it had changed substantially since my last visit—and I cursed myself for not having ventured here as soon as Darophon had indicated he was not responsible for some of the now missing features. Gone was the hollow beneath the hill in which Naschinne's body had been found. Also gone, any evidence of the party in the ruins. I had given someone the time and opportunity to sanitise places that, at the time, I had thought would always be available for re-inspection.

"How could they have got past you again?" I asked the Seraph wearily. It was about the tenth time I had asked the same question since we'd come back here, but if Sangael was irritated by the repetition, he showed no sign of it.

"I maintain what I said before, Azshael. It is not possible. The watch was doubled on the House as a whole and a member of my Order stood watch outside the First Herald's sphere all the time."

"What about inside?"

"The inside of the sphere was checked every dawn and dusk."

"Didn't do a very good job then, did they?"

Sangael pursed his lips and looked thoughtful. I turned and whispered to Lytta, my silent shadow.

"Is his blood running faster?"

"No," she replied although I knew from experience that Seraphs were very different to ordinary Angels, representing a higher state of Angelic development. I wondered if that meant they could lie with impunity and whether that was, perhaps, our evolutionary pinnacle; Angels who could lie so beautifully and deceive so perfectly that everyone would believe them and actually prefer deception to the truth.

"Is it not possible that whoever came here did so directly?" Sangael said.

It was an interesting thought and I wondered where it had come from.

"You mean straight into the sphere, without going into the House? Who do you know that can do that, Seraph?"

"No-one. I merely propose it as a possibility. I have been thinking about how the Succae female got here in the first place, and with several companions. I do not think it likely they could have evaded detection any other way."

He had a point of course, except for one key detail.

"Only the Angels that built it can re-shape a sphere. Isn't that right?"

"As far as I know, yes."

"You're saying that both the Succae and one of the Host came here directly?"

"I am just saying it is a possibility."

"How do you know that?"

"It remains the only logical explanation."

"It's not the *only* explanation. You could be lying."

Sangael shook his head and smiled.

"Why would I do that, Azshael?"

I didn't have an answer, so I turned and left.

Later, at the Red Roof, I sat in a corner with Lytta and tried to think through what I had learned. It was an amalgam of shreds and patches that on their own didn't amount to a great deal. Naschinne and Ischae had died in the same manner and had standing in Succae society, but after that, all similarities ended. Ischae had died alone in her own home, whilst Naschinne had died in the presence of others in Chorael's sphere. Neither had any obvious connection to Hostmann, although I supposed it was possible their paths could have crossed at some time or other. Neither had any obvious connection to Yggael or her possibly resurrected cult either, at least not that we knew.

"Rain," Lytta said quietly, bringing me out of my own mental labyrinth.

"What about it?"

"It is the one thing that connects the two killings. You and Ischae took it together for pleasure and so it seems, did Naschinne."

It was a good point and something I had not thought of before, but like the first drop of rain soon becomes a deluge, connections flooded into focus.

"Jasniz supplied Rain to Ischae and I. He also had me abducted and nearly murdered in a temple to your Old Gods. I feel it stronger than ever now. Whether he killed them or not, he clearly has answers we need."

Lytta nodded slowly, "I agree, and Succae somewhere are sheltering him."

So, I would have to go back down the Tether then. I felt my courage falter briefly as visions of the black toothed Priest who nearly took my life filled my mind. They were swiftly replaced, however, by Ischae's pale face contorted in death, and I felt cold sweat as undiminished rage coursed through my core.

Part Two

Chapter One

A serried rank of masked Ashai awaited us on the steps of the Shadow Citadel, a place of sharp angles and edges, cold and uninviting. Lytta slipped from the back of her Shadowdrake and marched past them as I landed beside her, my hands firmly gripping Nimrod, my war spear. I had opted to wear full armour too, not for any other reason than a healthy fear that we were both literally and metaphorically descending into a snake pit.

Sarzh stepped out of the shadows to greet us. I say us, but really his attention and words were aimed at Lytta and his tone bristled with negativity.

"Serrate, you honour us with your presence. How may I be of service to you?"

"We have questions for you, Lord of Scarpe, Ashai Prime."

Sarzh was one of those rare Succae, someone I could actually read, who wore his emotions relatively openly, at least for one whose race was generally enigmatic to a fault. He was also short, muscular and Karsz's right hand man, which made him seven shades of deadly in all sorts of ways. I could tell he was nervous about our appearance here, especially Lytta, of whom I could see he was wary. I very much doubted we were as welcome as she had predicted, but this was her world not mine, so I let her take the lead.

Sarzh led us into the keep, a pair of his Shadow Ashai bringing up the rear. He glanced backwards occasionally as we marched down wide sweeping stairwells into the heart of the citadel, and I saw revulsion in his eyes. Great obsidian doors opened ahead of us, and he stopped and turned, beckoning Lytta to one side. Their exchange was short but pointed in a dialect of Succae that I could barely understand. I saw the Serrate's fists clench, and she turned her back on Sarzh, who went on ahead, doors closing behind him to leave us outside.

"Something you said?" I inquired with a smile, but her face didn't soften.

"The Lord is having the chamber prepared," was all she said, and all she would say in the time we waited there. I could sense her frustration and guessed that she had taken whatever Sarzh had said as an insult. Yet there was more to it than that. It was bewilderment, I thought, a sense of alienation, something we continued to have in common.

Eventually the doors to the receiving chamber were thrown open, and hooded servants fell to their knees to form lines on our left and right. A few held offerings above their heads, and Lytta indicated to me that the right side was mine. The first Low-Nin I came to held a copper bowl filled with warm scented water, and I removed my gauntlets and washed my hands, taking in the surroundings. It was a high vaulted chamber, with the entire focus being the raised dais at the far end where Sarzh sat in a deep wooden chair. The air was heavy with incense, and a table laden with burners and the accoutrements of ceremonial welcome sat just beneath the Lord of Scarpe's seat.

I walked forward and knelt on a worn leather pad beneath the dais, removing tarnished silver greaves before doing so. Nimrod leant against my shoulder as I made myself as comfortable as I could. Lytta took her place next to me, her face concealed by a silver mask and lead shackles on both her wrists held together by a thin black chain. I had no doubt she could snap that chain in the blink of an eye should she wish to, and I wondered what kind of game Sarzh was playing with an entity who had no doubt seen many of his kind come and go. It felt like a powerplay, a reminder of who was in charge. If that were the case, it looked more like desperation to me, an act that made him look weak and clumsy. True power is wielded—it doesn't need to be pointed out in the process.

A staring match ensued, something I had observed before in Succae society, but never at this level. The Succae believe their lives, (such as they are for immortal vampires) are a series of challenges wherein their spirit can gain strength or be weakened by those they encounter. It is called the Game of Lao and Zi, and every Succae plays it all the time. The higher ranks do so to maintain their status. The lower attempt to attain a higher rank in their next incarnation. That Sarzh was willing to challenge a Serrate spoke volumes; he was either more powerful than he looked, or he was a fool. Either way, we didn't have time for games, so I came straight to the point, earning reproachful glares from both of them. Well, my Lao and Zi are just fine.

"We came to speak with you about Rain," I said, clearly surprising the Ashai Prime, who blinked in momentary confusion as he focussed his attention on me.

"Rain? The drug? What about it?"

"What it is, where it comes from, who uses it, and why. Those would be good starting points," I said with as genuine a smile as I could muster. Sarzh sat back in his wooden seat and the ghost of a sly grin played along the edges of his mouth making the sea of tattoos on his scalp writhe and twist as taut skin stretched even tighter.

"Would that be a personal interest, Ambassador? I am not here to be your guide, or your supplier." The barb stung but not that badly, so I decided to ignore it.

"It has become a focus point in the matter of the untimely demise of your master's concubine, Naschinne. As I am tasked with uncovering the truth, I suppose you could say it was personal, although given we all ultimately do the Vod's bidding, perhaps the better phrase would be 'mutual interest'?"

Sarzh grunted.

"Spoken like a true Ambassador. Very well, let's talk about Rain."

What followed was a discussion around the topic of Rain. It was clear in Sarzh's own self-important way that he wished he did know more, but in practical terms there was not much he told me I did not already know. Rain was a drug of leisure used originally by the High-Nin as a relaxant but had spread across Succae society in the past few years. The Vod officially frowned on its use by Low-Nin, but it was not thought to be addictive or dangerous, at least to the Succae. Its popularity had grown after the Accord, although Sarzh was vague in terms of actual dates, and it was unknown before then. So, the general message seemed to be that as long as it didn't cause any trouble, it was tolerated.

"What about its makeup? What is Rain actually made of?"

Sarzh shrugged. "I would have thought you would know more of that than I do but, in our language, the phrase means 'Fire and Water'. As far as I know, it has never been examined except by those who make it, and much of the Rain that is consumed is less than pure."

"How would you know that?"

"I remember when it first arrived among the High-Nin—people spoke of days of ecstasy. Hardly the case today, is it?"

"Suppliers? Who deals in this?"

"Probably the Low-Tsars," Sarzh said, the word rolling around his mouth like a sour grape. "When it comes to anything illicit, they are usually the source."

I had run out of questions and turned to Lytta as the room became silent. She was still staring at Sarzh as if their game of

Lao and Zi had never stopped. Sarzh looked suddenly agape in horror as he realised, and beneath her veil, I thought I saw the corners of her mouth crinkle in a smile.

Chapter Two

From previous experience, I knew Low-Tsars liked relative anonymity, purely as a mechanism of survival. These leaders of the Low-Nin were tolerated by the Vod on the basis that they kept the seething masses of the lower castes occupied, which meant no-one else needed to worry about them. Succae society was predatory by nature, and from what I'd heard it wasn't unusual for the status quo to be swept away at a moment's notice dependent on only the Vod himself. Over history, the Low-Tsars had clearly learned that to be available yet not easily found was a good policy.

"Any ideas?" I asked Lytta as we walked through one of the busy shadow markets near the citadel. "There is one I know called Tzir," she said as she took a shrunken white fruit from one of the stalls, allowing the seller to touch her hand in return. I watched as she drew the little energy that remained in it until it was a desiccated husk.

"He and I fought with each other," she went on to say, somewhat ambiguously until she saw me smirking.

"Is that how you say it?"

"I think alongside each other is clearer. If that's what you mean."

She thought for a moment and then nodded slightly. "Mostly that, yes."

"Where is this Tzir now? How do we find him?"

"I don't know, but I have heard his name mentioned around the outer edge of the city. I should be able to get someone there to tell me where he is."

"Well let's go then," I said, keen to be free of the confines of the caverns and labyrinthine tunnels of Scarpe's underground. She turned smartly on her heel, her braid nearly whipping me in the face.

"Not a place for you," she said, and I felt a flare of resentment flush through me. I was about to protest about having taken her places in my world where none of her kind would ever have been allowed, but she just put a finger to my lips, and I knew there was no point.

"If they see you, none of them will speak and we will learn nothing. It is better this way. Do you have somewhere you can wait for a few hours? You can return to the citadel and wait in my quarters if you wish."

It was an interesting offer, but I had other ideas and I told her I would meet her back at the market the following morning. Her eyes betrayed doubt about the wisdom of leaving me to my own devices, but I smiled reassuringly and told her to go. And so she did, her slender form disappearing into the ever dark of Scarpe's gloom.

It was quite a relief to be alone. I pulled my hood up and shuffled along with the crowds, rubbing shoulders with high and low caste Succae as I made my way back past the citadel square and down into the city's second tier. Only the top part of the citadel itself was open to the moon's thin atmosphere, along with what remained of the old settlements above ground, home to the poorest Low-Nin or those with good reasons to live above rather than below.

Off the central tunnels, hewn pathways led to residences that had been carved into the earth and rock, and I followed a familiar trail until I came to the towering manse that I had shared with Ischae, standing alone at the end of a narrow track. I peered over the lip to see the widening tiers of

Succae society below. The lower the tier, the darker it became.

I paused on the threshold, not certain if my actions were wise. I had not really planned to come back here for fear of awakening ghosts and demons, but on reflection, who was I kidding? They had been with me since the news of her death had come to me, and now I knew they would never leave until I had done whatever was necessary to find peace within myself. I reached for the cord around my neck and pulled it free. At its centre, an onyx ring had been bound and I untied it ready to push into the slot that would open the lock on the door. As soon as I put my hand on the stone frame, however, it gave under my weight and opened a crack. Surprised, I pushed again, and the door swung open further.

Dark shadows retreated as I allowed the corona of light that always surrounds me to grow. It revealed a familiar monochrome lobby, a place of black and white marble that stretched away to a wide sweeping staircase in its centre. I paused for a moment, allowing the full sweep of memory to catch up with me. For months, this had been my home, although at first it had felt stifling and cramped in comparison with my usual retreat. There is something about Angelic memory that is untrustworthy. Perhaps it is a survival mechanism of such long lives that our way is not to remember all the days we have known, but instead just selected highs and lows. Here had held both types for me, although most of the highs were eclipsed by the one great low that had turned a home into a tomb, a palace into a mausoleum, and a living space into a memorial.

I went from chamber to chamber in a kind of silent reverie, awaiting a deluge of sorrow that I expected would overwhelm and drown me in bitter tears. Yet it did not come. Instead, there was a curious feeling of intense detachment as

I passed quietly through each room and hallway. What was I seeking? Probably an act of closure in a place I had fled from when I should have stayed and sought answers to the identity of Ischae's killer. Perhaps those answers had once been here but now they were long gone, and in their place something sinister awaited me.

I was in our sleeping chamber at the top of the palace, the place where I had previously found my lifeless Succae love wrapped in a silken shroud before I realised something was very definitely wrong. I trod gently on the black sheets that still lay in disarray, pooling out from the bed itself, and it was then I saw the thin film of green dust that had gathered on the soles of my boots. It had laid its imprint upon the material, and as my mind realised it was there and had begun to process its meaning, I felt the world growing distant as I fell facedown into Ischae's bower. The world slowed as my face impacted with the bed and I fancied I could see more motes of green dust hanging in the air, each one the spore of a narcotic that held me fully in its grip. My eyes slowly closed against my will.

I awoke with a crushing feeling in my chest and a thousand tiny pinpoints of light exploding in my head. I tried to move, but I was firmly pinned and being crushed into the bed upon which I had fallen. I managed to spit out the silk sheet in my mouth, only to feel the weight upon me press down harder. Whatever was attacking me was bigger and heavier. I was not going to prevail in the weightlifting stakes. The pressure of the weight on me intensified and I sank deeper into the bedding, my mind racing, desperate to see a way out of my predicament. But I couldn't think of anything. Soon, I was shrouded in silk and linen, unable to see anything, although I could feel pain registering all over my body as the increasing weight crushed against flesh and bone. It was a horrible way to die, I thought, as the pain grew. I had been a fool to come back to this place of death and I prayed for a swift release from the agony.

The bed snapped in a sudden splintering of the ancient wood from which it was built. For the briefest of moments, I was separated from my assailant. I shot forward and spread my wings, ascending towards the chamber ceiling so that I could see my attacker below. It was a writhing mass of grubby flesh, sewn together at the edges with black stitching. The flesh was veined with green strands and had stretched in places to the point of separation, viscous fluid weeping from the resulting wounds.

From my vantage point, I could see the scattered tiles of the mosaic floor beneath which it had lain in wait. My careless step had disturbed the dust that I guessed had somehow brought it to life. Now it rolled from the remains of the shattered bower, its grotesque bulk somehow propelling itself forward. It paused for a moment, and the entire mass shuddered and grew. Strange bulges rippled below the monster's skin, and tears in its flesh widened as it pooled itself and grew vertically, blindly pursuing me.

Corrupted flesh reached out for me, and I narrowly escaped its tainted grip. I was wary of being herded into a corner and retreated towards the dark-glassed arches of the outer chamber. The creature shuddered again and grew in volume before pooling and rocketing upwards in a vertical spike. The move surprised me, and I was too slow to avoid the tip of my left wing being caught, breaking bones and sending me spiralling to the ground in an ungainly heap. The flesh creature's momentum punched a hole through the ceiling and the roof beyond. Another shudder and weeping wounds bled freely as the thing bulged ominously. It strained against its seams, cracks striating across the stone floor under its massive weight.

I saw Nimrod glinting in the broken bower and called it to my hand. It blazed through the air, and I caught hold of it as the thing shambled towards me. I pointed it at the hole in the roof and it hoisted me upwards, beyond the creature's smothering grasp.

I paused briefly on the roof. Pain raced through my wing from where the bones had been pulverized but were now healing anew. My respite was short, however, as the roof exploded around me, the beast in hot pursuit; a mindless, pulsating, and relentless ooze that would not be denied. I was sent sprawling over the edge, narrowly grabbing the hooked wing of one of the gargoyles that decorated the building. I gave its impassive stone face a sour look for having singularly failed in its duty to ward off evil spirits.

I felt the Flesh Beast roll across the roof and looked up to see it loom over me, pausing only to shudder once more. This time, seams split and the monstrous mass leaked clouds of green gas. Huge rents appeared as it quivered and rocked from side to side. I let go, falling in space as it exploded, the force ripping through the front of the building. We all fell together, the gargoyle first among the shower of heavy masonry that followed me swiftly to the ground.

Chapter Three

What the gargoyle lacked in perimeter defence, it made up for by acting as a solid protector against the bits of debris that bounced around us, and I was relatively unscathed by the time I crawled free of the wreckage. It was still hours before I was due to meet with Lytta, so I decided to go to the last place I had seen Jasniz before the night he had tried to harvest my organs.

The Rain Dens were over in an area called the Reaches, on the northern outskirts of Scarpe's surface. The Reaches were a by-product of the peace accord and allowed the High-Nin to indulge in the sorts of things that would normally be frowned upon or completely forbidden in their normally strict society. It had started as a shanty town, but time had turned many of the structures into something more permanent. Over the years, as traffic back and forth on the Tether had grown, my kind had found their way here too, some to observe, some to partake, and some to perform. It was a place of masks, cloaks, and few questions that Ischae had introduced me to early on in our relationship. Then, it was mostly to share Rain and to listen to sad songs sung by Succae Sirens whose beautifully brittle tunes stayed with you longer than you might wish.

Jasniz's Rain Den was on the corner of one of the last streets before dark, brooding structures gave way to the broken rocky expanse beyond. I was surprised to see a dim blue light hanging outside the door, the sign that it was open. I fashioned Nimrod into a golden sword and belted it to my side. I was certain that there was no chance that Jasniz was here, but that didn't mean that trouble couldn't still be found within.

Pushing past a velvet curtain that had seen better days, I entered the narrow doorway and looked down familiar worn stone steps. Already, I fancied I could taste Rain in the air, and for a moment I hesitated, suddenly uncertain if this was such a good idea after all. I closed my eyes and immediately I was back in chains, imprisoned in that dark antechamber with the ghosts of poor, sacrificed Angels beating uselessly against the walls. My addiction had nearly cost me my life that night. Did I really want to risk venturing down that path again? I examined my feelings and drew on the inner anger that had characterised my existence since Ischae's death. I knew I was stronger and more driven now. I had to find answers, and risking everything for that, was a chance I was willing to take.

Ischae had once described Jasniz's Rain Den as a 'womb with a view' and not without good reason. Everywhere you turned, heavy brocade curtains screened private booths from prying eyes. Silk and gauze hangings needed to be penetrated before you arrived in a narrow passageway that opened up into a wide semi-circular space with a small, elevated stage at its centre and a bar to the rear.

The heady atmosphere was thick with a mix of narcotics that the Succae patrons used for a variety of blood effects, adjusting their moods as a result. Blackbark could be smoked or chewed and had a calming, world-slowing effect. Red Dust was its direct opposite, pumping blood faster, leaving them excitable and animated. It was usually sprinkled directly on an open vein but could also be snorted. As for the relative newcomer, Rain, it could be taken any number of ways, but Ischae and I had mixed it in a frothy white concoction called Venii made of fermented fruit and mashed tree bark. Trust me, it tasted better than it looked or sounded.

I looked around and from what I could see, things had either declined under the new management, or it was just a slow night. A relatively youthful-looking High-Nin Siren sat cross-legged on the stage, pale skin visible through the slits in her dark red velvet dress. She had long dark hair that flowed over her shoulders and back like a black waterfall. She was staring at me, and as soon as she noticed me looking back at her, she turned her attention to the steel instrument that she had been adjusting intently. She fitted silver talons to the ends of three of her long, delicate fingers and began to make her instrument sing. The notes passed through me with a metallic ripple and as she bent the strings, so I felt them seemingly crawl up and down my spine. I smiled and nodded at her, but she made no recognition of my appreciation of her artistry. Instead, she looked distant, in a world of her own as she began to sing a murder ballad, her voice startlingly pure in its tonality. I turned my back on her and made my way to the deserted bar even though I was sure artistic angst was being sent my direction.

I peered over the bar and was surprised to see no-one there, just an open hatch that presumably led down into a storage space below. It's an old joke in the Flight—give a Succae a perfectly good hole and they'll dig two more beneath it. Okay, perhaps it's not that great a joke but you get the idea. A tattooed scalp suddenly appeared, coming up and out of the hatch. There was something about it that seemed all wrong until I noted the puckered scarring at the edges of each of the tattoos. They were freshly carved, still lividly red. Kurr looked up at me, finally aware of the shadow looming over him. He was short, wiry and lean, the skin on his face so taut that his eyes were like slits, his expression naturally ugly and sly.

"Bozz," he said, smiling widely to reveal a mouth of broken teeth. I smiled back, realizing that the Low-Nin servant that Jasniz had treated like dirt had enjoyed a sudden elevation in standing. I looked more closely at the black script inscribed in flesh and saw Karsz's house tattoo repeated in the swirling design. Not only had Kurr gained status but he had also gained a protector too.

"Is this your place now Kurr?" I enquired and he grinned back, arms gesticulating wildly as he confirmed what I thought.

"Yez Bozz. Yazniz go and no come back so I stay. Not want go dak no, no. Kurr speak Sarzz, Sarzz speak Vod and Vod take Kurr and place. See?"

I did see although I was surprised. I guessed that Kurr had been under Sarzh's influence a long time before Jasniz had disappeared. I wondered whether it was Kurr's information that had sent Lytta to my rescue that first night. It seemed unlikely that such a pitiful figure would spy on someone as dangerous as Jasniz, yet I was reminded of the Low-Nin's relative anonymity in their culture and their rapacious desire for status. Kurr had played a high stakes game and come out a winner, at least for now.

Kurr had always been quite animated, even in Jasniz's shadow. He had played the fool, always the butt of Jasniz's jokes and had often endured beatings that had shocked me. Ischae had led me out of the Den at times like that, knowing my instinct to intervene, but she would always say that unless I could adopt every Low-Nin there was, then such gestures would only worsen his lot. Low-Nin were that way for a reason, she said, and there was nothing that anyone could do about it. They were the lost souls, the undistinguished spirits that had no value until they themselves proved they were worthy of recognition. It was not something I could understand or relate to but it was also not in my gift to change the Succae culture overnight, so Kurr was left to his hellish existence until fortune intervened and brought freedom with it.

I spent some time talking to Kurr, and if Jasniz wasn't the topic of conversation, we got along fine. Whenever I brought his name back up, the diminutive Succae would scuttle off to check on his customers, leaving me alone, questions hanging heavily pregnant in the air. I couldn't blame him, for no doubt the Vod's protection came with a vow of silence. It was a given to Kurr that if the Vod wanted me to know something, a way to tell me would be found because that was the way of the High-Nin.

I leant against the cushioned bar and turned down Kurr's repeated attempts to sell me Rain. Instead, I drank unloaded Venii, its distinctive taste an initial sweet burn that slowly gave way to a pleasantly sour aftertaste. I was lost in thoughts and memories when the Siren came down off the stage and sat down next to me.

"I've been singing to you," she said, dark eyes locked in an accusatory stare. "Now I am thirsty and it's all your fault," she went on, crossing one long, lithe and shapely bare leg over the other, a very short velvet skirt riding ever so slightly further up her thigh as she did so. I couldn't help but smile and order her a drink.

Chapter Four

She said her name was Saaya as she led me to one of the Den's private booths. She was tall and elegant, her body more curvaceous than many Succae females, who tend to a bony gauntness that can become all too monotonous. Her face was painted white in the tradition of the Sirens, a small mouth framed in ruby lips. She had tied her black mane back into a tight bun, fastened in place by lacquered red sticks.

"I know who you are," she said, as she slid closer to me, "and why you're here."

"Is that so?" I replied a little too casually, given that I wasn't exactly sure myself. I was wondering what I was doing, that sense of being a spectator of my own life hitting me again.

"You're the one seeking Naschinne's killer, aren't you?" That got my attention.

"What would you know about that?"

"Everything and nothing," she replied enigmatically, leaning back away from me, and sipping provocatively from her goblet of Venii.

"Well, why don't you start with the everything and leave the nothing out?" I said, trying to be clever, but she neither smiled nor relaxed. Instead, she let a long silence grow uncomfortable as we stared at each other.

"Did you really love her?" she said finally.

"Naschinne?" I asked, perplexed.

"No. Ischae."

"With all my soul," I replied earnestly. She nodded and the silence returned in the all too familiar style of the Succae. I was about to give up when she slid back across the booth and kissed me voraciously. Whether it was the Venii or the melancholy of re-treading worn paths in desperate need of quenching, I cannot say but I yielded to the moment. I pulled her astride me and pushed her dress upwards revealing her naked body. Red flashed beneath her skin as her vampiric power stirred the blood inside, and it rushed to swell breasts and ooze from erect nipples that were thrust into my face. Her hair came down in braids that whipped me as she pursued ecstasy. I pulled her down and spread her legs wide. I freed myself from the constraints of my breeches, my sex engorged. Then I was inside her warmth, thrusting deep as slick streams of her blood cosseted my member. Her face became gaunt, the drain obvious in her features but she writhed and stared back, our animal-like grunts voiced in unison until I was spent. It was then I felt the reverse pull, as she drew life energy back from me. Ischae's pull had always been controlled but Saaya's was wild. I felt a surge of dozens of mortal years being stripped away and tried to free myself from her grasp, but her internal muscles clenched me tight, and the intensity of the moment was intoxicating, her gaze hypnotic. I felt weak as her body blossomed again and looked full of life before she suddenly let me go and I collapsed at her feet, weak and sated.

"I can see why she loved you," she said, straddling me again and leaning down to kiss me with lips now full and pliant. I avoided the kiss and she laughed.

"Feeling used, my poor little Angel?" She grinned briefly as she stood up and stretched languorously, the bounty of her refreshed body on full display. In a different time I would have felt lucky, but my single heart's staccato beat was a reminder that once again, I had walked blindly into trouble. She put her clothes back on and sat down, drinking deeply from the Venii, watching expectantly as I tried to recover what remained of my dignity.

"I was there when Naschinne was killed," she said, shattering an uncomfortable silence. Suddenly I was back in her velvet grip again.

"You were?" I said, almost surprised that my mouth was still working. She nodded and went on.

"Before you ask, though, I don't know who did that to her." I could see her shrink inwards as she visited with a difficult memory, "but I know she got what she wanted."

"What she wanted?"

"Yes," she answered quietly, and I felt a reluctance creeping in to her demeanour as if she had begun to question the sense of talking to me.

"What did she want Saaya? Please, tell me."

"To find her *Maz's* killer," she said finally, using a Succae phrase that implied parentage. It's not as clear-cut or as simple as that but I understood Saaya's meaning.

"Her mother was murdered?"

She looked at me askance and then realisation dawned on her face.

"You don't know, do you?"

I was confused. "Know? Know what?"

"Ischae. Ischae was *Maz* to Naschinne. That's why Naschinne was doing what she was doing. Ever since Ischae's death, she's been doing whatever she could to find her killer."

I felt like my wings had been cut off. How could someone that I had shared everything with have kept something so important from me? I was beginning to question everything I knew, including whether my relationship with Ischae had really been as deep as I had believed. The enigmatic shroud of manners and honour that wraps Succae society had never felt more alien to me than at that moment.

Saaya's mouth was moving but I wasn't listening anymore, and it was only when she got up to leave that I came back to the moment.

"Where are you going?"

"To play," she replied as if I had said something ridiculous.

"No. We need to talk further. I need to know what happened on the day Naschinne died."

"I've already told you," she said, her voice low but cold as ice. "She found what she was looking for and look what it got her? I shouldn't be talking to you. You have no idea how far this goes." I rose and blocked the exit to the booth. "All the more reason to tell me everything you know. I walk with the Vod's personal warrant so you can either answer to him or answer to me," I said, my voice quivering with suppressed rage. She surprised me by laughing caustically, a short derisive bark. "Do you really think you and that ancient ghost were sent to find the truth? Let me tell you…"

I wish she had. Yet, those were the last words she spoke.

It was a Chakkar that decapitated Saaya; a thin discus of gold and steel, finely honed around the edge. I doubt she saw it flash through the air before it severed her neck, head falling forward to the floor in a lifeless heap. Her body took one step to the right before faltering, its elegant frame suddenly ungainly and deformed.

Nimrod sprang to my hand, and I charged out into the den. I nearly crashed straight into Kurr who stood at the entrance, mouth agape. He pointed up the stairs and I hastened that direction, the word 'Angel' following me. I pursued as fast as I could but outside only darkness awaited, cold laughter hanging in the broken, bloody night.

Chapter Five

Kurr's Den emptied faster than a sinking ship but in a far more orderly manner. Even in a crisis, the Succae are polite. Hooded Angel patrons tried to avoid catching my eye as they also melted away into the night to leave me standing alone outside.

Part of me wanted to join them and leave someone else to clean up the mess and placate the angry ghosts. However, it was my actions that had disturbed the shades in the first place, and whilst the night's events had been terrible, maybe they were an indication that we were on the right track.

"I go get Ashai," Kurr said quietly. "I walk slow." I got his meaning. Once Succae authority arrived, I would be excluded from any further investigation. Kurr was giving me valuable time to look around.

I went back to where Saaya's decapitated body lay still and silent. Dark energy oozed from the otherwise clean and precise cut. I repressed the surge of anger that coursed through my veins and instead focused on the hunt for any clues her killer may have left behind. I took my long knife from the scabbard on my belt and carved into the leather seat. I found the thin Chakkar buried in the wood of the booth. It was a marvellously penetrative weapon for something so small. It was light and of exceptional craftsmanship, clearly a weapon of the Flight. Of course, a weapon is a tool that can be wielded by anyone who cares to master its use. It was further back in one of the silk entry veils that I spotted something far more revealing; a feather that had been dyed black. I realised that I was holding my breath as I pulled it free of where I was, certain it had to have been placed by its carrier. It was the calling card of a ghost.

Chapter Six

Kurr was good to his word and the Ashai that came with him clearly didn't see the need to rush to the scene of a dead Siren, especially with the killer fled and gone. However, there was nothing more to find and I was pretty sure I knew what message he was sending, a warning as unsubtle as my glowing spear.

The masked Ashai were efficient and polite in escorting me to detention in a nearby watch tower. Their gestures were open and unthreatening, and I did my best to assure them that I was neither the killer nor likely to run off. I heard Sarzh's name invoked several times, but he never came to question me. It gave me time to think about what I had found.

In my younger times, when my skills as a hunter and scout for the Flight had become superlative, I was sent by the Heralds to serve in a group that called themselves the Halokim. A literal translation would be 'avenger' and our task was to hunt down and extract retribution from anyone who had struck an Angel down in combat.

To begin with, the work felt worthy, almost necessary for the rest of the Flight to do its duties. However, the leader, Kael, had an odd way about him. I do not like to look back on this time, but the discovery of the feather left me little option. It is safe to say that we all enjoyed our work too much, especially Kael who glorified what was really nothing more than extra judicial murder. Our tradition was to dye wing feathers black with each Angel revenged, and we became notorious. I left the group disenchanted and concerned that many of those we had killed had been convicted on nothing more than hearsay, uncertain eyewitness identifications and forced confessions. It was clear that Kael didn't really care who we killed among a given enemy.

Kael had been disappointed when I left, but he didn't try and stop me. He thought I was squeamish and undeserving of the honour of the Halokim. Personally, I thought he was insane, and was unsurprised when reports in the early days of the Succae Wars placed him and the rest of the group as casualties in one of the early great battles on the surface of Cerule.

Now I had to wonder whether Kael had been doing something else with his time, keeping the Halokim secret from the enemy. I also wondered for whom this black feather had been placed? I doubted Saaya had killed an Angel, but then I also doubted that Kael would question any order to kill an enemy if it came from the right person. She had clearly been silenced and an Angel had been her assassin. Just what had I stumbled upon?

Chapter Seven

Lytta's face was surprisingly expressive when I finally related what had happened since we last met. She would not let me speak until we were on the trail that wound back to the surface of the moon and on the path to Low-Tsar Tzir's compound, beyond the Twisted Wood.

"It was only one night," she said, shaking her head in exasperation. "What do I have to do to keep you out of trouble?" she added and all I could do was shrug and smile.

"I guess trouble has a way of catching up with me," I said, finding her reaction bizarrely amusing.

She rounded on me, her braids nearly lashing my face and I could tell she didn't find anything funny in the situation at all.

"Everything you do reflects on me, the same as it did on Ischae. Do you understand?"

I sort of did, but I also didn't like being treated like a child, so I said nothing more and walked on moodily.

Narrow cave paths soon gave way to a steep, wide upward slope that led to an exit to the surface. The exit was dense with brambles and other spiky flora that wanted to snag, pull, and tear at me. Lytta's slender and sinuous body seemed able to bypass the fibrous fingers whilst my bulkier and more armoured frame was clearly everything they were waiting for and could not bear to part with. Naturally I was too proud to ask for help and Lytta did not bother to wait for me, marching on ahead at her usual relentless pace. Reluctantly, I converted Nimrod into a machete and hacked my way free. The plants recoiled as the bright blade burned through them, and I thought I heard them hiss in anger.

By the time I had caught up with her, Lytta was standing at a crossway marked by an ancient, gnarled tree. I fancied I could see a face in its dead trunk, often the sign that a God had once favoured this woodland. Yet the Succae had killed all the Gods of this place, so if it was, it was the afterimage of one long lost. I wondered if his equivalent was one the Flight had met, and if so, was he perhaps at root in the Horta Magna? Lytta saw me thinking and put a delicate gloved hand on her hip. It was an unexpected move, almost insouciant. She smiled and I smiled back. Then, I realised it was not me she was looking at. It was the assassins behind me.

Chapter Eight

There were six of them, all clad in Ashai armour. The only things missing were their screaming face masks, replaced by a simple dark head-wrap, from which only the whites of eyes could be seen. They had fanned out behind me, emerging silently from the dead thicket around us, and I fancied these were no Low-Nin pretenders seeking advancement. These were the real thing, full blooded warriors with an enemy at bay.

I took a cautious step back as Nimrod became a spear again, and raised my hand in placation, but they leaped past me in a sudden, swift move, and I knew they were not here for me or at least, not right away. As they had moved so had Lytta, and now the two sides faced each other, bodies tensed. The Ashai were mostly sword-wielders but here, two held long spears that ended in a slim axe blade, and another held a military flail, an iron capped shaft with a heavy spiked club on the end of a solid foot long chain. They advanced slowly until Lytta spoke.

"I am the Serrate," she said her voice strong and resonant.

"We know who you are," said the swordsman closest to her.

"You know who I am but now I will tell you *what* I am."

I have never forgotten those words, delivered as they were in an even, almost conversational tone. Maybe it was because she focused on me as she spoke them, her eyes reassuring me that this was something for her and her alone and that I was not to interfere.

"I am the Sixth Succae Spirit of War. I am the Watcher in

the Well and High Executioner of the Inglorious Dead. I have slain gods, cleansed fields of battle and fed upon the spirits of the heroes of our enemies. I have one wyrd and that is destruction. There is but one certain outcome to your challenge and that is final death, for I will crush your bones into dust and drink your soul dry."

If the Ashai were impressed or frightened by Lytta's words, they didn't show it. Instead, they shared glances with each other, and the swordsmen drew their blades. I had witnessed fights between the Succae before and had some sense of what to expect. Like all Succae life, duelling has its own stages of ritual. First comes the *Osi*, an acknowledgement of the enemy. Only after *Osi* can a participant withdraw. Of course, this costs significant loss of face and honour. Second, the *Gata*, a taking of stance which allows each side to gauge the other. Sometimes, the *Gata* can last for minutes, hours, even days have been known. Then the fight, *Tambo*, ensues.

In this case, Lytta did not really bother with *Osi*, although she would say her verbal challenge was enough to satisfy the purists. The *Gata*, however, shocked everyone, including me. Calmly, her face set in a thin smile, she walked towards her assailants with palms up, hands empty. The Ashai tensed visibly in their martial stances, blades quivering. Then she stood still for a moment, before collapsing, albeit elegantly into a cross legged position, head bent forward, white pale neck exposed. There was a moment of confusion among the would-be assassins. She sat there and did not move, and the three swordsmen decided to take the initiative. One raced forward, two hands holding a long blade that now came down in an arcing strike that would sever her body from shoulder to sternum. The second leaped high in the air, blade turned downwards so that it would plunge straight through the top of her head and exit from her mouth. The last sped past her, leaping in a turn designed to bury his blade in her back.

As a species we are blessed with sight beyond the mundane. My kind can see many planes of existence at once and it was with this special sight that I saw the Sixth War Spirit of the Succae in all her revealed glory. Colours and shapes blurred in a sudden motion, a many legged rainbow tigress with a draconic tail flying tattered colours behind her. Everything was shifting and changing at once so this is the best description of what I remember seeing, but on no account can I swear to its total accuracy. Her stylised tiger's face was set in a snarl but alongside that I fancied I could see the hooded heads of a dozen snakes spitting and striking.

She took the charging swordsmen first and his body undulated as she slammed into him, pushing his own smaller spirit out, screaming as she went. Now in control of his body, she pulled his strike and turned it into a one-handed sideways slice that cut the second swordsman in half at the waist, his descending sword falling into her left hand as the two pieces of his body fell on either side of her inanimate shell. Her killing cut continued in a full circle, parrying the third Ashai's blow before it reached her back. She threw the blade in her second hand at him, and it flew handle over handle until he staggered backwards with the weapon buried in his chest, staring incomprehensibly at the seeming betrayal of his own companion.

The other three went down just as fast in a series of possessions, executions, and shocked faces. At the end of the battle, her spirit hovered free of those now dispossessed and she kept her promise. She called them all to her, dark tendrils tying their spirits and pulling them into a growing vast dark maw that devoured them entirely. It was chilling to watch and a reminder that perhaps we had been fortunate that Vod Karsz had chosen to agree to an armistice.

"So, do you want to tell me what that was all about?" I asked as Lytta's body jerked back into life.

"Sarzh," she said with a slight smile.

"The Ashai Prime just tried to kill you?"

"No not really. More a test of skill, I would say."

"All because of that dumb game?"

"Yes. He has done what his honour demanded he do."

"What? Wasted the lives of six of his best soldiers just for a bit more Lao or Zi?"

She sighed. "Lao. No-one of standing wants any more Zi".

I looked around at the devastation and for once, found myself speechless.

Chapter Nine

It was some more hours of travel before a true pathway began to reveal itself again. Lytta slowed her pace and began to move more cautiously. We came across evidence of habitation—an occasional way camp and more interestingly, a shrine to Kora the Beggar, the lowliest of the seven penitents that the Low-Nin venerated and appeased in the hope of a better tomorrow. It was clear that the shrine was regularly in use, and offerings littered the site. On closer inspection, they were small, sad things, a well-worn button, a feather, a broken eggshell. What Kora did with these small devotions I had to wonder, but I had no doubt that they were the sincere leavings of those who had almost nothing else to offer. They were also open offerings to a pagan goddess and not something you would see in Karsz's capital.

Soon, the path gave way to a wider trail, and it was clear that the tangle had been cut back. Suddenly we were in the midst of a village and wary Low-Nin hurried out of our way. Lytta ignored them and walked on to greet a large group of armed men and women who had appeared at the head of the trail.

They were clad in a wide array of colourful *yukes,* martial robes that clad the body and torso but left arms and legs free for fighting. Most were barefoot but some wore boots or sandals that had thick wooden platforms. The only common features were the tattoos on their hands and arms, a sign that they had sworn to service. In this case it was a weasel that coiled around the arm, presumably Low-Tsar Tzir's identifying sigil. They had the swagger of a group that were unused to challenge, and they fanned around us in what I thought, given what I had just witnessed, was an incautious manner.

Lytta waited for a moment and then pointed to a squat man with a bulbous nose. She moved forward and the bravado seemed to fall away as the others parted in front of her. She lent down to whisper words in his ear, and he visibly blanched and took a step backwards. In the hushed moment that followed, I didn't know what to expect but he spoke harsh sounding words and the group around us fell to their knees. Lytta moved among them allowing each a chance to touch her hand.

As a group, we went on together up the trail, the squat man whose name I understood to be Bharzo, leading the way. Lytta walked slightly ahead of him, with the rest of the group flanking her and glaring at me superstitiously. It was probably fair. If there was anyone they hated more than the overlords of their own kind, it was us, the invaders.

We arrived in what I took to be the equivalent of the village square. There was a well-house in the centre and beyond it, an ornate set of heavy wooden gates that linked to red stone walls on both sides enclosing an impressive set of buildings. This would be Tzir's hold and accommodation for his followers.

Bharzo hurried to the gates that swung open on his command, beckoned Lytta on, and we passed over a bridge beneath which clear water flowed, populated by large golden fish that swam in lazy circles, occasionally coming to the surface to taste the air before suddenly disappearing in a colourful swish of tail and fins. More tattooed followers crowded around us as we made our way through this inner village until we arrived at another pagan shrine. This God I recognised as Zarrat the Judge, one of the Guardians of the Succae Hell. His statue was of a dark, robed man with a distinctive square headdress, sitting on a wide stone throne within a roofed mausoleum. Zarrat was a plenary figure who was supposed to honestly evaluate the souls of his worshippers and was a common incarnation of a spirit we had met before in hundreds of cultures. Again, he was supposed to be dead and gone, but the shrine here was in good condition, his scales full of votive offerings.

Bharzo pointed to a long rectangular building that had been painted black, and Lytta paused a moment, her head bowed in quiet respect. Her lips moved in a silent invocation before she signalled me to join her. I moved to her side but felt the bristle of disapproval in growled murmurs and sharp intakes of breath. Bharzo shouted more harsh words after Lytta shot him a glare and the group fell silent. She climbed up lacquered steps and into one of the Succae's Houses of the Dead.

The sweet but cloying smell of incense hung heavy in the air in the Dead House's lobby. It was said to be an opiate for the vampiric wraiths who would acclimatise to their disembodied state before returning to the Well. Two wide panel doors stood in front of us, one marked for Low-Nin and the other marked for High. In between, a broad wooden bowl had been set on the floor, along with several personal items that I presumed to be the former possessions of the dead; a wooden thorn necklace and an iron spearhead in one pile, and in the other, a jade ring and a blackened fish knife. Lytta showed little interest and slid the panel door open.

Inside, the air was thick with more narcotic smoke that lazily oozed from ornate iron spheres that hung from the rafters. The bodies of two Low-Nin were laid out on benches. One bore the tattoos of the Low-Tsar whilst the other's skin was unmarked. Somewhere, deeper in the building, I heard the sound of a panel door in motion, but no-one entered the room we were in.

On closer inspection, it was clear that something was odd about the bodies. Strange holes no wider than my finger appeared to have punched through flesh and bone to the point that you could see all the way through from entrance to exit wound. Each body bore multiple marks of the same type of injury, and I wondered exactly how these Succae had ceased to function, as there was no obvious reason for their demise. Lytta lent close and inspected the holes on what was presumably one of Tzir's guards. She sniffed the wound before inserting her finger in the perfectly round hole and then pulling it out.

"Do you have to do that?" I asked, my voice seeming loud and out of place in the hushed, smoky gloom. She stood up and put the same finger in her mouth and I was about to express my revulsion when the door to the chamber from the opposite side opened and the Low-Tsar arrived.

Tzir, clad in a monochromatic *yuke* with a red, dragon-headed mace in one hand, was flanked by armoured guards who wore almost full sets of Ashai armour - a crime that any Vod would almost certainly punish by death if those beneath were Low-Nin pretenders. It was a bold display and clearly intended to send a message. Here, we'd play by Tzir's rules or regret it.

One of the guards advanced on Lytta, who had shown no interest in or recognition of the new arrivals. I was about to speak when Lytta suddenly turned and in a blur of motion took the guard's weapon from him and vaulted over his head to land with the bare blade up against the Low-Tsar's neck as the others looked on in stunned silence. To his credit, Tzir didn't flinch.

"Hello Lytta," he said.

Chapter Ten

There was something about Tzir that was immediately likable. Perhaps it was the nonchalance with which he regarded our presence in his halls, or because his animated familiarity around Lytta bore all the hallmarks of prior intimacy. Whatever it was, I warmed to him straight away.

"An Angel and a Serrate," he said, once his guards had left to man the exits and only the three of us and the dead Low-Nin remained.

"Now that's something I think it's safe to say you don't see every day."

Lytta had returned to examining the bodies and waved her hand, as if our presence should be as normal as the wind blowing through.

"We need your help with Rain," I said, but Lytta steered the conversation back to the Low-Nin again.

"Where did you find them?"

Tzir smiled at me apologetically, and I knew my questions would have to wait.

"The lakeside underground. The fisherman had been missing for a few days, so I sent Krat to look for him. When he didn't come back either, I sent a larger group under Bharzo's lead, and he found them both, apparently washed up on the bank. It looks like they drowned, and the lake's Blindfish fed upon their bodies."

"So maybe one killed the other in a fight over a Blindfish,

and in remorse the other killed himself? Is that your stupid conclusion?"

Tzir's eyes narrowed. I imagine it had been a long time since anyone had spoken to him that way.

"The nature of these wounds are far from normal and were not caused by any Blindfish," Lytta said.

"There is Necrene residue inside them meaning some *Necrote* has slipped free and needs stopping before it causes wider damage. It would seem it is a good thing we came when we did. You should burn these bodies in case whatever it is laid anything inside."

She turned to leave signalling me to follow and like Sariel's obedient Sunpup, I did.

"Oh, and Tzir? Next time you lie to me, I suggest you remember who I am and what I can do to you."

I am not sure what she really meant by those words, but from Tzir's insouciant grin, it was apparent he had chosen the best possible meaning.

Once we were outside, I quietly asked her why Tzir looked so happy.

"Tzir is compromised and is pleased that I reacted the way I did. Whoever is listening must be someone more important than a Low-Tsar, otherwise he would not be so wary. That can only mean an Ashai or higher, in which case they already know who we are, and that I would recognise the state those bodies are in."

"That means someone got to him before we did."

"Yes. That was his way of telling me to be careful. The High-Nin apparently think the Lower castes are stupid. I am feeding their existing beliefs."

"What about the bodies. You said a *Necrote* did it. What is that?"

"Your kind probably call them *Hegosz*," she said. In truth,

I had not heard that word before either, but I understood the meaning. Something that was beyond our mutual control had escaped and needed putting down.

"How did it escape?"

She didn't answer immediately, instead donning her gloves and walking on in search of Bharzo.

"That's what I'd like to know," she said softly.

Bharzo agreed to take us back to where the bodies had been found, and it turned out that Tzir had not been completely lying. The Lake was underground in a cavern where the inner icy core of the moon met with warmer currents to create a melting spring.

"How far does it go?" Lytta asked Bharzo who shrugged and pointed off into the darkness. I sighed and increased my corona until light flooded the cavern. Black, cold water rippled out from the ragged shoreline, the surface dotted with the pale upturned remains of dozens of small Blindfish. It looked bleak and unwelcoming.

Lytta placed a hand on her sword hilt and waded down into the water. I decided, after a brief experiment to fly as far as was possible and accordingly, hovered just over the surface as we moved further into the lake. It was fine for a while, but soon Lytta's head disappeared beneath the water and the stalactites that hung from above like so many pointing, pale fingers, grew longer, forcing me down into the inky black waters as well. The cold seeped in, momentarily disorienting me, dimming the brightness, and I felt for a moment that the dark murk itself was alive and trying to extinguish my light, roiling, and bubbling at the edges. Beneath me it was hard to gain purchase, the soles of my boots slipping and sliding on the dark slimy rocks below.

Even with my aura, visibility was poor, and I could just about make out Lytta's form to my right as we progressed deeper into the cavern, passing through a narrow passage where the water, carried by an invisible current, gently pulled us into an underwater forest of skeletal, twisted ebony trees, their thin and spindly spiked branches thrusting towards the surface. They looked like supplicants on their knees in repentance, a congregation of diseased souls.

The lakebed fell away before us, down into a deeper gloom and I did what I could to increase the level of illumination around us. Maybe it was a mistake, but it also saved me, as just in time, I saw the spiked tendril that snaked out of the dark water and tried to impale me. I narrowly avoided its deadly thrusting point, only to see three more follow in its wake. They came at tremendous speed, and I spun Nimrod in a circle that narrowly deflected them all. They were grotesque things, bloated, scarred and ugly appendages with a heavy and sharp bone spur at the end. All along the flesh, sucking mouths with thin arrays of needle-sharp teeth opened and closed, and I propelled myself upwards, anticipating that their next move would be to try to encircle me and pull me down to wherever the creature's maw was waiting.

Below me, I saw Lytta take my place and I shook my head in frustration. More tentacles lanced through the water, and I watched as her silver blade blurred in a myriad of cuts that left them all severed, the detached remains sinking towards the lake floor in an inky trail. I felt a pulse of pressure then, as if something large had dropped into the water and we were feeling the resulting swell. The water below Lytta roiled and churned and I saw her head down into it. I shook my head in disbelief, but I knew I had no choice but to follow.

Deeper we went, and as we did, more attacks of increasing numbers of tentacles came our way. Again, Lytta's blade-work was equal to the task, and severed tendril after tendril as we finally came to the rocky bottom of the lake floor. Ahead, she paused at another cavernous entrance and turned my way. She was trying to signal me when a huge pulse of darkness spread through the water and engulfed her. I heard a strange sound, like air rushing through a discordant pipe, and every fibre of my being felt terror pulse through my veins. It took a moment to gather my faculties, ignore the urge to flee. Instead, I pointed Nimrod in the direction of the cave mouth and held on to the glowing spear as I shot forward in pursuit.

Nimrod speared through the black gloom until I saw a shaft ahead going upwards and I broke the surface, spread my wings, and continued upwards. The *Necrote* was a massive, squat, ugly island of flesh that bulged and warped in a disgustingly misshapen manner. Hundreds of pustular mouths shrieked obscenities in a hundred languages, a cacophony of noise that was as intimidating as it was horrific. Over its bulk, wide eyes blinked, and a thousand orifices leaked a black discharge. Then there was the stench, the beast wrapped in a haze of yellow gas that burned my eyes and throat and made me gag.

The thing moved, suddenly and unexpectedly rolling sideways, and propelled a pile of evil looking muck in my direction. A small amount splashed on my breastplate and immediately discharged tiny white spiders that scuttled across it, seeking the seams and joints that led to my warm flesh. My armour glowed red hot, and the arachnids squealed and popped on its surface. I looked for any sign of Lytta but could not immediately see her. The mound launched a dozen tentacles in my direction, spikes transforming into bigger mouths with an array of jagged teeth. Nimrod became a great shield and I parried them, although the force with which they impacted sent me flying backwards and into the rocky roof. I saw a gigantic jagged split open in the creature, a pair of jaws, the likes of which I had never seen. At that moment Lytta appeared out of the black water and vaulted onto the creature's mass, her blade jamming the jaws open.

"Fire! Now!" she yelled and without hesitation, I transformed Nimrod into a fiery spear and hurled it with all my might. The weapon struck its target and I looked on in horror as the creature swallowed it whole, jaws snapping shut. Lytta leapt and caught her blade as it was catapulted vertically under the force of the creature's closing maw before she fell back into the water.

For a moment, I paused in shock as the creature rolled around, seemingly unhurt. Then, a ripple of flame as flesh pulsed, and from its orifices expelled gas that was on fire. I realised what I had to do and called Nimrod back to me. The monster's entire form shuddered as the weapon pulled itself through the proto-flesh, inch by agonising inch until it was airborne again and came back to me. The body split and rents opened wide across its fleshy expanse. Faces seemed to press against the creature's skin, mouths stretched wide in screams as fire licked and melted flesh. Dozens of tendrils waved in the air as the beast shuddered and subsided, small internal explosions rocking the body until the whole thing was ablaze, yellow rivers of fat dripping down its now still flank. The flesh was still popping and blistering when I left it.

Chapter Eleven

By the time I got back to the lakeside, only Bharzo awaited me. Lytta had apparently gone on ahead. I was tired, cold, and wet after the exertions of the fight and Bharzo bombarded me with questions about the beast. In some ways it was a good thing that he would talk to me so readily, but I was in no great mood for conversation. Something about this place gnawed at me, a feeling of being constantly on edge that the vanquishing of the *Necrote* had done nothing to allay.

Our return to the village was relatively low key. Bharzo soon had his followers around him again and as a group, they escorted me back over the bridge and into the inner compound where Tzir's would-be Ashai pointed me to a wooden longhouse.

Inside, it smelt of wood and incense and I was left alone to explore. The structure was square, one of four longhouses that enclosed a partly covered ornate garden which I peered down on from a balcony above. At its centre was a steamy pool, vapours gently curling upwards like pale ghosts in the night. Despite my best efforts, I was still cold, and the thought of a warming swim was appealing - until I realised I was not alone. To my left, at the top of the square, I saw the red burn of a smouldering pipe and could just make out a figure sitting still in the shadows. I wasn't certain that they had seen me, and so stayed where I was, mirroring the stillness. Then I saw Lytta rise to the surface of the pool and walk up the steps. I wanted to call out to her that she was being watched but it felt wrong to break the silence and so the words died in my throat. Her naked, athletic body might also have been a factor; the incredible tattoos that adorned her back and shoulders, too. On the right, a black and red wyrm whose tail wrapped around her upper thigh, its ropy snake-like body coiled up her arms and shoulder. On the left a stylised pouncing tiger that came all the way down her back, its extended claws raking her buttocks. She stood for a moment to settle her braids before stalking back to the longhouse opposite mine and I realised I was holding my breath. I looked back over in search of the other silent observer but there was no sign of them, the balcony empty and cold.

I found a bed that was laid with soft skins and smelt of loam, and before long, restless sleep found me. I was back with the Halokim, flying through a shadowy forest as a dozen Necrene beasts pursued us. I could see our leader, Kael, ahead, his bright spear burning brightly, weaving through blackened trees whose skeletal limbs wanted to snag and stab. I did my best to keep up, but wherever I flew, trees grew thicker, and branches pulled and tore my wings until I crashed into decaying undergrowth, the soft ground giving under my weight. The earth pulled me down, thick corded vines holding me tight. Down into haunted black caverns where my light would diminish and fade. I called for Kael, but he never came back for me. Then after a while he did come, but he was as pale as the Succae, and I could see he had become one of them. I struggled against the vines as he approached, my one heart beating wildly. At his command they released me, and I fell before him, twisted and broken. He lent in close to whisper, but I never heard what he said. I looked into dead eyes as a knife was driven into my heart and read the silent words on his lips, "For Duma".

I awoke with a start to find the skins of my bower scattered around the chamber and myself cramped in an alcove of the ceiling. Bharzo was looking up at me in bemused surprise, a bundle of clothes under his arm.

"Hmph," he snorted. "I suppose if I could fly, I would sleep that way, too. Here, I bring you fresh clothing and Tsar Tzir invites you to join him in his hall when you are ready." I nodded and landed gently, trying not to show that for some reason, I had managed to rattle myself by dredging up the most terrifying shade from my past. I closed the door so that Bharzo wouldn't see me shaking as I got dressed.

I was surprised that no-one paid me much mind as I entered Tzir's hall. It was packed with his Low-Nin followers and what I guessed were the more important members of the surrounding villages that were under his care. They were well into their cups and poisoning their blood in a good way by the time I was shown to a seat one bench down from the top table, the space reserved for honoured guests of the Tsar. I suppose I had earned that privilege, and it was a welcome reminder of how open and friendly the lower castes could be.

Lytta looked down and briefly acknowledged me, but didn't smile, her attention seemingly focused elsewhere. She looked, if not anxious, then vigilant and a little irritated, probably by the proximity of a concubine who was quite literally all over Tzir himself. It made me look again, and I realised something was missing—the black armoured Ashai. Initially I had just presumed they were among the Venii-and-Kii-swilling crowd, but that felt out of place now, and wrong. Then again, maybe the dream had put me on edge, chasing shadows.

As the event progressed, entertainments were brought on, a band of Sirens whose musicianship was beyond compare; a group of clowns who were raucous and amusing, interacting with flesh balls that had minds of their own; actors performing speeches from impenetrable Succae tragedies. (All their plays are tragedies).

I sipped Venii and took it all in. After a couple of attempts to pull Tzir from his companion - or his companion from him - I gave up on the idea of asking my questions about Rain for the time being, and instead watched my ever-intense Serrate watch everything and everyone else. She knew something was wrong and I kept coming back to that feeling I'd had since we had arrived here. It had never truly ebbed, even after the Necrote was dead. Eventually Lytta looked at me with an expectant stare. I took it as an invitation to join her and I moved to her side.

"There's something not quite right," I said, and she nodded slowly. "That thing. It was no accident it was here when we arrived was it?"

"No. I don't think so," she said in a soft whisper. "I think it was meant to kill us but they underestimated our power." I was about to say more but she rose abruptly and left the room and the look she gave me as she left indicated it was best that I didn't follow. Yes, there was something amiss alright, and I had the feeling it wouldn't be long before I was face to face with it.

Chapter Twelve

Tzir retired about an hour before the rest of the hall were falling into stupors of their own making. I left the hall and took to the air and flew into the dark sky over the mountain that Tzir's fortress nestled beneath. Below me I could see the clowns herding their flesh balls back up a steep path that cut into the mountainside behind Tzir's hall, a path that was invisible from below. It made me think about the Flensers, the pagan flesh crafters whose cult I had discovered was far from dead. I had always assumed the flesh creations were remnants of the war but now I wondered if the Flenser's cult was still active. It was a worrying thought, especially here, where I had seen so much other evidence of pagan worship. There had been more than a few flesh creations in service to Jasniz too. Did that make him part of their cult and could Tzir be hiding him here?

I watched from above as the clowns disappeared into a tunnelled passage and decided to follow them. I swooped down from above, landed on the rocky pathway above the tunnel and waited for them, but they failed to emerge on the other side. I dropped down to ground level and peered into the gloom of the tunnel, only to taste the smell of burning pitch emanating from within. I stowed my wings and crept in to find another entrance that went deeper into the mountain, recessed into the tunnel wall. It wasn't concealed, but then it wasn't that obvious either, and I imagine that in the dark, you could easily walk or fly past it if you didn't know what you were looking for.

Initially, it was more a set of caves and caverns that interlinked with each other, and I watched the clowns skip and hop over rocks and then drop down out of sight. I followed as stealthily as I could and took flight vertically to hover in the shadows of the cavern ceiling. Beyond, a wooden bridge that had seen better days stretched across a deep abyss to another rough-hewn entrance, but this one was guarded by the black-armoured Ashai with whom Tzir had greeted us. They occupied a strong defensive redoubt, protected from above by overhanging rock and a thick wooden latticed gate that blocked the exit from the bridge.

The guards seemed less than impressed to see these unexpected guests and refused to open the gate until one of the clowns stood forward and took something off his neck to show them. The Ashai passed the item among themselves briefly before opening the gate and cautiously letting them pass through. It was clear I couldn't follow, so I used the moment to quietly slip over the edge and fly down in search of another way in.

It didn't take long to find, and I landed on a stone promontory some hundred feet below the guard point. Below me, I could see ice in a slow-moving stream, presumably the same source that fed the underground lakes a few miles away. There was a thin crack in the stone face here, just wide enough for my slender, unarmoured form to slip through. I emerged on a slim ledge that looked down on wide-hewn steps that were dimly lit by torches. On closer inspection, the holders were large, crudely moulded hands, made of puckered flesh that had blackened and blistered in places where the flame had presumably guttered too low and burned the flesh itself. I heard steps and shrank back into the ledge's shadows as the clowns made their way down the stairs, their flesh balls bouncing ahead of them like demented pets.

I flew quietly ahead and above them, and sought another viewpoint, crouched atop a tall stone archway that was shrouded in shadow. They passed below me, annoyingly silent in their purposeful strides. Ahead were a pair of great iron doors, guarded by another group of armed Ashai. Here again, more interrogation and another display of the totem around the leader's neck led to massive doors eventually swinging open to let them through. This time, however, the Ashai refused to return the 'key', the lead halberdier keeping it for himself. The clown took it in his stride and didn't look that concerned. It gave me the chance to see the amulet for myself, and what I saw made my remaining heart beat a little faster. Fashioned and embossed into an oval pendant made of blackened iron, the shape was unmistakably a feather. The black feather, the symbol of the Halokim.

By the time I returned to my quarters I could feel the weight of the expectations of the dead laying heavily upon me. I could feel the outrage pouring from their contorted, drained, and severed bodies and I knew they couldn't be at rest until someone had delivered justice to their shadowy killers.

Clearly there were pieces of a jagged puzzle missing, although I believed more than ever that cabal was at work on both sides of the tether, but their identities and their purpose remained a mystery. It came back to Jasniz, the one real conspirator who had been foolish enough to show his face to me. I felt certain he was a follower, not a leader and I wondered now if Ischae had known that too. Had she used the cover of our relationship to get closer to whoever gave him his orders? In so doing had she played her hand too early and paid the ultimate price?

I also kept coming back to Saaya's last words, insinuating that the search for Naschinne's killer had been handed to the two individuals least likely to solve it. The more I thought about that, the likelier it felt to me that such a cynical move was most likely the work of my kind alone.

I felt more resolved than ever to get to the truth and tear down those that were responsible, but fitful sleep only brought the shades of the dead to me. I could see their mouths stretched wide in silent screams as I was helplessly re-shackled to the dissecting table. A masked Flenser cut my remaining heart out and threw it to one of the juggler clowns as my wings slowly beat their last, feather and bone clattering against cold, hard stone.

I awoke with a start to hear hammering at my door. Before I could get there, it burst open and black armoured Ashai quickly surrounded me.

Chapter Thirteen

"Only the Excelsis is always right." That's a Flight saying that means assuming you're right all the time means you're bound to be wrong. In this case, it was the Ashai I had judged incorrectly. They were the real thing and not Low-Nin in armour. It begged the question - what they were doing hanging around with a Low-Tsar and his followers? I was intrigued and followed the orders they gave in brief guttural phrases to go with them whilst leaving my armour and weaponry behind.

Soon we were back on the road to the hidden citadel within Tzir's mountain, except that rather than going down we were going up. A grand set of wide, winding stairs led to a set of gates that led out into a moon garden whose beauty was breath-taking.

Avenues of small ornate trees that glowed in the ambience of the moonlight illuminated the deep bowl-shaped crater into which this surprising arboretum had been placed. I was escorted down an avenue and over an ornate bridge, beneath which black waters rippled gently in an astral breeze. Small lanterns bobbed in the water, each slowly floating on a current that clearly flowed back past me. I was kind of distracted, and didn't notice the Ashai had stopped, so I stumbled into the guard in front of me. To his credit, he barely moved as seven feet of Angel bashed into him, although I felt the tension in all my escorts as a black shadow stalked out of the night ahead of them.

"I will take him from here," Lytta said. It took the Ashai a moment before they separated ranks and I was pushed forward.

"What's going on?" I asked her as she turned sharply and bade me follow her, my Ashai escort following a discreet distance behind us. Initially she said nothing, just pointed ahead as the path rose, leading to the banks of an ornate lake at the bowl's centre. It was a surprising expanse with a formidable residence seated on a small island in the middle of dark water.

Lytta turned and looked at me for a moment. I could see her eyes narrow as she studied my face for what felt like an eternity.

"What is it?" I asked, bemused and she turned away and shrugged.

"Just tell the truth," she said, and I wasn't sure whether she was really talking to me.

She walked to the end of the jetty where a long, engraved leaden bell had been secured to a metal post. Until recently it had clearly been under water as its surface was slick, the markings on its sides long faded and now indiscernible. I was beginning to feel uncomfortable. This was not Tzir's residence, but someone else he was probably protecting. The question was who and what influence they had over Lytta. I was in the wrong place to suddenly be alone with no allies and I began to wish I had made more of a fuss about Nimrod staying with me.

Lytta rang the bell. Its tone was deep and sonorous, and I felt its power resonate within me. It had an ancient sound, the sort that belonged in temples and could bring the faithful to their knees. I watched the water as it began to stir, and four giant figures emerged from the black water. I had heard of their kind before, but this was the first time I had ever seen them. The Succae called them *Golakki*, spirits of heroes and leaders of vanquished enemies bound into stone and destined to a lifetime of servitude. In their own way, the Succae saw this as being an honourable fate, recognition of a worthy adversary.

Black water ran in streams away from the stone giants' bodies as they lumbered into position to haul a stone walkway into place. Each one had been painstakingly carved, to be what I was sure was an accurate representation of what they had looked like in life. One was a kilted man with long warrior braids. Another was completely bald and clad in plate armour. A third was female and looked like a sorceress, such were the arcane markings carved on her body. The last I recognised as a representation of Yggael, a snake-headed woman with stylised serpents crawling all over her body. The one thing that united them all was the lack of facial features. Each one had been left blank, a deliberate reminder of the fate of anyone that stood against the Succae. Your fate was to be forgotten.

Lytta pointed ahead, and I walked across the bridge to the banks of the house on the lake. There could now be only one occupant of this place, but that answer only raised even more questions that I hoped I would shortly have the answers to. This could only be home to a Vod, and I was certain it wasn't Karsz.

Chapter Fourteen

Lytta waited on the steps and indicated I should go on. I could sense her feelings of unease, something that I shared. I had heard stories before about the unpredictable nature of Vods, whose control over their people was so absolute that ill-chosen or misspoken words could sometimes have dangerous, even deadly consequences.

I walked into a shadowed hall that was empty except for a glowing bronze cauldron which filled the immediate area with the smell of woody incense. I passed beyond into quiet hallways and desolate chambers before passing to the far end of the structure and down into an ornate garden, where a tall muscular man, stripped to the waist and clearly still vital, was digging a wide plot in the ground. He wore a wide-brimmed hat and paused to take a long look at me. He took a drag from a white pipe that was carved in the shape of a dragon's maw, white smoke swirling away into the darkness. His face was expressionless, skin so taut across his face that all lines and marks of the passage of time had gone, the great inked patterns that decorated his skin barely visible. It gave him an odd symmetry with the Golakki that served him outside, but more importantly, it marked him as ancient, in Succae terms at least.

"So, you're the Angel ambassador?" he said, his voice deep with resonance.

"I held that title a long time ago," I said. "Now, I am

appointed as my Prince's emissary."

"Emissary? A grand title for an assassin."

I paused for a moment and looked at him directly.

"Pretty poor assassin that comes unarmed."

"I hear your kind need no ordinary weapons. You wield fire, don't you?"

It was becoming clear that whatever he had heard came from a biased and out of date source. My abilities with fire had been seriously curtailed by the long addiction to Rain. That said, I didn't really want him to know more than necessary so I stayed silent.

"Yes. You think we're fools, don't you?"

I shook my head emphatically.

"No, indeed. Far from it. Different yes, but foolish? No."

The Vod smiled briefly, and fixed me with a dark-eyed, unwavering glare.

"Who sent you to kill me? I am no threat to your Prince."

"Kill you? I did not come here to kill anyone. I came here to speak with the Low-Tsar about Rain. I did not even know you were here."

He paused for a moment and looked past me. I turned around and saw Lytta standing in my shadow. How she had got so close without my senses reacting worried me. Her hand was on the hilt of her blade.

"That is what she says," he said, bending down to retrieve something from the ground. "Explain this then. It was found in your quarters."

He handed me the same token I had seen bring passage to the entertainers at Tzir's feast, the black feather mark of the Halokim.

"If you knew anything about me, you'd know I would never keep that token with me."

"Yet it was found among your belongings."

"Planted among my belongings. Look, I was once what you suggest but that was a long time ago. Long before your kind and my kind even began their fight. I left the Halokim, the group this insignia represents. It was poor judgement to join them, and I was relieved to leave them behind. For a long while I believed they perished in the early battles of our conflict here, but recent developments suggest I may have been wrong."

"So, you want me to believe you are a reformed assassin?"

"I was a soldier then. I am not one now. I want to avoid any more wars."

The Vod lent on his shovel and nodded, and I felt Lytta brush past me.

"Then there is no need for this grave that I have been preparing. Neither for you nor for me." He reached for a grey doublet and Lytta handed him a soft fur robe that he wrapped around him.

"I told you," she said, and the Vod's demeanour visibly softened.

"Let us hope you are right my precious first Serrate," he said and then I knew I was in the presence of Dursc the Enlightened, father of the modern Succae and creator of the secular society that had turned its back on the rapacious conquest of dozens of worlds.

Dursc and I talked for some time as he showed me around his night garden. He was surprisingly talkative for a Succae, and a keen intellect. The laws of succession meant that he had taken no part in our wars on Cerule, and he seemed relatively out of touch with Karsz and his current court.

"Karsz was an Ashai when I was Vod. Just a rank-and-file warrior," he mused. "Although even then he had a reputation for martial ability and ruthlessness."

"So, you're not hiding from him here?" I said.

"Hide? Why would I want to hide?"

It was a good question, and I didn't really have an answer.

"It just feels like you're hidden away. Why aren't you in Scarpe? Surely, you'd still like to have influence?"

"I am here because my family is here, and I owe them my protection."

"Tzir? Tzir is your progeny?"

"Not exactly. I am his protector, and he is mine."

"Having an honour guard of Ashai at hand must be useful for you both," I said, and he smiled knowingly.

"It has its uses."

"Does Karsz never come and speak with you?"

Dursc laughed softly. "Come now, Ambassador, you know better than that. That would be a sign of weakness. The Vod knows all, rules all, is all."

It was not so far removed from the way the Flight was run, although Prince Anael had often sought counsel from his heralds and generals, at least until the war here had taken its toll. In recent times, I'd heard it said that Trinity Palace had become a quiet place.

"Come," Dursc said, leading us back into the villa which was suddenly full of life. Ashai stalked the halls or stood vigilant as servants busied themselves around the former Vod, and empty chambers were made habitable again; soon we were seated in high backed armchairs sharing a spiced, warm drink called *Aerbe*.

"Lytta told me why you are both here. Frankly I'd be surprised if Tzir could tell you anything useful. Whilst we do not exactly hide away here, it is true that little of the outside world bothers to make its way to these gates. I have asked Tzir to come and speak with you. Give you whatever answers we have."

I smiled, but there were things I wanted Dursc to know before Tzir arrived and so I pushed on.

"I have seen signs of veneration of the Old Gods here. I thought you banned their worship?"

Dursc sighed.

"That is not entirely true," he said, leaning forward and sipping from his cup. "All I did was to break up the cults of those who I believed were taking us down the path of destruction."

"Like Yggael the Serpent?"

"Yes. Her cult was poisonous in all senses of the word. Its secretive nature had drawn all manner of plotters under her wing and her powers had grown as a result. Her followers believed they could control us from the shadows, but I took the precaution early on of seeding informants among her Priesthood. It was still a battle to remember with Yggael herself though."

"Is her spirit imprisoned? I assume that is her likeness in the Golakki outside."

"Yggael was destroyed. It is her High Priestess, Lakza, who is bound within that Golak."

Dursc then turned the questioning back on me and I told him why I was here, about the deaths of Ischae, Naschinne and Saaya, and what little Lytta and I had discovered.

"I remember Ischae well," Dursc said, and I saw the warmth of remembrance in his eyes. "She was a fine intellect and a brilliant *Locux*," he said, musing into his cup - which Lytta promptly refilled without being asked.

Suddenly, I was transfixed. I had heard that title before although never in association with Ischae, and its meaning was opaque. At face value it meant a speaker or representative, but to the Succae it had a mystique of its own—agent or spy might be a better definition.

"It was indeed Ischae who helped us bring down the Serpent Cult as I remember," Dursc continued, and I felt a chill of recognition as more connections seemed to fall into place. I looked at Lytta, but her attention was focused outside.

"It's strange. I mean she was here not long ago. Appeared suddenly and then disappeared again. We barely exchanged a word."

"What did she say?"

Dursc thought for a moment but before he could answer, the door was opened, and events took over.

Tzir was flanked by two of Dursc's guards when he entered the hall. I noted that Lytta had moved between the former Vod and these new arrivals as if in defence of his body, but if Tzir noticed, he didn't react. Instead, he knelt in front of her, asked Dursc to forgive his intrusion and handed Lytta a sealed scroll that bore the stamp of Karsz—an armoured fist.

She read the contents swiftly and I saw, for the briefest moment, what I took to be a look of annoyance.

"Problems?" I asked, and she shrugged.

"I must return to the city," she replied.

"But we've only just got here."

"Did I say *you* had to return? These orders are addressed to me and me alone."

"And what am I meant to do whilst you're gone?"

"Nothing," she replied smartly. "Nothing at all. Take him."

The Ashai drew their weapons as Lytta backed away to guard Dursc, but I was in no position to fight.

"What is this all about Lytta?"

"The Vod commands your death. I will return to the citadel to find out why."

"You question the Vod's command?" Tzir said, a little too eagerly for my liking.

"I saw no messenger and have only the word of a Low-Nin that this message is genuine," she replied evenly. "Before I kill an emissary whom I have sworn to protect, I need to be certain I am carrying out the Vod's actual orders."

I could see Tzir's face flush in frustration. This clearly wasn't in the plan.

"No-one will harm this ambassador until I return," Lytta said, her words largely addressed to Tzir, "or they will answer to me."

As Dursc's guards closed in, the former Vod stared at me, his smooth face expressionless. He beckoned to Lytta, and she lent down for the briefest of exchanges.

I was hustled out the door as they both stared at me, a look of accusation on their faces.

Chapter Fifteen

I was not the only one to be surprised at the terms of my incarceration. I could see Tzir was angry at the impassive nature of Dursc's honour guard who, despite his protestations, returned me to my quarters rather than to his preferred location—a dungeon beyond the brass doors of the hidden fortress. Frankly, I was with Tzir. I would like to have had the chance to see beyond those great brass doors and whatever secrets the Low-Tsar kept behind them. I was beginning to wonder how much Dursc really knew about what was going on around him and whether his island retreat had really become a gilded prison cage. Still, I was reunited with armour and weapons which gave me some level of reassurance, and I settled down for a while to await developments.

As it turned out, I did not have long to wait, and within a few hours, there was a knock on my door after which an Ashai guard entered, followed by a tall man shrouded in a hooded cloak. The Ashai left and the hooded man revealed himself to be Dursc.

"My apologies, ambassador," he said, "but some level of artifice is necessary in these circumstances."

"What circumstances?" I asked. Dursc shook his head, and for a moment he looked as old as I knew him to be, his face crinkled in lines of consternation and concern.

"I fear both you and my Serrate have fallen into

something bigger than the murder of a concubine. Such things should not be handled this way."

I had been thinking the same things and I told him what Saaya had said about low expectations before she was silenced. Dursc nodded.

"It has that feel about it. That your competence and her alienation would combine to give the appearance of the matter being handled appropriately whilst in reality, you would get nowhere. It looks like they have underestimated both your suspicious nature and her talent for tenacity. You have come too close to something and now they are trying to stop you."

"That would explain the Necrote we encountered when we arrived. They must have known Lytta would have no choice but to investigate and confront the beast. They were obviously hoping it would devour us and solve their problems. But why would Karsz set me up this way?"

"Who said he did?"

"The order to execute me had the Vod's seal!"

"That does not mean it came from him."

"You said before that the Vod hears all, sees all, is all. Remember?"

"I do. Yet he relies on the counsel of others, the eyes and ears of others. That is why Lytta must return to the Citadel and establish the truth."

"That could get her killed."

Dursc nodded sagely. "Yes, it could. Disobeying a real order from the Vod is punishable by death. Yet she is one of our history's most illustrious Serrates and as such she is responsible for not taking actions that reflect badly on her Vod. This is a sensible precaution, especially given what the letter said."

"What did it say?"

"I will come to that. First, I must talk to you about Ischae and issue an apology."

"Apology?"

"Yes. You were a guest in my home when you were arrested. I should have intervened, offered you *rezort*."

Rezort implied sanctuary, certainly the right of any High-Nin with the force to support it. This was again a matter of honour. By not intervening, Dursc had lost Lao to Tzir and gained unwanted Zi, which would be lessened by my acceptance of his apology. I knew that the longer I considered his offer the better it would be for him, so it was a few minutes before I accepted his apology. Dursc smiled gratefully and continued.

"Ischae spoke highly of you," he said, and I was relieved to hear that said by another Succae. After all that had been revealed, I was beginning to worry that she had got close to me for reasons other than attraction.

"When I saw the Vod's letter it reminded me of something. A discussion she and I had when she was here. A conversation I had forgotten."

"What about?"

"A place on Cerule. A city."

"Which place?"

"Saindrescan," he said with a finality that made it sound notorious. It was not a name I immediately recognised, and I certainly couldn't remember Ischae ever mentioning it to me, so I shrugged.

"It means nothing to you?"

"Not as far as I can remember," I replied.

Dursc paused for a moment in considered thought.

"Ischae only mentioned it briefly, but I find it odd that it should come up again, now, and in such circumstances."

"The Vod's letter mentioned Saindrescan?"

"Indeed so. It said, 'following news received from Saindrescan, I now order you to sever the soul of Ambassador Azshael who I name assassin.' Quite specific, eh?"

"So I have enemies on the surface. It does not especially surprise me."

Dursc smiled briefly.

"I do not think that likely."

"Why not?"

"Because Saindrescan is a dead city. It has been so for a long time. One of the first places destroyed in your Judgement War against us."

"If it's dead then why did Ischae mention it?"

"She wanted to confirm if it was built on an historic site."

I could feel pieces of the jigsaw coming together in my mind.

"It's where you and the Serrate confronted Yggael isn't it?"

Dursc looked at me directly and nodded.

"Yes. Yes, it was."

Chapter Sixteen

I could really have used Sariel's help unravelling Saindrescan's past, but she was too far away, and I didn't have the time to spare. It would be quicker to go there and see for myself. I thought I was aware of most of the Flight's key engagements, and the fact I didn't know this one gave me cause for concern.

With Dursc's information on the city's location, I took flight and broke free of the moon's thin grip to soar into space, Nimrod carrying me forth into the starry darkness like a shooting star. Unlike some of my kind, I have always loved the freedom of flying in space, alone in the vastness of it all. I admit that even with the vacuum burring at the edges of my protective aura, I probably spent too long admiring the view of Cerule below, which was at once both awesome and terrifying. Awesome because of its inherent bounty and terrifying because of the extent of the damage we had wrought upon it in the war. There was no question in my mind that Cerule was on the path to destruction, tearing itself apart from the inside, and I could see huge red rivers of magma, like bloody open wounds, bleeding profusely across the planet.

I entered the atmosphere in a blaze of fire over the smallest of the continents, a set of three broken landmasses too large to be classified as islands, although given that they sat in an emerald sea, I suppose that is what they were.

Dursc had told me to look for an inlet that led up a river into a bay on the northernmost landmass, and it wasn't long before I had my bearings and descended through wild storms that sent angry, white-capped waves surging against the shoreline.

Saindrescan was tiered into four distinct sections carved into the side of a mountain. The Port and lower city sat below the main citadel, which stood atop a plateau guarded by great sandstone walls. This was itself divided into an outer and inner ward.

I landed on a worn jetty in the lower side of the city, where once busy port side wharves now stood silent except for the sound of heavy rain hammering down on ancient stone. Further on, the remains of abandoned ships waited for crews that were never coming back, decayed and spindly rigging looking like so many spiders' webs. Lesser vessels had already been sunk by the might of the seas, watery graves marked by debris or the occasional rotting mast top.

Rain gusted around me, and visibility was poor, so I flew upwards and landed atop the great sandstone walls of the upper citadel that were scarred, shattered and broken in places. From up above, what would no doubt have been teeming streets full of life, had a sad orderliness about them, as if bereft of purpose without the lives to fill them.

It was not the first dead city I had seen, and before, I had maintained a sanguine sense about them but now, I realised that a deep melancholy laid within, along with a lingering pang of doubt as to the righteousness of our cause. I quickly reminded myself why I was here and looked again for any reason as to why Ischae would have come here, and indeed, mentioned it to Dursc.

I dropped down into the outer ward and walked along the rooftops of buildings that nestled close together, watched only by the eternally vigilant eyes of the windows of empty and abandoned homes. I was glad of the sound of the rain around me, otherwise the silence of the place would probably have been overwhelming. I stalked vacant alleyways and thoroughfares, peeked inside homes and shops long left silent.

After a while, I developed a nagging feeling that I was missing something. Perhaps the answer lay not in something I could see but rather in something I couldn't.

In the inner ward of the citadel it was much the same story, except the residences of the High-Nin were much grander and the avenues wider. I reached a central square dominated by martial statuary, and a palace flanked by ancient temples. The rain began to ease and within a few minutes, as I stood beneath Dursc's statue, it had stopped completely. It was then I realised what was missing. The judged.

Judgement is a physical process that frees the spirit and leaves ashes or other vital essences behind. I could understand that, over a century later, the remains of those who had been caught outside when the Flight arrived would have been washed away or scattered to the winds, but what about those who had been inside? I looked around and made my way across the rain-slick square to the Palace.

It was a grand rectangular structure supported by hexagonal columns whose edges, whilst worn, still had a sense of being finely honed. I certainly wouldn't want to collide with them at speed. Great leaden doors embossed with scenes of martial prowess were caved inwards, buckled as if struck by a giant fist, and I had to squeeze through their twisted remains to emerge in a cool, quiet hall.

I paused for a moment to take in the environs. I had the impression that this was a place of reflection - a retreat rather than a functional building of state. Unlike the Succae architecture I knew, where the aesthetic was purely martial and austere, this spoke of artistry and sophistication. The stone floor was covered with chunks of debris. The walls were damp, the remains of colourful murals only vaguely discernible. In later chambers, rotting tapestries and torn hangings drooped sadly and water dripped through cracks, falling in droplets from the broken roof.

I wondered if the city's residents had crowded in here as my brother and sister Angels lit up the sky. Had they really expected to escape? No, of course not; they had expected their Vod to fight and his Ashai to drive these winged invaders from their sight, back to wherever they had come from. They were Succae. Why would they expect anything less?

I stood in the great hall of the Palace and thought about that arrogance of faith. It reminded me of the worst moment in my early days in the Flight and our own civil war. Eventually, we called him the Fallenstar, but he had many names both before and after that ill-advised rebellion. None would say it now, but back then, he was widely considered the brightest of the Archangels, a Prince of Princes. If I close my eyes and let the world slow around me, I can still feel the golden warmth of his aura, hear the mellifluous tones of his voice.

What happened next, I do not intend to rationalise or explain. I have said before that Angelic memory is unreliable and with the amount of Rain that was still making its pernicious way through my system, it is true that I was sometimes prone to hallucinations and a level of delirium. It is just that he and I have a connection, and I swear that sometimes, I can both hear and see him. It is impossible of course, but there; I have said it. Maybe it is because Nimrod, my golden lance, was once his and a part of him is imbued within it. I remember using that against him, pinning him to the ground as others well beyond my ambit came to chain him for the Judgement of Excelsis.

Maybe it was because I had bested him that he smiled at me as he and his conspirators were thrown from grace. Whatever the truth, I can only say I felt his presence at that moment and that I believe it was he who led me to the awful truth of Saindrescan.

Chapter Seventeen

I have never seen the actual moment of an individual's judgement. That is between Excelsis, and the soul involved. I have witnessed the aftermath, of course. The moment of ascension to the divine is like watching a cascade of thousands of tiny stars blazing in the firmament. I am told it is a moment of ecstasy so pure that no other known pleasure can begin to rival it. Imagine the sum of all your positive sensual encounters and multiply by a thousand, and you might skirt the surface. There is not meant to be any pain, even for those judged unworthy of redemption. We were told that there is no pain or suffering either, and certainly not a tortuous death wreathed in pain-etched agony.

Yet that is what I guessed had happened here at Saindrescan, when intuition or something else told me to look beyond my natural sight. It was in the realm of spirits that I saw the residue of Succae souls like so many unwashed stains on the stone floors and walls of the Palace.

It took my breath away, their shadows twisted and contorted in the same shapes as the bodies of Ischae and her child Naschinne. I made my way back through hall after silent hall to see more twisted and contorted shapes packed into every corner. It was clear that as many of the populace that could get inside to seek shelter had done so, and that the Thrones and Powers had come and destroyed them all.

I could feel my heart hammering in my chest as the

sickening realisation dawned. It was within our gift to murder in this way. Fair battle with armed enemies that resist judgement is one thing, but the wholesale slaughter of innocents is entirely another. I slumped down against a wall and wept, tears streaming down my face as the nobility of my purposed existence proved nothing more than a false idol, an edifice of my own construction that had taken an eternity to construct and literally a blink of a third eye to shatter.

Questions sparked like a chain reaction, each one piercing my heart like a barbed arrow. Personal questions came first - had Angels murdered Ischae? What if I knew them? Could Camael have been involved? Ischae knew him as my friend, so she would have let him into her presence. He must have known how she died was within his gift, yet he had done nothing to change my previous belief that it had to have been a Succae assassin.

Then wider questions—was our purpose truly noble? Did Excelsis allow the means to be the end, no matter the suffering? I was drowning in self-loathing and lost in anguish. I suspect that is where I would have died had it not been for the Fallenstar's voice inside my head, the last words he had said to me before the fall—"Screw serving vengeance cold. I'll take it hot and right away."

Chapter Eighteen

They came creeping in the dark, the four Angels sent to kill me. It was a stray piece of stone that one accidentally knocked with the toe of their boot that gave them away. It was the briefest of touches, but in my heightened state, it was as good as ringing a giant bell, and I retreated to take cover behind the base of a broken statue as they advanced. Part of me wanted to submit, to end the anguish, but that is not how I was made. No fire ever wants to wane when it can burn brightly.

I suspected they were the Halokim reborn, but clearly standards were slipping since my time in the group. We never made mistakes. They came into view flying inches above the ground, two abreast on opposite sides of the hallway. A tactically poor decision given Nimrod's powers, but then I doubted anyone had bothered to warn them of that important detail. I shaped the Fallenstar's weapon into a slim discus approximately five feet wide and hurled it with a strength enhanced by cold fury and rage at the pair on the left. I saw one of them react, bringing his spear up to parry, but the thin blade cut straight through the haft and went on to slice them both into two pieces. There was a brief gasp as life left them both, upper torsos sliding backwards as their lower bodies took a step forward before collapsing. I saw the motes of fire burn briefly against the pale walls as their souls were released.

To their credit, the other pair reacted swiftly, both flying upwards to gain a better view of their target. I sprinted in the direction of Nimrod, and one threw his spear straight away, missing me by a hair's breadth. I heard it slam into the wall beside me, chips of debris flying as the golden spearhead pierced stone. The other waited a moment before launching his projectile, the javelin gaining a silver sheen as it left his hand. I tried to duck and turn, but the weapon went straight through me, the icy haft cauterising the wound as it went. He had aimed for my remaining heart and missed only by a fraction. One piece of information they presumably had been given!

It hurt like hell and would take time to heal because of the sealing effect of the ice, but I kept going, focussing on staying on my feet and only just managing to reach Nimrod in time, as the assassins were hard on my heels. I fashioned a great shield as the pair breathed in and blew icy shards at me, seeking to cut and freeze me in the blast, hailstones as large as my fist bouncing off the edges. I held fast and pushed back, smashing into the pair with the shield and forcing them backwards. They went with it, making acrobatic dives and turns in mid-air as they tried to put distance between us. It was a good tactic for the one whose javelin had lanced through me, but the other was a fraction too slow. He paid for it as I reshaped Nimrod into a halberd and thrust it forward and up, twisting the blade as I went so that it sliced a surprised face in half, crunching through flesh, bone, and brain.

My final assailant gave me a black look as Nimrod regained its normal shape and I realised that we knew each other. He was one of Darophon's strong-arm gang.

"Who sent you?" I said as he drew his sword, a long, curved blade that blazed into life and sent shadows scurrying around the blood-stained hall.

"You should have stayed in your mistress's bed a few hours longer Azshael," he said, "then we'd have got you both. You're already dead Ambassador, a dead Angel walking. You just don't know it yet."

He may have said something else but by then the blood pounding in my ears blocked everything else out. I probably should have just wounded him so that he could be interrogated but as it was, I cut him to bits and took my time about it, too. I left their bodies in the temple, a suitable sacrifice to the long departed Succae dead of Saindrescan.

Chapter Nineteen

I was about to leave the dead city when it occurred to me that my assassins had to have come from somewhere nearby. There was no way they could have followed me as I descended to Cerule without my noticing, although I suppose they could have been told where I was headed. That would mean Dursc had betrayed me, and I didn't believe that was likely. No, it was far more probable that they were already here and I had stumbled across them. I'd come wandering into their web like an innocent fly ready to be devoured by so many spiders.

If they were already here, then there had to be a reason. What were they guarding or keeping safe? I resolved to find out and began searching the Port city for any sign of a hiding place I hadn't noticed on my original scout. I spent hours looking through sewers and canals, and in the Palace and Temple for any hidden areas, but to no avail.

Perplexed, I sat down near where the Angels' bodies were piled on a white marble plinth and thought for a moment. It was then I noticed the dried remains of a reddish mud on the boots of one of the dead. I inspected it and noticed the way it had splashed and stained the leather. Wherever this one had been, it had been muddy and wet, for the soles were still damp and sodden. I inhaled the scent and tasted Cerule's ocean.

I took flight and began to look around the coast for signs of caves, quickly finding several higher up the headland. I looked for the one that was least accessible from the perspective of a climber without wings and made entry as cautiously as I could.

Inside, I descended through a spiral of twisting passages that led to a cavern that fed into the sea. There, stacked away from where green water swirled and eddied, I could see barrels secured in netting. Half my height and twice as round, there were about thirty of them, all marked with the words *Sanguis Pluvia*, a phrase I had never heard before, but which loosely translated as *Blood Rain*.

Certain that there was no-one else around, I made Nimrod into a hatchet and broke one of the casks open. The liquid inside was thick and opaque, a whitish grey gloop with a pungent aroma that was distinctively acrid. It was also familiar, and it took my senses a while before I could place where I had smelled it before. I broke into a cold sweat as memory took me back to the time and place where I had lost my heart, or more specifically, to the chamber in which I had been imprisoned as I awaited my fate. I had thought it was just my imagination that had heard so many Angelic souls entrapped in that ghastly prison, but now I was beginning to wonder.

I kicked the cask open so that the contents rolled down the slick cavern floor in a white river, to swirl among the spume of the thundering waves. I watched with a sickened fascination as the identifiable remains of several glistening white hearts swirled within the green water before falling to my knees and retching noisily as memory finally identified the smell and the taste in my mouth. It was Rain.

Chapter Twenty

I stood atop the headland for some time and stared at the waves crashing on the shore below. The sea was angry, green water churning and frothing, spitting white spume against the rocks. I could see the red magma boiling in the depths below, the slow process of the crust tearing itself apart. Yet that process was also generating new verdant islands, magma quickly turning into the bedrock of ultimately short lived but fertile land.

As below, so above. I could feel my hands clenched around Nimrod's haft. It was a rictus grip, my muscles tensed, as red-hot anger coursed through my mind and body only to meet the ice of my cold and logical intent, resulting in new bodies of thought. In years past, I would have gone straight to Darophon and beat him to a bloody pulp in search of answers, but I had learned over time to allow the mist to clear and only act when the labyrinth of truth and lies had been successfully navigated.

There were things that didn't fit. Darophon was an intriguer of course, but intriguers very rarely made the mistake of leaving trails that led straight back to them. The Heralds work on the principle of deniable involvement in the influence over outcomes. You felt their presence, never saw it. No, Darophon was more elegant than that. He had also come to me early on and deliberately sought me out to tell me he was not the enemy, at least not this time. It looked like he had more faith in me than I had thought. He had my measure. He knew that if there was a chance to find Ischae's killer, it would be motivation enough for me to stay straight and find answers.

I had been selected to fail, but not by Darophon, which meant the presence of one of his foot soldiers among the troop of my would-be assassins was an attack on him as well. That was intriguing. I thought back to our conversation and his words about the armistice. I had taken that to mean he was in favour of its end, but I was now wondering whether my own defensiveness had obscured a subtler message. That he had, in fact, been trying to warn me. He had been right about Naschinne being more than a concubine, and maybe I had been right about the abuse of Chorael's sphere being a message to him. Darophon was one of the most powerful and influential individuals in the Flight, but such standing came with its own set of challenges, and it took constant vigilance to survive.

I went back to the beginning. I thought about my rescue and Lytta's intervention. The Vod had brought her back for reasons that, on the face of things, made sense. Yet, if Karsz was behind a Cabal, that reason made less and less sense. Why put such a powerful entity into play when you can't be sure of controlling its actions? I understood the incredible ties of loyalty and obedience that the Vod commanded, but my experience of Lytta suggested she was more her own person than not. Of course, whether Karsz knew that before he brought her back and rebound her in flesh was not something I could know. Karsz did not strike me as a likely suspect anyway. The Succae way was generally more direct, and I could not imagine Lytta being set up to fail, whatever Saaya had implied before she died. It was a frustrating puzzle. I could see the pieces moving but the overall picture was still a phantom image at the edge of my sight,

I watched the dark green waters churn below as my mind wandered, I noticed something strange carried by the white-capped waves crash against the rocks. It looked like a wrapped corpse whose bindings had unravelled in the tide. It was oddly incongruous and the only body I had seen in the environs of the quiet necropolis of Saindrescan, so I spread my wings and flew down to take a closer look.

It took little time to pull the body from the waves, and I carried it back to the headland for closer inspection. As it turned out, it was still fully wrapped, just a stretch of its binding that had frayed. It had the qualities of silk, a tough yet light and tensile strand that looked as if it had been used as a tether.

I drew my boot knife from its scabbard and cut the woven bindings to reveal the body within. It looked like a Succae male, with pallid skin and tight features. He was hairless, the skin smooth and curiously unworn or marked in any way. I was so used to seeing tattoos all over Succae bodies, it came as a kind of a shock to see such a blank canvas, and for a while, I just stared at it, totally transfixed. Then, my gut began to clench as I looked back out at the ocean. A deep sense of foreboding began to grow within me as I started to realise that Saindrescan's true secrets might lie beneath its surrounding waters rather than on land.

I took flight and headed out to sea. Directly ahead a couple of miles away, I could see pillars of steam where a new island was taking shape, and I flew around it before soaring down to skim the glassy green waters on the way back to the headland. I couldn't make out much, so I took the plunge, dropped into the cool water and headed down into the depths.

Chapter Twenty-One

Visibility became poorer the deeper I went, and the numbing coldness shrouded me in an icy caress. Part of me was tempted to head to warmer waters where the magma was leaking into the sea, but I suspected my task lay closer to shore.

Before long, an underwater forest came into sight, long strands of weeds swaying in the invisible flow of the current, and I swam into their gentle embrace. There was a kind of melancholy beauty about them, timeless dancers of the depths that moved in perfect synchronicity with the planet. I went deeper in and headed downwards for the forest floor. Nimrod's golden haft glowed brighter as the dark fathoms pressed in around me.

Lower down, the forest grew denser and thicker. I could feel my light fading and I knew that I could not spend too much longer here in this dark, hostile environment. I pulled at strands of the weeds with my spare hand and they softly drifted away like a regretful lover, until I could see the sandy seabed below. For a while I walked along the bottom, the sand sucking at my heels as I went, until I finally found what I was looking for.

They were ghostly white visions, the white bindings of their shrouds luminous in the gloomy depths. Each body had been tethered and bound to several strands of seaweed, and there were dozens all around me. I knew what I would find, but I cut through the bindings anyway to reveal another Succae face, eyes closed, skin unmarked, unlined and inanimate. A blank canvas waiting to be written on, but to what purpose? With heavy heart, I thought I knew, and I now understood the real secret of Saindrescan's Necropolis; that it wasn't a city of the dead at all. Rather it was a centre of the waiting dead, a mustering point for a replacement army.

I was about to leave when I saw another group of white shapes, tightly clustered and tethered to a skeletal coral reef. They were bulkier than the others I had seen but the shrouds were just as tightly bound. I approached and slit the bindings on one of them. It was an Angel, one of my brothers. His face a death mask of unlife. His arms were folded across his chest in gentle repose, but I could see his chest bore the scars of violation in the areas where his hearts had once been. Someone, a flesh crafter I presumed, had filled in the holes and I surmised these would be infiltrators, wolves in sheep's clothing who could get near to those that mattered in the Flight command. It made me sick to the core.

I headed for the surface, and as I trod water in the moon-drenched sea, I realised why Lytta had been brought back. It wasn't anything to do with this or with me. In the same way I had been relied on to fail in my task, so she had been brought back to succeed in hers; to lead the Cabal to the one Succae they couldn't get access to. Dursc.

Part Three

Chapter One

By the time I arrived back in the black sky over Dursc's moon garden, all I could see was the press of battle. Ashai swarmed everywhere, their black armour like the chitinous mass of some giant insect that undulated and swayed to the sound of the cries of battle.

The focal point was around the steps of the main residence where the bodies of the fallen already lay in piles. I saw Dursc briefly, as a bright spear lanced sharply through the heads of several attackers that fell back before him. Then he was gone again, moving with a speed that belied his years. Away to the right, bodies rippled and surged as Lytta moved through them, possession after possession, the spectral Tigress shredding and mutilating as it went. I wondered if her body was secure inside the building or whether it was just another apparent corpse buried under many others.

I heard a shout below me and looked down to see one of the Ashai in blood-red armour, like that worn by the warrior commanding the assault on Hostmann. Bowmen ran to his side and suddenly the air was full of arrows, and I had to quickly ascend to avoid their deadly points.

I soared over the house and round the lake to see Tzir and several members of Dursc's honour guard hard pressed on all sides, a shrinking pocket defending the lakeside of the house from being overrun. It was such a surprise that I had to look twice to confirm what my eyes had already told me. If anything,

I had expected Tzir to be leading the enemy assault, not a spirited defence. I fashioned Nimrod back into a great golden shield and called down to Tzir to make space. To his credit, he hardly flinched, just shrank back slightly to allow me to take his place and push the melee line backwards. Ashai attackers stumbled and were then trampled under the push and sudden shove as I put all the strength I had behind the weight of the shield.

Perhaps it was my arrival or that Dursc had not gone down easily, or perhaps Lytta's literally soul-destroying powers had affected the attackers' morale, but the combined effect shattered the Ashai assault, and they broke, lines of troops literally vanishing into thin air. The red-clad Ashai was last again and turned to acknowledge us with a swift flourish of his blade and a bow before disappearing. Dursc, his skin almost black with Succae blood, turned to me and said one word: "Snakes".

Chapter Two

"Snakes everywhere," Dursc said again, through sharp teeth gritted so hard I could picture them fracturing and breaking apart. For a moment I was lost, all my senses seeking a new threat until Tzir fell to his knees and bared the back of his neck to the former Vod. It was then I understood Dursc's meaning and the understandable venom of his tone.

There was a moment of absolute quiet and I tensed, awaiting Tzir's sudden demise at the edge of Dursc's great blade.

"Why did you betray me, Tzir?" Dursc said as the Low-Tsar stayed still, eyes facing the ground.

"*Prizz*," Tzir said, and if he said it once, he said it a hundred times in a rushed mantra of unexplained confession. Dursc shook his head in slow disbelief as did I. *Prizz* was a practice that was only common among the Low-Nin, a way of rationalising their status and allegiances to the higher caste. In essence, it meant that a Low-Nin could have obligations to numerous masters if, at the time the obligation was made, it didn't conflict with another one already in practice.

"Who?" Dursc said quietly, but Tzir said nothing in response. Lytta's body stirred; she suddenly rose to her full height and in one swift motion, the silver blade she carried blurred through the air in a strike that would have separated Tzir's head from his body, but Dursc casually waved his hand and she stopped short, the edge of her weapon only a hair's breadth shy of Tzir's exposed neck.

"*Prizz* it is then Tzir," Dursc said, his gravelly voice devoid of emotion.

"No longer will I see you. You are released from my service."

Tzir said nothing, but his face was distraught as Dursc's guards removed him, leaving Lytta and myself alone in his presence.

"Let us inspect the dead," Dursc said, striding out on to the battlefield that had once been his gardens.

Dead Ashai littered the manicured lawns, slumped and lifeless beneath the ornamental trees. "Citadel soldiers," Dursc said after he had turned a few over and examined their markings in detail. "These Ashai swear loyalty to the Vod and Marshal alone and follow only their orders. They obviously weren't expecting to have to deal with all of us," he added, looking at Lytta and myself.

"Why did you return, Lytta?"

"I read my orders in more depth and realised they were not signed by Karsz. As far as I am concerned, it is only the Vod's direct command that I must follow. Anything else is optional."

"Including orders from me?" Dursc said with a ghost of a smile.

"Yes," she replied simply, with no further explanation.

"What about you, Ambassador? I didn't expect you to return here at all."

I talked then for a while about my discoveries in Saindrescan and the attack by the Halokim. Part of me was wary about revealing that I knew about the army that slept beneath the waves off Saindrescan's coast but given I had been right about Dursc being a target of whatever Cabal I had uncovered, it seemed counter-productive to keep anything from those that I hoped were now my allies in all this.

Dursc sat down slowly, suddenly looking less vital.

"That must be what Ischae was referring to when she talked

about the waiting dead. I presumed she was speaking prosaically not literally." I could see the sadness he bore; the responsibility for her death that weighed as heavily on his shoulders as it did on mine.

"Peace is only secured by preparing for war," Lytta said quietly. It was a military truism, but Dursc shook his head.

"That presumes your enemy is also aware of your strengths. This is preparation for annihilation and a violation of the Accord we agreed. A Vod is worth his word, or he is worth nothing," he said, and his voice trembled with rage.

Dursc had a point, but I couldn't help but wonder if Karsz and his supporters would feel the same way. It was easy to uphold ideals of leadership and be critical of those who fail that test when you're not the one under attack.

"They're being staged and animated here," Lytta said, and we both turned to look at her sharply. "I have seen blank bodies in the vaults below and at least one Flesh Crafter as well."

"So Tzir is a part of this Cabal then?" Dursc said wearily.

"I'm not certain that's the case," I said, "but he must know at least one who is. I do not believe a Low-Tsar of his standing would allow such things to take place in his hold without at least being aware of them."

"He has declared *Prizz*. It allows him to stay silent on the matter."

"To other Succae, yes that's true but not necessarily to me. If I can convince him to talk, perhaps I can give him a way out of this mess."

Lytta nodded. "Until now, Tzir has been your loyal supporter and we have faced much together. I would rather know to whom his debt is owed than not."

Dursc sat silently for a moment and then stood up.

"Very well," he said. "Say whatever you need to say to get answers but whatever the outcome, Tzir's time in my service is over, as is my time here. It will not be long before whoever sent these troops sends more than we can handle."

We returned to Dursc's villa, and his few remaining bodyguards stood watch whilst he collected a few personal items and mementos. Lytta went to summon her Shadowdrake and I had the chance to talk with Dursc about Ischae.

"Was she working for you when she was killed?"

"Yes, she was. She was my emissary during the later stages of the war. At that time, it felt to me that we were moving backwards. You see, in times of serious threat, it has been my experience that our society either unites or fragments, and from what my agents were telling me, it was the latter rather than the former that was happening."

"So, you were advising peace talks?"

"Yes, or at least a truce to give both parties a chance to consider such a path."

"What did Karsz say?"

Dursc looked at me solemnly. "No Vod likes the thought of admitting weakness any more than your Archangels like the thought of defeat."

I thought back to the way Darophon had described the Accord as a truce and one that could end anytime, and now his words sounded more and more like a warning than a threat.

"So he was against it?"

"I would say he resisted the concept for some time; really until the retreat to this moon."

"Why change course then?"

"I think because of Ischae. In my service as an emissary, she spent much of her time mixing with the High-Nin and gauging their opinions. That was useful, but survival in the High caste dictates stating categorical support for the Vod, or at least saying so with credible conviction. It was, however, her attention to the Lower castes and discovery of their return to worshipping the Old Gods, especially the more voracious ones, that I think got Karsz's attention. An invading enemy is far easier to fight and identify than a hidden one that lives and thrives within. I think Karsz understood that he was losing the belief of the people, no matter how strong he himself might be. We reserve the right of challenge to any and all, so Karsz would have been concerned that a challenger with the powers of a deity behind them might have proven too much, even for him."

I paused as Dursc carefully rolled up an intricately woven wall hanging and placed it into his knapsack.

"Did she ever talk to you about a Low-Nin called Jasniz?"

"No. It is not a name I know. Why?"

"He's seriously involved in all this. We knew him as the owner of a tavern where we would spend time. I'd say he was a Low-Tsar in everything but name."

Dursc raised his eyebrows.

"Ischae? In a tavern? If that's so, then it wasn't for entertainment. I think she was watching this man, building a picture of who and what he really was."

I tried to think back to when we had first visited Jasniz's tavern—probably only a few months before Ischae's death and a few months after Rain had first started to circulate. It felt like Ischae and Jasniz had known each other well before I was invited, but perhaps that was part of her cover. Her ability to listen meant people were all too willing to talk, and I had to include myself in that.

"What about Rain?" I asked as Dursc packed his final memento mori.

"What about it?"

"You know what it is? What it's made from?"

Dursc looked at me, his eyes piercing but unreadable.

"I do now," he said after a long pause. "Not before."

"But why?"

Dursc shrugged, his shoulders knotted with muscle.

"It must be a weapon," he said simply, "a tool of revenge."

"Against us? But it only has power over your kind—to me it's just a narcotic."

"Are you sure of that? I thought Yggael was vanquished, yet I saw her powers being used on the field of battle just a few hours ago. Is everything just the way you understand it to be now, or could it be that just like me, you don't know everything?"

Dursc smiled and I had to smile back. He had a point. The picture was coming together but it was still a jigsaw.

Lytta arrived then and signalled for the former Vod to follow her. In the garden I could see the Shadowdrake's immense form silhouetted against the moon.

"I'll get Dursc to safety and then I'll come and find you," Lytta said. I smiled appreciatively but something in her tone reminded me of the day we'd left my side of the Tether. The anniversary of the Accord would be only hours away by now. It had to be the Cabal's target, although who they were, who they were planning to kill and how were still all unknown. I needed answers—and quickly.

Chapter Three

It didn't take me long to find Tzir. He was alone, sitting on a stone bench next to the Moon Garden's ornamental gates, his face a study in misery.

"Go away, Angel," he said, although his voice was soft, and his tone lacked conviction.

"Might not be the best of ideas. Pushing away the one hand that could help you."

Tzir looked up and fixed me with red eyes that were full of blood.

"Help me? How could you possibly help me?"

"That depends, doesn't it? I mean I know you have declared *Prizz* which means no Succae can demand any answers from you. I'm not one of your kind though, am I? You can talk to me without breaking any vows you might have made, can't you?"

I left the question hanging and Tzir's silence spoke volumes as I saw him thinking through the implications.

"I'll even help you out —I'll do all the talking. All you need to do is nod when I'm right. How's that?"

"What do I get in return, Ambassador?"

"My promise that I will do what I can to get Dursc to reconsider your position."

Tzir looked at me and shook his head in resignation before sitting upright again and regaining some of the poise and posture that I had seen when I first arrived in the presence of the Low-Tsar.

"Go on then," he said quietly. "Speak and I will listen."

My first topic was Rain. I could see Tzir nodding in confirmation at what I already knew of its composition and effect, and I had a feeling he had been involved in distributing it.

"It was made here, wasn't it?"

Tzir looked momentarily uncomfortable but then set his jaw and nodded.

"Were Angels brought here to be harvested?"

"No," Tzir replied with some level of indignation. "I would never have agreed to that."

"How can you be sure?"

"I never wanted any part of the war. I just wanted to keep my people and my network safe."

"Rain is not just another narcotic, is it?"

"Not now, no."

"What do you mean by that?" I asked, slightly confused.

"It has changed since it was captured at Saindrescan. The basic ingredients might stay the same, but the chemistry has been adapted. It is no longer the weapon your kind used on us there."

I was so shocked that I was momentarily speechless. Surely that couldn't be true. We had built a biological weapon from our own body parts to destroy a city. Tzir saw the look on my face and laughed softly.

"What? You didn't know? They called it the Silver Rain. Beautiful at first, and magical. It stimulated our spirits, gave us a sense of unbelievable euphoria for a short while. Then, once it had gone through the skin, it pulled the essence from us, drew the blood out in a horrible, choking death."

"How do you know this?

"I was there," he said simply. "Fortunately, I was not in the city but in the smuggler's tunnels beneath the city's docks. My crew managed to weather the Silver Rainstorm underground and departed before your Angels began their sweep of the city."

"If it was so effective, then why didn't we just continue to deploy it? If what you're saying is true, we could have quickly won the war."

Tzir nodded calmly. "You'd think so. From what Ischae told me, the results, however, were not effective. Silver Rain destroys the essence of being Succae. You are here to judge souls, but Silver Rain destroyed everything, our entire being. It made an impression, but ultimately, it was not going to help you achieve your 'judgement'."

I didn't know what to be more appalled about—the fact that the Flight had slaughtered a city to make a point or that we had been made to carry on fighting and dying when there had been an alternative. Yet these were the fine points that separated Heralds from soldiers. I was just surprised that Anael would have sanctioned such a terrible act.

"You said the chemistry has changed. Why would you allow something so lethal to be distributed to the population at all?"

"It is not the same now. It has been distilled into something less potent."

"For what purpose?"

"It's a blood stimulant. A narcotic. You should know—I understand you were quite taken with it not so long ago."

I smiled and Tzir took it to be a rueful one, clearly believing that he had caught me out. In truth it was a victory smile. In his efforts to impress me, he had made a minor slip. Something small yet revealing, and I was almost certain I now knew to whom Tzir had sworn his allegiance before Dursc.

"So Jasniz had no other purpose for it, other than to make a profit as befits his Low-Tsar status?"

"Not that he ever said," Tzir replied casually, not realising he had just betrayed his own vow of silence. I paused, and he swiftly realised what he'd said. He visibly deflated, all the arrogance and posturing snuffed out in an instant. To his credit, he must have realised that confession was the only viable path left available to him.

"He's up to something but I swear I don't know what, and by the way, Jasniz is no Low-Tsar. He's a High-Nin masquerading as one of us, a Servant of the Well."

Ischae had mentioned these supposedly mythical individuals before, High-Nin avatars of the Necrene source that animates all Succae. Before the Enlightenment, they had acted as agents to the High Priests of the Succae's pagan cults, and even the Vods had feared their talents to inspire and lead insurrection from the shadows.

Had Jasniz taken it upon himself to lead an insurrection against Karsz? Had he found sympathisers among the Angels who hated the truce just as much, and was that how the Cabal was born? It was beginning to make sense. Jasniz had spent years building to this, allowing time for a new army to be ready to deliver an unexpected, possibly decisive blow once the Accord was over.

"Where is he now, Tzir?" I asked, and his eyes looked down the steps towards the lower citadel.

"It's too late, Angel," Tzir said, standing up and removing his armour and weapons.

"What do you mean?"

"The last shipments left for Scarpe several days ago."

"Shipments of what? Rain?"

Tzir said nothing. Just drew a thick bladed silver dagger from within the folds of his martial juke and knelt in front of me. I hadn't witnessed a Succae honour-death before, and it took me by surprise.

"If you have any care for me, take my head," Tzir said, and before I could protest, he had plunged the blade into his sternum with an audible gasp. He drew the blade along and then jaggedly upwards, folds of flesh falling away. I confess that I was momentarily stunned at the suddenness of his actions. I wish now I had acted quicker, but he pulled the blade right to reveal his rib cage before Nimrod sliced through the air and ended his agony, his body slumping backwards, black blood pooling out slowly around him.

Bharzo was waiting for me beyond the gate. He must have been one of the masked soldiers that Tzir had brought to Dursc's defence, and he greeted me with unexpected warmth.

"Tzir's not coming," I said after the exchange of pleasantries. Bharzo sighed and nodded his head.

"I thought as much. Did he die well?"

I didn't really know the answer to that, but I recognised a soul in need of comfort.

"Yes," I said.

Bharzo nodded and grinned "He'll be back then, and a High-Nin as well. The Well rewards."

The Well Rewards: it was one of the Succae's most important principles, the belief that a humble life held in service as a Low-Nin would eventually be rewarded by a return to life in the Higher caste. A soul could be returned to the Well many times before achieving this honour. I remember Ischae being scathing about the belief, which she held was born out of hope rather than truth. Yet for the Low-Nin at least, it was a pillar of existence.

"Here," Bharzo, said, unwrapping an intricately fashioned, star-shaped piece of metal and handing it to me. "Tzir said to make sure you got this."

I turned it over in my hands. It was heavy and only just fit my palm. In the centre was a dial that could be turned to reveal a series of spikes that would emerge and retreat, depending on how far the dial was spun.

"What is this?"

"It's the key to the Lower Citadel," Bharzo said.

I paused for a moment and said a silent thank you to Tzir. I realised now that he had known his outcome from the moment he had decided to maintain his vow to both the High-Nin he had sworn to serve. Nothing I could have said or done would have changed that. In Tzir's case, I hoped Ischae was wrong and that the Well would indeed reward as expected.

Chapter Four

Once I had found a suitable set of Ashai armour to disguise myself, Bharzo led me down towards the gates of the Lower Citadel. I was surprised to see them unguarded, albeit firmly closed. Bharzo indicated the recessed mechanism and I slotted Tzir's key into position, hearing a distinct whirr and click as bolts locked into place. Bharzo pushed on the gate, which swung open with surprising ease, and we moved inside.

Stone steps led down into a great vaulted chamber that was dimly lit by central cauldrons, where fires dwindled and the hot coals within glowed red like rats eyes in the night. The cauldrons had clearly not been tended to for a while and vast areas of the chamber lay swathed in shadow. Bharzo and I advanced quietly down the steps and into the chamber. It looked as if the guards had used this area as a barracks, but it was deserted now.

At the end of the chamber, another set of steps spiralled down into darkness. Bharzo hesitated as I tentatively began to make my way down, body hugging the wall.

"It does not smell good down there," he said. I sniffed the air, but aside from a stale mustiness, could sense nothing untoward. I could see he was nervous and decided to let him off the hook. He had probably done far more than Tzir had told him to.

"Why don't you stay here? Secure the exit."

He breathed an audible sigh of relief and nodded swiftly.

"Yes! Good plan. Bharzo will stand watch and make sure

you can make a quick escape if needs be." He saluted me and quickly retreated into the dimly lit chamber. I turned up my aura, light leaking from the black carapace like armour, and made my way down.

I passed through a stone archway and found myself in front of a solid wooden door banded with metal. I could see sigils inscribed on the wood, and various rough-hewn votive offerings piled in the vacant eye sockets of skulls that were stacked, top down, on both sides of the doorway. Most of the offerings were snake shaped and I thought I had found my way to where Yggael's cult had been brought back to life. I pushed against the door, and it gave way with a low creak.

I stood in a cavern and heard skittering as a dozen Dead Men's Hands approached me, like a pack of so many white spiders. They were flesh creations with eight fingers and a single wide eye embedded in the back of the hand. I was clearly not who they had been designed to serve, and no sooner had they appeared than they skittered back off into the shadows.

There was a power here. I could sense it with every fibre of my being. I was used to hunting deities, and I could sense the presence of one nearby, giving off waves of angry malice. It had to be Yggael herself. I advanced cautiously through more caverns until I found her, shackled and subdued, surrounded by hundreds of her dead children, the lethal green snakes that had nearly claimed the lives of both Sariel and I in the ambush at Hostmann's former residence.

I stayed in the shadows awhile, monitoring the massive viperine shape that writhed in the dark pit below. She was restrained by great shackles that bound her within a warded circle, magical runes of imprisonment carved into the lip of the pit's wall.

Her serpentine body was scaled and black, ending in a long tail that coiled beneath her. Her humanoid torso glittered green with occasional flecks of yellow, breasts small and pointed. Her face was a curious mix of humanoid and reptile, strangely compelling and beautiful in its own sinuous way.

Green snake eyes with yellow irises wept bitter venomous tears of frustration that spattered below her, pitting the ground with their acidic touch. Her head, crowned by a writhing nest of Lishi, was secured by a solid metal yoke that had been placed around her slender neck. Each of the seven lesser viperine heads strained and pulled in different directions, desperately tasting the air with forked tongues for a clue to a way out. I had no doubt this Gorgon Goddess, at the height of her powers, would be a formidable opponent.

"I can see you Angel," Yggael said suddenly.

"Even when you're hiding, your light is brighter than anything else here, so there's no point lurking in the shadows." For a moment I felt pretty foolish, forgetting that I was in the presence of a power, and I emerged slowly from my useless hiding place, drawn on by her voice, which was sonorous, yet inflected with weary sadness. Even in a diminished state, deities are not something to be taken lightly, and I was painfully aware how alone and potentially vulnerable I was. I decided on a show of force, a reminder of my potential, and Nimrod amplified my luminance in a brilliant blaze of light that lit up the chamber as if a hundred candles had suddenly burst into flame.

"What have you come here for? To kill me?" she asked, and her voice sounded subdued and defeated.

"I'm not one of the Halokim," I said, thinking she would get the reference, "so no. I'm not here for that."

"That's a shame. I would happily return into the darkness now. I am sick of being abused in this way."

"Abused?"

"Can't you see? Each time they use my powers for their own, they call my children forth. Yet in this prison there is no space, and when I move, they are crushed and die. I am killing my own infants, my precious Lishi." She screamed in frustration and the seven heads screamed with her as the snakes on her head seemed to writhe in agony. Acid venom sprayed the walls to leave smouldering, pitted marks on the stone.

"Free me, Angel," she begged, and I felt the siren power of her voice. Yet, this was hardly my first dance with a serpent goddess, and I stood impassively as she wailed.

"You would surrender for judgement? Final judgement this time, Yggael traveller of worlds?"

She looked up at me and nodded sorrowfully.

"Yes. Yes. Any fate is better than this."

"How did this happen to you?"

"I was a victim of my own vanity. They devoted worshippers to me and gave me just enough power to lure me back to this world when your war ended. I was vain enough to believe they truly needed and wanted me here. They promised me a great temple, a movement that would crown me as their Queen of Queens. Of course, I came, only to find Angels and their mastery of fire. They burned my children, forced me into this pit. At first, I thought it was an Angelic plot, that my Succae worshippers would come and rescue me." She slumped downwards and coiled in on herself.

"Then what happened?"

"They came alright, but not to worship. Rather, to abuse me, to milk my veins for venom and draw my powers from me. They cared little for the consequences."

I was thinking about what to do and how I would get her back to the Tether when she screamed again, this time in obvious, agonised rage. Her head shook briefly, and I could see dozens of small green and black snakes fall and cascade off her slender shoulders. Small bursts of green light erupted around the cavern as the Succae used Yggael's stolen powers of travel.

I took flight and retreated into a shadowy cove, watching as a dozen black-armoured Ashai arrived, led by a familiar face. Jasniz.

Chapter Five

The Ashai with Jasniz spread out quickly to search the dark corners of the cavern, but clearly the news of my intervention had not reached their ears as they concentrated their search on the ground, rarely looking up above them. A group of four soldiers left the cavern to have a look above, but I heard Jasniz tell them not to go too far.

I had positioned myself behind several stalactites in the cavern ceiling above Yggael's prison. It was a perfect spot to see and not be seen, out of reach of both the goddess and her captors. Jasniz had taken his helmet off but was otherwise clad in dark red armour, emblematic of one of the senior ranks of Ashai, and he casually strode to the edge of Yggael's pit. I was tempted to put Nimrod straight through his head and wipe that casual smirk off his face, but I needed to be sensible. He had information I needed, and I had to find a way to get it out of him before indulging in any revenge.

"Not long now Yggael," he said, peering down at the goddess, who had retreated against the pit wall to avoid her fallen offspring, who even now writhed beneath her, blindly seeking her warmth without realising the danger of being crushed beneath her serpentine bulk. "Soon this will all be over, and I can let you depart for somewhere else, somewhere where you're truly wanted."

Her face contorted into a sneer. "I don't believe you Jasniz the Liar. You have come to end me."

"End you? Well, there's a thought," he said with a smile, and walked away to speak with some of his men who were busy moving equipment from a hidden cache that I had failed to notice in the brief time I'd had to look around.

I heard a buzz in my head and realised it was a telepathic message, which could only come from one person in this place. I lowered my mental defence to allow Yggael's voice to come clearly into focus.

"I claim sanctuary, Angel. I will surrender to your Archangel, accept my fate, and become a shadow, a forgotten shade. I will answer no more entreaties, accept no worship. Be the false idol your creator says I am. Just save me!"

"I'll do what I can, goddess," I said. Thanks, Yggael. Great timing.

Jasniz's soldiers had moved barrels to the edge of the pit, and I recognised Hostmann's markings on the side of several of them. I had a bad feeling about what was to come next when the patrol suddenly came running back.

"What is it?" Jasniz said, as one of them ran up to him.

"Dursc's troops. I saw a group of them moving down this way."

Really? Had Bharzo suddenly managed to impersonate a group of soldiers? To be fair, he was a big unit, but hard to mistake for more than one man. It was a useful distraction, though, and one I knew I had to take.

"Be ready Yggael. I am going to need your help if we're going to come out the other side of this more or less intact."

"More or less?"

"Just being optimistic," I replied caustically, and then I swooped down from the shadows and into the flickering light.

Chapter Six

Nimrod blazed into light as I came into land, my wings buffeting both the barrels and the Ashai immediately surrounding Jasniz backwards. Several soldiers were blinded and sent sprawling, but Jasniz and his three closest cohorts - who were clearly veterans of Angel warfare - had quickly turned and linked arms so that the effect was muted. For a moment I hoped that Jasniz, dazzled by the radiance of light, hadn't recognised me, but it was a hope quickly dashed.

"It's Azshael!" he shouted retreating behind the three Ashai who had now quickly drawn weapons and were moving to encircle me.

"Aim for his hearts! He only has one."

The ones I had temporarily dazed were quickly recovering and I realised I was outnumbered, eight to one.

The Ashai attacked in a worryingly co-ordinated manner, blades slicing past me, and I was forced to take flight again and take refuge over Yggael.

"Stop playing with them," she said, ever so helpfully, in my mind.

"Oh, I'm sorry. Do you want a give it a try?" I replied, my words laced with suitable sarcasm.

"Break these chains and I will," she said, quite earnestly. Well, it's hard to turn a polite request from a goddess down, so I did as she asked. I dropped down to Yggael's head height, ignoring the screams of warning that were rocking round my mind.

Call me proud, but at that stage, I would rather have been paralysed by her than killed by Jasniz or his stooges. I thrust Nimrod into the metal yoke around her neck and pushed with all my might. For a moment it stood firm. and then I felt some movement and heard the squeal of metal bending and breaking. I gave one final twist and the yoke suddenly fractured and fell away, the shattered lock crashing down into the pit below.

Yggael, uncoiling, launched herself upwards to tower over the pit wall. Her whole frame shuddered, and she showered the Ashai below her with an emerald green mucoid spray. They recoiled backwards, but Jasniz leaped forward and kicked two of the barrels over the lip of the pit wall. I had a very bad feeling but there was nothing I could do. I just watched them sail out into space and then plummet thirty feet or so to crash open and cover the stony pit floor in a crimson wash.

The next thing I heard was screaming. Ashai were screaming as first armour and then flesh melted away in the acidic spray. In under a minute, they were nothing more than steaming puddles of white bone. Yggael's hooded viper heads emitted a strange whistling sound before she herself began to tremble and scream. It was a horrendous sound, and I was momentarily transfixed as I saw what was happening.

Yggael started to convulse and began haemorrhaging. Dark green rivers poured from her mouth, eyes, ears, and nose. Her chest was similarly awash, blood flowing freely from her nipples. Within seconds she just seemed to collapse and coil in on herself, a vibrant divinity drained and desiccated into a barren husk, lying silently in a dark pool of her own blood.

The intoxicating scent of strong red wine enveloped me, and I recognised it immediately as Hostmann's creation. This must be why they had used him—to create a wine that would mask the taste of Rain or whatever toxic version of the drug that Jasniz and his cabal had refined over time. Having seen what it could do to a goddess, I had little doubt of its lethality.

"I can see you're impressed, Azshael," Jasniz said, his voice echoing around the cavern. Yggael had helped even the odds. It was just him and me now, and I knew only one of us would get out of this place alive. I switched senses, seeking the shifting vampire wraith inside him, and I saw him standing back by the remaining stack of barrels. He was uncoiling a long chain with a knife point at one end and a spiked ball at the other. It was a weapon called a Serpent's Rattle but, in the Flight, we had nicknamed it 'The Hunter'. It had been one of the Succae's more lethal weapons, smashing through wings and pulling us to the ground where the bladed end would quickly tear through flesh and spell doom. The only good thing about it was that it was hard to master and only a few elite Ashai could wield them effectively.

"You know," Jasniz said as he wound the chain around his body and casually walked towards me. "There was a time when I thought you and I would be working on the same side. That's why I had Ischae bring you down to the tavern. To observe you, sound you out."

I felt my blood rush and my corona pulsed a darker shade. Jasniz laughed.

"Surely, you've worked that out by now, Ambassador. Ischae was originally part of our little conspiracy."

"You're lying," I said, but something moved in the depths of my subconscious. It was like feeling the wash of a Leviathan's wake as it cruises through the depths.

"Oh, no. I assure you that in this matter at least, I am telling you the truth. In fact, you have me to thank for your rather ill-timed romance. I told her to get close to you and she did as she was told. Unfortunately for her, and now for you, she did her job rather too well."

"Why would Ischae want war? She spent all our time

together working to make the peace last."

Jasniz drew closer and then sighed audibly.

"It's not always about you, Angel. Ischae may not have wanted war, but I can tell you that she did want a change of Vod. If that meant war, then it was, for her, an acceptable price for the removal of Karsz."

"So Karsz is not behind all this, then?"

Jasniz laughed and shook his head.

"Well done, Ambassador. You always were quick on the uptake. Before the war, Ischae served the Vod. Or perhaps, serviced the Vod would be a better choice of words. He is a voracious man with strange appetites, but as you know, Ischae was a strong woman, a concubine capable of dealing with his more vicious side. Or perhaps I should say 'surviving'?"

I couldn't tell if he was baiting me, trying to goad some sort of emotional response. Yet there was no malice in his tone. If anything, it was tinged with some level of melancholy.

"I admired her greatly you know," he said, "especially after the Vod chose Naschinne to join his harem. It was the one thing she begged him not to do as she was released from his service. You understand they were..."

"Like mother and daughter, yes."

"Indeed so. She made no fuss, left his service with her head held high and did her best to prepare Naschinne for what was to come."

"If you admired her so much, why did you have her killed, Jasniz? What secrets was she about to reveal?"

Jasniz shrugged his shoulders.

"Honestly, Azshael, I had nothing to do with it. It is my understanding that Angels assassinated her, so it was almost certainly a warning to you."

"How do you know that?"

"Naschinne told me. It's why she was on your side of the

Tether when she was murdered. Her *maz's* death touched her quite deeply. She was driven to find answers."

He carried on talking, drawing closer. His tone continued to be reasonable, but I stopped listening to the words, as it had got to the point where they really didn't matter. His only purpose was to get in range of using the Rattle and I had known that from the start. Jasniz was cleaning house and there was no way I could be exempt from that process.

"I made a promise," I said, and Jasniz stopped suddenly, his words abruptly cut off. "So it doesn't really matter what the truth is, does it? You're an accomplished liar, those lies kill people, and you care little for the consequences. I made a promise to avenge the dead and it starts with you."

That was what I wanted to say, but Jasniz attacked as soon as I interrupted him. He launched the knife end of the rope straight at my face, but I spun Nimrod's haft and caught the chain so that it wrapped around my spear, the tip of the knife slicing through my cheek. I yanked Nimrod backwards with all my might, and Jasniz made the fatal mistake of hanging on to his weapon. To be fair, maybe he was tangled up in it and had no choice, but I like to believe he made an error of judgement in his final moments. He'd already made a bad choice trying to kill an Angel of Vengeance in the first place. I pulled him off his feet and watched him tumble into the same pit where Yggael had died in such horrendous agony. For a moment he dangled in space, and our eyes met as I slowly turned Nimrod to a vertical position and the Rattle's chain slipped down the haft to join its owner in the deadly, poisonous stew that waited below. He and the vile wraith within him both died screaming.

Chapter Seven

I returned to the Horta Magna via the Sky Gate, alarming the small number of guards led by Pellandriel, one of the few female Powers Anael had allowed in the Flight. Pell and I went back some way, and her long copper hair, bound in gold circlets, framed a perfect visage and cascaded down a toned, athletic body that I had once known in all its glory. Now it was bound in silver armour, and golden eyes regarded me with suspicion.

"The Sky Gate is out of bounds, Azsh. Of all people, you should know that" she said with an exaggerated sternness.

"Yes," I replied with an insouciant grin, "I can see you're overwhelmed with travellers."

Pell put a graceful, gloved hand on an even more gracefully curved hip and smiled thinly. "You know, I could have you detained for this transgression. Leave you rotting in a cloud cell until I finally remember to let someone know you're there."

"You mean you'd do anything to get me alone Pell? I'm flattered."

"Don't be," she said firmly, that graceful hand pointing to the exit. I took the hint and left before Pell's mood changed from playful to something a little less pleasant.

I had chosen the Sky Gate because it was the least populated entrance back to the Gardens. I was hoping that Pell might have had information on any news that might have been doing the rounds, but her brevity and brusqueness told me that I was still a persona non grata. That was confirmation that nothing substantial had changed which had to mean there was still time to upset the Cabal's plans.

I quickly descended the seven hundred and seventy-seven steps of the Sky Gate's watch tower, past the platform of the Golden Horn where Throne Angel Cacophon waited patiently to fulfil his duty of notifying the Upper and Lower cities (via fanfare) should the Sky Gate finally receive word from Excelsis or visitors from another Flight. It promised to be an event that would both literally and figuratively shake our world.

The streets of the White Citadel seemed quieter than usual, and I made my way as unobtrusively as possible to the cloistered buildings of the Halls of Records and the Scriptorium, where I hoped Sariel would be hard at work. Her cell was empty, however, her lectern tidy and her pens and inks safely stored away. I felt a familiar clench in the pit of my stomach that told me something was wrong, and I marched down the hallway, only to be intercepted by Narinel the Wise.

For as long as I could remember, Narinel had looked old. I was sure it was an affectation, but then you didn't get to be called 'wise' without good reason and constantly looking the part couldn't hurt.

"Can I help you, Ambassador?" he said in a deep and measured voice, the words long and drawn out.

"Actually, perhaps you can," I replied, and Narinel raised his eyebrows.

"Perhaps?" he said, as if the word itself was an insult.

"I was looking for Sariel. Do you know where she is?"

"That is interesting. I was just coming to find her myself. She has been absent from her duties now for two days. I was hoping that she had returned."

"Apparently not. I've just come from her cell and there's no sign of her - and her tools are stored away." Narinel paused for what seemed like an eternity. I could see he was considering whether to tell me something or not, and in these moments, there is nothing one can do except wait for him to decide. It's like watching paint dry.

"You know, she was a bit quiet after Darophon's men came to see her."

"When was that?"

"About three days ago," he said fixing me with a rheumy gaze.

"You're sure they were Darophon's?"

"Well, I didn't recognise them specifically, but they were wearing his colours."

"Do you know what they talked about? What they wanted?"

"I don't, I'm afraid. She said it was personal business."

I couldn't imagine what personal business Sariel would likely have with Darophon, and even if she did such an open approach was only proof of one thing—that they wanted her to be seen with those wearing Darophon's marque. If there was one thing the Heralds generally were good at, it was disguising their hand in any action and covering their tracks. This just felt seven shades of wrong, although it had been Darophon's men who had come after me on Saindrescan. Perhaps he was playing some kind of shadow game?

"Now I think of it," Narinel said suddenly, "they did make quite a fuss. It was like they wanted to be seen here. Not very Herald-like, is it?"

Like I said—slow, but wise.

I headed straight for Darophon's tower, but the landing was closed and shuttered. The same was true for many others of the Heralds and I could only assume that they were in session at Trinity Palace. I was about to leave when I saw a glint of light over to my right. It was Benazzar's tower and clearly he, or someone there, was signalling me.

Chapter Eight

It is said that some of us have voices in our heads that speak up and give a warning when heading into dangerous situations. Mine is annoyingly quiet and that's about the only defence I have for walking into the trap that had been set. Well, that and the fact I am attracted to shiny things and that I trusted Benazzarr implicitly.

He smiled at me as I came in to land, quickly beckoning me into the shadows of his bell tower where a savage blow from a heftily swung bell knocked me flat and barely conscious. I was aware of weapons and armour being taken, and my wings, hands, and feet being bound before my dazed and confused state passed. When I came to, I was lying on one side and looking up at Benazzarr and Kael, my former mentor and leader of what I now knew had to be the revitalised Halokim. Several of his masked companions lurked in the background and seeing them from this angle made me realise it had to have been one of this bunch who had been witness to my heart being taken. Joy.

"Well, well, Azshael," Benazzarr said, looking down at me with his kindly, innocent face, "this is a bit of a pickle isn't it?"

I was about to grunt something unpleasant, but Kael kicked me heavily in the guts and all the air flew out of me.

"Yes, yes. Quite a pickle. I suppose I should be impressed with you doing so well, but I suspect you know by now that is not at all why I picked you and recommended you to the Prince."

I was tempted to interrupt but Kael was still looming over

me, so I said nothing and Benazzarr the Watcher, my former friend, carried on.

"You see, Azsh, you were picked to fail. I rather expected you to flounder about and do nothing of import, but then I suppose that does fail to take into account your misplaced sense of honour."

"Why?" I asked, risking another of Kael's vicious blows.

"Oh, I think you already know that don't you? The Accord is nearing the end of its usefulness. The longer we wait, the more likely our enemy will have the resources to give us a damn close run and we don't want that, do we? No, far better that we get this thing resolved so that the Flight can move on."

"Resolved how? If we can win, why did we stop fighting?" I said, between carefully taken breaths.

"It's all in the scrolls, Azshael. It certainly took some finding but it's all there. I think we have Darophon to thank for finding it. Of course, he did his best to conceal it from us all, but he's not the only one with eyes in the Scriptorium."

I looked up at him, and clearly, he saw the lack of understanding in my eyes.

"It's not about winning, Azshael. It's about acceptable retreats. The Succae have clearly changed, so let them carry on their small lives on their dying planet. The Seventh Flight is more than one Angel."

"You're going to murder Anael?"

Benazzarr just smiled and said nothing. Kael pulled me upright and dragged me to the ledge of the Watchers tower.

"Sorry about this, Azshael. You can blame me if you like. It was a rare error of judgement to involve you, and for what it's worth, I'm truly sorry for both you and your friends. Sariel just couldn't resist telling Camael, and we really can't have any loose ends lying about now, can we?"

"This isn't over, Ben," I said coldly, as Kael pushed me over the edge with a cheerful smile.

"Oh, I rather think it is," he said dismissively as I began the long, fatal descent to the ground below.

Chapter Nine

I reckoned I had about seven minutes of deadfall before a sudden rendezvous with the ground would end my existence. In the first minute I tried to stay calm and test my bindings. Unfortunately, nothing had changed in terms of Halokim efficiency, and I discovered I was securely and tightly bound.

In the second minute, I fell past the grey walls of the Citadel's Upper Landing and on into white clouds. I tried shouting out in case anyone happened to be on the walkways but honestly, it was half-hearted, as even I didn't think that by the time an alarm had been raised, anyone could catch up with me.

In the third minute, I began to ponder the reality of my possible death. Since Ischae's murder and my own subsequent decline, I suppose I had kind of tip-toed around the edges to see how close I could get to actually stepping over that line. In that time, I thought I didn't want to go on - and yet here I still was. It wasn't exactly a ringing endorsement of existence, but it was its own truth to a greater extent.

In the fourth minute, I was lost in the clouds and shrouded in their ethereality. I pondered my purpose and whether this was how things were meant to end. I weighed up the value of my life and wondered whether I had achieved anything, any great plan that I could look back on now and be content with. My answer wasn't very satisfactory.

In the fifth minute, with the lands below beginning to come into sight, I raged against the world and my place in it. I screamed and howled in anger and pain that was both primal and primitive. I spat curses on everyone and everything in a stream of verbal name rage that eventually left me breathless and spent.

In the sixth minute, the Horta Magna and the Lower Landing grew in scope and detail, and when my breath returned, I marvelled at the beauty of it all. I felt brief euphoria until a strange peace settled in at around about thirty seconds from impact. I managed to turn so that my back was facing the fast-approaching ground and I was looking back up at the sky. I closed my eyes, whispered a prayer of thanks, and waited for whatever came next.

Chapter Ten

Ten seconds from impact. "Azsh! What are you doing?"

I opened an eye to see Pellandriel flying beside me. I think I must have smiled, as she smiled back. "Falling," I replied innocently, and I saw the flash of the copper sickle she had long ago adopted as a sidearm. Bonds loosened and melted away as Angelfire raced across the bindings and I felt my wings unfurl. Pellandriel swooped upwards and held out an elegant, gloved hand that I reached for in desperation.

Five seconds from impact in a deserted part of the Garden, our hands met, my grip tightened, and I dangled below her as she hauled me to a shuddering stop, just inches from the ground. I giggled maniacally, and she frowned at me and let me go. I was so surprised I hit the ground and fell over.

Pell came swiftly down to land beside me.

"What just happened?" she demanded, amber eyes sparking.

"I don't think there's time to explain," I said as I picked myself up. "I got thrown off a tower by an old enemy."

"You got thrown from Benazzarr the Watcher's tower."

"How did you know that? Were you following me?"

Pell's face flushed slightly. It was nice to see that even a Power could catch herself out.

"Yes, I was."

"Why?"

"I was asked to keep an eye on you if you came through the Gate."

"By whom?"

"Darophon. He didn't mention someone might try to kill you, though. If he had, I'd have stayed a bit closer. What is going on Azsh?"

Before I could answer, I heard distant peals coming from the bells of the Trinity. It meant that Prince Anael was abroad, no doubt heading to the Accord anniversary celebrations at Vigil Keep.

"Pell, there's no time to explain. Do me a favour and get word to Darophon to try and slow things down and tell him from me that his instinct is right."

Pell eyed me suspiciously, and it was obvious that I wasn't telling her the full story. If I told a Power that Anael's life was under threat she would have to take action, and that would scatter the Cabal. With everything I had been through, I was keen to catch as many of the conspirators as I could.

"Please, just trust me."

Pell fixed me with a stony glare and then relented.

"Very well Azshael. Where are you going?"

"I left something at the Inn. I'll join you at Vigil Keep as soon as I can."

Pell nodded and took flight as I headed to the Red Roof. I just hoped I could get there in time.

Chapter Eleven

It was quiet at the Inn, doors closed, and windows shuttered. The Feast's outside preparation tables were deserted, tools left out in the open. I landed as softly as I could and made for the east end of the building where Sylvenell had her private quarters.

I peered in through the slats to see her tightly bound and gagged in an armchair that was close to the front of the building, with a view over the Inn's courtyard. She was not alone, however. Kael had left one of his followers standing watch, weapons at the ready. I had enough respect for the Halokim's abilities that I knew she would be dead before I could make a difference, so I needed to look elsewhere for a way in.

At the other end of the building, the upstairs bedchambers were empty, and using Pell's sickle I went to work, first on unhooking the shutters and then on cutting away the lead in the frame of the casement window. With some difficulty, I managed to squeeze into the chamber and placed the thick pane of glass quietly on the bed. I heard a door closing nearby, and flying a couple of inches off the floor, I swiftly moved next to the doorway, weapon at the ready.

I heard the door next to mine being opened and closed again and braced myself. The door opened into the room, and the Halokim guard's eyes widened in shock as he saw me. I drove the point of the sickle up under his jaw and pushed with all my might so that the blade cut through tongue and on up into the brain. His curved sword fell from his hand, and I just managed to catch it on the broad of my foot before it would have clattered onto the wooden floor. It all happened so fast, I doubt he knew much about it.

I donned the screaming-faced mask he had been wearing and made my way to Sylvenell's chamber. The guard there spotted my deception too late, and the sword and sickle did their grim task quickly and efficiently. I freed Sylvenell, who smiled serenely and gave me a demure hug.

"Where's Cam?" I said as she stood up and smoothed her dress, moss green against her pale flesh.

"In the hall. They made him drink something and he passed out."

"Sariel?"

"Not here I'm afraid."

"How many?"

"Six. I heard them say they're waiting for their leader."

I got Sylvenell to describe where she had last seen everyone and where the Halokim had stationed themselves. I had taken care of two of them, and four remained. It was stiff odds and would need the element of surprise. Fortunately, the Red Roof Inn had attracted some useful occupants over time - none more so than its Landlady herself.

Chapter Twelve

When I approached the Inn from the front courtyard, the door was opened swiftly, and one of the masked Halokim waited in the shadows, his hand beckoning me in.

"I've come to negotiate," I said, showing empty hands.

"Oh really?" he said quietly, "Well, why don't you come in and we can talk?"

He sounded reasonable, even-toned, possibly friendly, but I had once worn that mask and I knew it was all a ruse to get me inside and under control. I went with it, even gave him a smile as I walked in and swiftly walked on into the Inn's main hall, my welcomer's protest lost on his lips. I had to be sure that nothing had changed from Sylvenell's description.

The Inn's population was gathered around the stage where Ysabeau sat and stared at me intently. Her hands strayed towards the strings of her harp as the Feasts snickered and whined a welcome, but the nearest guards gave Papa a push and levelled a spear at Ysabeau and she thought better of it, pale white hands returning to her lap. The worst sight was Camael, who sat stoically in a big armchair by the hearth with one of the Halokim standing behind him, a drawn blade nestling close to his throat.

"Not much of a party, is it?" I said, and the Halokim looked at each other as if I was mad. Well, at that moment it was perfectly possible I was. Taking out elite assassins by surprise was one thing. Facing them down when they had time to react was something else. I heard the guard who had been my doorman call to his companions upstairs, not knowing of course that, in this life at least, they would not be responding. There was a long silence and I looked first at Cam and then at Ysabeau. She met my glance, and I looked down, hoping that she would understand that I was looking for confirmation that her mother remained undiscovered. She smiled thinly, and I experienced the briefest moment of elation as I triggered our bid for release.

"Grow!" I shouted, just as I felt the Halokim behind me strike with his sword, which leapt into flames as he took flight and slashed in a body severing arc. I threw myself prone, hurling Pell's sickle at Cam's guard.

"Mother!" Ysabeau screamed as the Halokim near her lunged forward, aiming to impale her with his spear. The Hyena gods snarled into action, Papa throwing himself on to their guard as Mama bared her fangs and leaped forward.

I flew up as the flaming blade narrowly missed me, and green vines exploded through the cracks in the wooden floor. Colour was everywhere, and most of it was red. My copper sickle clattered off the wall as the Halokim cut deep into Cam's neck, blood spurting down his body in a sickening torrent. I looked into his eyes and was surprised. I didn't see fear, anger, or pain. Instead, I saw relief and happiness.

Nearby, the glittering green spider goddess had snared the spearman and disappeared back below the stage with him entangled in her deadly embrace. Mama Feast's mouth widened and slammed shut on the head of the Halokim who had thrown Papa Feast against the far wall of the Inn with a sickening crunch. He had fallen into the trap and missed the more dangerous foe. She swallowed his head whole.

Two down, two to go, and everywhere, vines were twisting and ensnaring, entwining the surviving Halokim in an ever-tightening embrace. Not that it stopped them from trying to kill us of course. The swordsman sliced through tendril after tendril, fire from the blade racing along the vines, blackening and curling them as it went. There was a distinct popping sound and an acrid smell in the air, and I knew Sylvenell would be in pain, all this growth a true extension of her own body. I looked over at Cam as the swordsman flew directly at me, sword pulled back and ready for the coup de grace strike. Cam seemed to be in a state of grace as the knifeman sawed through the corded muscle and flesh of his thick neck.

"Cam!" I shouted desperately, and his eyes turned my way and blinked.

The world slowed down. I watched Camael's Angelic form shift and slide, as though he was made of liquid. His would-be assassin stumbled back in shock as the edge of his blade lost its bite and purchase. Cam's form shimmered and shifted into something giant and spectral, great wings outlined against the dark wooden ceiling. For a moment, the world shrank inwards, time and space around the Halokim visibly warping. Then, in an accelerated pulse of light, it expanded and stretched outwards, bodies twisting, warping, and ultimately separating as they were devoured in motes of fire that sparkled briefly before fading away.

It was remarkably still and quiet in the aftermath except for Mama Feast, who cradled Papa and wept.

"Where's Sari?" I asked.

"They took her away," Ysabeau said quietly. "They said something about insurance, in case you prevailed here."

That sounded like Kael, always prepared for the next step. Yet, he had personally seen me go to my presumed demise from Benazzar's tower, so perhaps Sariel's life was already forfeit. No. The more I thought about it, the more I believed she was still alive. Kael was insane but his was an organised, cold, and calculated madness. He didn't willingly dispense with anything that could prove useful and I was sure Sari fell into that category.

"Syl is rooted," Cam said, his voice painfully loud in this confined space.

"Mama, take Papa down to the cellar," I said, as green shoots were already wrapping themselves around his broken body. He was still alive and if anyone could heal him, it was Syl.

"What now?" Cam asked, his form shrinking and becoming more solid.

"We need to get to Vigil Keep and prevent an assassination," I said, picking up the swordsman's golden blade from where it had fallen on the wooden floor.

"Who are they going to kill?" Ysabeau asked.

"Everyone I think."

Chapter Thirteen

Camael and I flew with grim purpose towards Vigil Keep. Below, the ornate parks and lawns of the Horta Magna gave way to a patchwork quilt of managed wilderness. Like much of life in the Flight, it was an illusion.

"I never knew you were capable of such destruction," I said to Camael, and he looked at me askance.

"What are you talking about? You have seen me in elemental form before."

"I wasn't talking about just now. I have been to the city of Saindrescan on Cerule and seen the horrors we unleashed for myself."

Cam went silent and shook his head.

"You don't understand, Azshael."

"Don't understand what? That they all died the same way Ischae did? That you knew that and never told me? All this time, I thought it was them, that the Succae murdered her, only to find out it was bloody well us all along."

"It wasn't like that, Azsh," Cam said, his voice deepening. Dark clouds gathered around us as if the process of recalling unwanted memories had an associated physical manifestation.

"First of all, I was a soldier then, same as I am now, and I followed the orders I was given. You may have left that all behind now, but even a Power does not question his Archangel's commands."

"Anael ordered the slaughter of a city? I find that hard to

believe. Or did the Heralds give the orders and you assumed they came from the Prince?"

"I believe it is called a chain of command, Azsh." I was about to protest, but Cam raised a huge hand and came to a halt, hovering in mid-air.

"It is true. I would have done what I was commanded, but that city chose to die before we could do anything."

"What do you mean?"

"The Heralds received a deputation from the city. Their leader was defiant and said we would take Saindrescan, but they would keep their souls and we would be haunted as a consequence. It was early in the war, and we had yet to truly understand their Necrenic powers. They returned, and the Flight elements that were there were arrayed for Judgement. The Voices spoke to the wind and sent messages to every mind in the city."

Cam stopped and his tone quietened.

"I remember the sound. It is something I will never forget. It was like steam through the mouth of a kettle pot, a slowly building scream that initially sounded like one very loud voice, until you listened more closely and realised it was hundreds, thousands of voices unified in anguish and pain. It can only have lasted a minute or so but that was the longest minute that I can recall. Then there was silence. Blessed silence."

I didn't know what to say so I said nothing, mainly as I now felt foolish for assuming the worst of my own kind.

"The Heralds said they poisoned themselves. It was a statement of resolve, proof that they would never surrender even one Succae soul for judgement." I thought back to what I had seen at Saindrescan and wondered whether any High-Nin had perished there that day. Could that be the real 'secret of Saindrescan' that Ischae had uncovered; a mass sacrifice of the Low-Nin? We flew on together in silence as I thought things through. Camael had a stoic nature, and whilst I hadn't exactly apologised in so many words, a nod and a conciliatory smile had put us back on track and defused the tension between us.

Ahead, the defensive spine of un-scalable peaks called Vigil's Teeth that cordoned the Horta Magna from the Tether came into sight. In the centre, nestled deep in the mountainside, stood the grey walls and towers of Vigil Keep, and we could see the Flight's banners and the flags of Karsz's House flying side by side.

"That's Pellandriel's signal," Cam said suddenly, and a few seconds later, I picked up on a red glint coming from the top of the eastern tower on our side of the Keep. I wasn't sure how Cam knew it was her, but sure enough, as we drew closer, I could see her floating in the air, wrapped in her white cloak, the Red spear she had named Revelation casually emitting small red sparks that glittered and faded away.

"About time," she said with her usual sardonic smile. "What happened? Did you decide to walk?"

Cam sighed, but I decided it was best not to get into a slanging match, especially with a Power. Those are arguments that just can't be won.

"Have they started?" I asked, keen to get back to the problem in hand.

"No. I managed to convince Darophon to delay things and buy you some time. He went over all the protocols with the Heralds again in fine detail to ensure they are all in place. I believe that work is due to end shortly."

"Any sign of Benazzarr?"

"No. He's not here. I'm sure of it."

"That's worrying. I would have expected him to be on hand. Varael?"

"Oh yes, he's here. He's in the Pavilion below."

Sure enough, I could see Vigil Keep's commander standing

on the newly built steps that went up into the tented Pavilion. It was a grand affair, white and gold trimmed on the keep side, and black and red dressed on the opposite representing Karsz's banners. His attention seemed understandably diverted, Heralds fretting and talking at him from all angles, galvanised no doubt by Darophon's unexpected intervention. I almost felt sorry for him. Almost.

"I can't see Sari," Cam said.

"I think Kael has her or maybe Benazzarr himself," I said, and Cam growled menacingly, massive hands tightening into balled fists. At the same time, I saw the Heralds around Varael disperse as he signalled the Tetherside gatehouse where Voices waited with long golden horns to sound the fanfare that would signal the arrival of Karsz and his delegation.

"We're running out of time," I said as Varael's command was actioned and the musicians blew their horns. "Cam. Check the Tetherside of the keep. We need to get Sariel to safety before we can take any further action." Cam nodded and strode away along the battlements as Pell frowned at me.

"You can't put a Cherub's life ahead of the Prince's," she said, and I could feel my face flush with anger. Was that what I was doing? Probably. The Archangel could look after himself, but that didn't excuse my lack of concern for him.

"You're right," I said, "but I need you to buy us as much time as you can."

"How am I going to do that?"

"You're a Power, Pell—use your imagination!"

She gave me a sour glare as I headed off in search of the one person I thought I could still count on in this place—my former Sergeant, Inias.

Chapter Fourteen

I descended the steps of the eastern tower and went out into the courtyard, where the great and the good of the Flight, dressed in ceremonial uniforms, were waiting to be shown into the Pavilion. I was likewise attired, in a white tunic and scarlet sash that marked me as a diplomat, and it made me invisible to the few guards that Varael had stationed on this side of the fortress.

I soon found Anfial, chief steward of Trinity Palace, in the Keep's Great Hall. The place was busier than I had ever seen it, but Anfial took everything in his stride and was as calm as I had ever known him.

"Looks like you've got your hands full," I said as he smiled at me.

"One feast for two distinct tastes, Ambassador," he said, "but you know all about that, don't you?"

I did. The Succae's feeding habits could be distressing to witness for those less exposed to their culture and I noted that Anfial had worked to bring in several living plants and fruit trees that could be consumed one way or another by anyone. It was a solid diplomatic solution, albeit a bland one by Succae tastes, but more importantly, it also ruled out the likelihood of the food being poisoned.

"Have you seen Inias?" I asked, and the steward looked at me with renewed interest.

"Is there a problem?"

"No, no," I said trying to sound casual. "I just have a

message for him from an old friend." Anfial eyed me cautiously but decided whatever intrigue I was about was my business alone.

"Last I saw him, he was manning the Tetherside gatehouse, but that was some time ago."

I thanked Anfial and took my leave, and once out of his sight, followed the trail of his staff down below the Hall and into the cellars, where various produce was being plated and carried up to the tables in the Pavilion. There were hundreds of wine casks, all the same shape and size as I had seen with Jasniz. For a moment, I considered trying to destroy them all, but I knew that Varael's men would stop me long before the task was complete and that being taken seriously afterwards would be an issue. Besides, what if the wine I was after was elsewhere? I had a feeling that wherever it was, Kael was too. Too much had been staked on this one moment for anything to be left to chance.

I headed back up into the courtyard and round the keep towards the Tetherside Gatehouse, trying to stay on the covered walkway. I tried to keep myself from looking over at Varael, but I couldn't resist, and typically, at that moment, our eyes met. Then something strange happened - I saw him signal to the Western Tetherside Tower. It was a brief, casual gesture, as hidden as Varael could manage, and no sooner made, he turned away. I paused for a moment and looked in the direction of the Tower, but I could see nothing strange or untoward, yet Varael had piqued my interest. Whether it was a concession between rivals or a gambit to lead me into a trap, I wasn't sure, but at least I was going in with my eyes open.

Vigil Keep was a place I knew like the back of my hand, and I was mentally picturing the layout of the Tower as I made my way up the stairs to the Western battlements that connected the Garden and Tetherside towers. As I emerged into the sallyport which stood exactly halfway between the two, I was surprised to see my former adjutant, Inias, standing over the body of a dead Angel.

"Something you want to tell me?" I asked, and he spun round, his face clearly anxious and vexed.

"He tried to kill me," he said. "Just like that, out of nowhere. All I asked him was what he was doing here, and he just drew on me."

I patted Inias on the shoulder and looked down at the fallen Halokim's mask and sword, both of which I quickly appropriated for myself. It was a definite improvement on having just Pell's sickle at my side.

"Don't worry, Inias. Trust me, you did the Flight a favour." Shame it wasn't Kael, I added in my head, but then it would have likely been Inias's body that I would have found. Besides, I owed Kael a special kind of payback, which was long overdue.

"Have you seen Sariel, Inias?"

I had to say it again before he responded, lost in his own thoughts.

"No, I haven't," he said, and I saw his eyes briefly meet mine before his gaze darted away. I remembered what Lytta had said about both the guardians of Vigil Keep being liars and realised the truth of what I had stumbled across.

"So, was he about to kill you or me?" I asked.

Inias looked at me, and I could see the guilt writ large on his face.

"Probably both of us, but me first," he said quietly.

"I suspect you outlived your usefulness, Inias. That's the problem with conspiracies; the more people you involve, the more loose ends there are to tie off. Did Varael recruit you?"

"Yes," he replied, and from what I could tell, he was telling the truth. That didn't square with what the Commander of the Keep had just done, unless of course he was diverting me into an ambush.

"Are they in the Western Tower?" I said, nodding Tetherside. Inias shrugged.

"I don't know, Azsh. That Tower has been shut down on Varael's orders for a couple of days, but there have been so many people from both sides of the Tether coming in and out, a small army could have sneaked in there and I'd be none the wiser."

It was true. The Tetherside towers had extensive vaults beneath them.

"What about him?" I said, pointing to body of the dead Halokim. "Where did he come from?"

"He was hiding up in the roof here," Inias said, pointing upwards. "I only just heard him in time."

I looked up - and Inias made his move to try and kill me.

It was a brief fight. Inias was no slouch as a fighter, but he was not special, and Kael only chose those few who could be defined as artists of violence to serve in his precious company. Thinking me distracted, Inias had drawn his dagger and planned to literally stab me in the back. Transfixed, I would have been vulnerable to his sword which would have dealt the killing blow. It was a soldier's attack, brutal, functional, and unarguably effective. Against an unprepared enemy that is.

In truth, nothing had looked right to me from the start, and I had kept an extra foot of distance away from Inias, leaning slightly towards him so that it gave the illusion of being closer. When he made his move, I moved straight into his body and smashed the golden mask into his face. He staggered backwards, and I moved with him, smashing him back into the wall. Under the force of the impact, the dagger fell from his grasp, and I caught and spun it in my hand so that the handle was in my grip. I drew the sword from my side as Inias shook off his initial daze. I looked at the Angel I had personally selected, trained, and mentored for years. He had served me faithfully and I would have counted him as a friend. There could only be the one reason for his betrayal, and it made me sick to the pit of my stomach.

"Advancement?" I asked as Inias drew his own blade.

"Can't be a guard forever, Azshael. You know that."

I did, and for Inias' sake, I made it quick.

I emerged out on to the battlements and looked around for Cam, but I couldn't see him. I did spot the Voices making their way to the Tetherside gatehouse, presumably ready to provide a fanfare for the official arrival of the Vod and his entourage. Whatever Pell had done to delay events, it looked like it had swiftly run its course. I wondered if Lytta was among that coterie and if so, would it be better to wait for her, but with Kael apparently tying up loose ends, I didn't like what any delay might mean for Sariel.

I approached the Western Tetherside tower cautiously, trying to stay within the darker cover of the crenellated walls. At the last minute, I shot swiftly upwards, hoping to surprise anyone hiding at the top of the tower, but it was thankfully empty.

I moved to the doorway and peered down the stairless shaft to the floor below, only to see darkness and no sign of life. So, it continued until I reached ground level, and the steps that led down into the vaults below. Outside, the Voices made the Vod's arrival known, and I knew I had to hurry.

I was surprised at the lack of sentries here as I took the twisting stairwell down into the lower vaults. Here, I quickly came upon chambers stacked with barrels that looked recently supplied, but it was impossible to tell their origin as they were marked only with the steward's sigils. I moved on, heading deeper into the castle's depths. Away from the noise of the surface, deep in the buttresses, it was eerily quiet, and I was aware of every scrape of boot on stone. I couldn't help but imagine Kael waiting in the darkness, my own weapon ready in his hands to deliver an ironic epitaph to my existence.

Yet it didn't happen, and finally, I rounded a corner to see pale yellow fingers of light seeping out of a closed door to what I knew to be the master chambers of the Reeve, Head Steward of the Keep. It was a position untaken in my time, Anfial having been capable enough to man both Anael's palace and cater to the smaller needs of Vigil Keep. I doubted anything had changed under Varael.

Options were limited, given the situation. I could either charge in and improvise or try for a more subtle approach and see if Kael was of a mind to negotiate—or at least talk. He had been surprisingly taciturn in front of Benazzarr, something it had taken me until now to realise. I donned the screaming mask of the dead Halokim, hoping it might give me some kind of an edge, approached the door and eased it open, stepping into the light.

Chapter Fifteen

The chamber was cast in gloom. The illusion that it had been well-lit was due to a storm lantern placed on the floor facing the door. I could feel Nimrod close by, its power calling to me. I picked up the lantern and cautiously headed down the short flight of stone steps that led into the main room, shining the light ahead of me. It revealed a barricade of barrels at the far end of the chamber, and at once, I saw Kael's purpose. Much like Jasniz had done, he would use the tainted wine as a weapon to deny the ground to any attacker.

I looked up and saw a vaulted arched ceiling with just enough room to manoeuvre in flight. It was a good plan, and I was sure Kael had practised combat in the tight spaces above. I took flight and headed straight upwards to see over the obstruction, and what I saw made my remaining heart skip a beat. There was Sariel, lying on a wooden table. She was dressed in the simple white muslin skirt and chemise of her order, blonde tresses splayed out beneath her head and her hands were closed in apparent devotion. Nimrod had been laid beneath her body, and whilst it stirred at my call, Sariel was clearly enough of a weight to keep it in place. For a moment, I lost all care for my own safety in this place and landed straight by her side.

"Sariel?" I whispered gently.

"She can't hear you, Azshael." It was Kael and I turned to see him standing almost directly behind me.

"What have you done Kael?" I said, feeling a mix of fear and anger flush within me.

"That? She's just drugged. Wouldn't stop whining. You know what Cherubs are like. Frankly, I don't understand the appeal, except for the obvious, but I didn't think you were that way inclined," he said with a thin-lipped smile.

"They are called friends, Kael, but then you wouldn't understand what that means, would you? The only person you care about is yourself."

Kael smiled in a manner that showed his teeth, and that whilst the halls were lit, no-one was necessarily in residence. I put my hand on Nimrod's haft and felt the cold edge of Kael's black sword—known simply as 'Thirst'—at my throat.

"Let's not do anything hasty," Kael said evenly, and I carefully turned to face him.

"Last time we met, you tried to kill me, Kael. Why don't you just get on with it, or are you hedging your bets? What did Benazzarr promise you? A restoration of the Halokim?"

Kael shrugged but said nothing.

"You really think that's likely to happen? Anael banned the Halokim years ago. You and your followers are criminals, charged and convicted in absentia. It is just his judgement that awaits you."

Kael nodded. "All true, Azshael. At least, under Prince Anael."

It made sense. Kael's only real hope for redemption lay in a new regime for the Flight, but I guessed Benazzarr would quickly dispense with him once things had changed. No-one trusts a madman with their secrets, and it now looked as if Benazzarr had more than a few skeletons in his closet. I thought for a moment, and realised that even in his insanity, Kael was thinking the same thing.

"What's the plan, Kael? You kidnap a Cherub, try and kill an Ambassador and you think everyone's going to forgive you?

You're involved in a plot to kill an Archangel! The best thing you can do is surrender to me now. Show mercy, and I promise I will speak on your behalf. It's Benazzarr who is the architect of this plan isn't it? You're just a soldier following orders."

I could see Kael thinking, but the sword's edge hadn't moved, and I wondered whether anything I was saying was getting through.

"You're a survivor, Azshael," he said suddenly. "I'll give you that. It was what made me think you would make a good member of my Order. Yet you talk far too much. You're not dead because it doesn't suit my purpose to kill you. Yet."

So that was it. He was merely playing for time, the usual cautious assassin, waiting to see which way the game was going before playing his hand. To be fair, when he had pushed me off Benazzar's tower, he probably hadn't expected to see me again. I was a wild card, and for once I was not alone. I decided to push him.

"Don't you get it, Kael? No-one is coming. Inias murdered your man in the hope of promotion, and I took care of *him*, so who does that leave?" I saw a slight tremor in Kael's face. I guessed the news about Inias came as a surprise.

"Do you think Benazzarr himself is going to come for you? He's a Watcher, and they don't worry about underlings."

"I am not an underling!" Kael shouted, and I felt his blade begin to bite into my flesh. Yes, I pushed him. It wasn't a good idea.

Chapter Sixteen

Kael's blade sliced through my flesh. It was so sharp, I barely felt it until the familiar warmth of pain began to register. My blood cascaded from the gaping wound, and I could see dozens of tiny spectral mouths open across the surface of Kael's sword. They yawned wide in anticipation of the red rain coming to quench their terrible thirst.

I stumbled backwards, crashing into the table with such force that it went over, sending both myself and Sariel's unconscious body to sprawl in an ungainly heap. Kael followed swiftly in a leaping attack, and I just managed to avoid being impaled as the deadly tip of his sword sparked as it impacted with cold stone.

I flew upwards, calling Nimrod as I went, but my weapon was stubbornly lodged beneath Sariel's body. Kael followed, and we bounced around the architraves of the vault in a deadly game of cat and mouse where he was decidedly the analogous feline. Time was on Kael's side, and he switched from propelled thrusts to a series of wide, scything attacks that were less deadly but harder to dodge, and my wings were soon bloody from small but deep cuts that bled profusely. I knew this couldn't go on forever and that it was time for drastic action.

Gritting my teeth, I launched myself directly at him just as he came at me, and we collided in mid-air with a bone shuddering thump. Kael tried to adjust his blade at the last moment so that it would run me through, but his timing was just off. Instead, Thirst was knocked from his hand, tumbling to clatter on the floor below. As we plummeted to the ground in a winded spiral, Kael had the presence of mind to draw a jagged-edged dagger from his boot, and proceeded to stab me with it several times. By the time we crashed into the stacked barrels, I was bleeding profusely, my right wing severely damaged and unusable from where I had tried to cover up.

Barrels cascaded away under the impact of our fall, and several splintered open, covering the flagstones in a slick wash of rich claret. I instinctively rolled towards Sariel whilst Kael went the other way, flying into the recesses of the vault. I knew I was badly hurt and could feel the processes in my body working their magic. It was slow, though, powered by only the one heart, and I had the sinking feeling that it wouldn't be quick enough to stop Kael.

I scrabbled forward on my hands and knees, reaching for where Nimrod still lay, trapped under Sariel's unconscious body. I turned her over and had one hand on Nimrod when Kael smashed into me from behind. I fell forward, my head cracking against the cold floor and I slid forward in a dazed heap.

It was probably seconds, but it felt like an eternity before I could properly focus again, and when I did, Kael stood over me, Thirst in his hand. He reached for a pouch at his belt and produced the Halokim's calling card—the black feather. He smiled triumphantly.

"You know, Azshael, part of me was disappointed when you left the Order. Yet now, seeing you like this, I realise I made a mistake in ever letting you join in the first place. You are weak! Weak-willed, weak in mind, and weak in body."

Kael had always been my better with a weapon in hand, and I was a fool for thinking I could stand toe to toe with him. I did look him in the eye as he droned on about my failings, my litany of misdeeds, and my descent to the broken Angel that now lay sprawled below him. As it was, I was proved almost instantly right when I stopped Kael in his tracks and said:

"You talk too much."

Chapter Seventeen

Now, I am not a quitter, yet at that moment, lying in a pool of my own blood with every part of my body screaming in pain, I knew I was beaten. Like much of the Flight's rank and file, it is rare for any of us to ask for help from a higher power. This is because we know we have already been gifted abilities that let us burn so bright that the risk of our candles occasionally burning out unexpectedly is quietly accepted as part and parcel of service in the engine of Judgement.

Yet there are times when I have found myself praying for the miraculous, however unlikely the chance of a response. This was one of those moments. I'd like to think it was more on Sariel's behalf than my own, but the reality was mostly an instinct for self-preservation and the chance to see the look of murderous triumph wiped off Kael's face. It was not the first time I had been in such a dire circumstance, but this time someone heard me, and a miracle occurred. My prayer was answered.

The Golden Horn has an unmistakable sound, and when you hear it, it vibrates through every inch of your being. It is the breath of Excelsis itself, the perfect note that delivers an ecstatic reverie it is impossible to ignore.

Kael was poised over me, Thirst ready to be plunged into my throat and drink deep, but the siren call of the Horn had him as gripped, as it had me. We stared at each other, lost in the moment, and then the wakened Sariel plunged Nimrod through Kael's left heart from behind. The spearhead emerged from his chest with the glistening organ impaled on the blade. I remember being briefly disappointed that it wasn't black.

Kael gasped, and his face contorted in agonised disbelief, falling to his knees as his body briefly shut down. Sariel quickly withdrew Nimrod, gobbets of flesh and gouts of blood coming with it. She lined up a follow-up thrust for Kael's second heart when I heard myself shouting, "No!"

I don't know why I stopped Sariel delivering the killing blow to someone who would certainly not have shown me the same mercy. Maybe I was weary of seeing dead Angels, or perhaps seeing my own agonies reflected in Kael's face was too much to bear. Either way, I knew I really didn't want the responsibility for Kael's death to be on either our hands or our consciences.

Sariel looked at me as if I was crazy but seemed happy enough to hand Nimrod back to me. The weapon gave me strength, and in short order, with Sariel's help, I was standing again. Kael continued to convulse on the floor, and I decided to leave him to it.

Chapter Eighteen

By the time we emerged from the tower's vaults, the Keep was in turmoil. I could already see the roseate trail of Anael and his closest allies in the sky as they headed back to the Citadel. I looked around and saw Camael hurtling towards me.

"Azsh! You look like Hell! What happened to you?"

"It was Kael," Sari said, saving me the breath. She glowered at Cam with a kind of 'where were you?' expression on her face but if Cam noticed, it washed off him like so much summer rain.

"Where's Karsz?" I said, and Cam pointed towards the confused-looking Succae dignitaries accompanying the Vod.

"They're not happy," Cam said, and I could see confusion beginning to turn into anger as rumour of Anael's sudden departure became obvious fact. The situation was complicated by the disappearance of most of the Heralds and the wary way that Varael and his guardsmen were lining up around the Vod and his entourage.

I spotted Vachs, one of the Succae court and a Lord of Protocol. He was an apparently elderly man, his lean and gangly frame disfigured by a curved spine that, given his height, always made him look as if he was leaning towards you in inquiry. Dressed in a purple *khot,* a martial robe, and the standard Succae garb when out of armour, he was presently prodding a bony finger with a long-lacquered nail at Varael. It all had the potential to go dramatically south very quickly, so I moved forward, shouldering my way past a couple of guards to stand in front of

Vachs.

"Ambassador?" he said, clearly surprised to see me.

"Yes," I replied somewhat unnecessarily, although to be fair to myself, I hadn't thought much beyond physically intervening at that moment in time.

"What are you doing here?" Vachs said.

"He brings news," Varael said in such a calm and assured tone that I was almost sure he was right.

"He does?" Vachs said, looking as confused as I felt. I fumbled for words, caught in indecision as my brain held a hasty debate as to whether truth or lies would be the best pathway to resolution. Whilst that vexatious argument was taking place, events on the ground overtook me as I saw Karsz being handed a long-stemmed glass of red wine.

To this day, no-one is sure how I got past the Vod's entourage and knocked the vessel from his hand, but I did. I can still see it sailing gracelessly to the ground, surrounding Succae and Angelic eyes wide in surprise as it thudded into the turf, spilling its crimson contents over green grass. I had certainly diverted attention and created my very own, much worse situation by personally assaulting the Vod. The moment of shocked silence that followed seemed to last an eternity. Then all hell broke loose.

My eyes met Karsz's, and a silent understanding seemed to pass between us as the Vod's entourage belatedly intervened and we were propelled away from each other. I could hear Varael barking orders and felt Angels around me trying to both push me forward and pull me back. One of the Vod's honour guards had also grabbed me, and I was at the centre of a bodily tug of war. I initially offered no resistance and became a marionette doll as a result, flopping about this way and that in the press of the melee, depending on who had control of my 'strings'.

This went on for several seconds until I saw the flash of a

blade near Karsz. I managed to shout a warning, and the Vod's honed martial senses must have done the rest. He turned and caught the assailant's wrist, the sharp tip of the short blade just an inch or so away from his neck. It was one of his own Black Guards, and he snarled in anger as he crushed the man's hand and turned the blade back in on the attacker and buried it in his chest. He finished the move by kicking the man in the midriff to send him reeling to the ground, and the Vod's other Guardsmen disarmed the man and pinned him with the butts of their spears.

The assailant's wound was far from fatal for a Succae, but within seconds, the soldier began to convulse and scream in agony as the poison that had tainted the blade went to work within his body. Soon, the vampiric blood that had sustained and animated him poured from his eyes, ears, nose, and presumably every other exit from his body and oozed down his face to pool darkly beneath his twitching form. Unsurprisingly, all the Succae looked on in horror and took an instinctive step away from the lifeless corpse and the ever-expanding pool of blood.

"What the…" Varael gasped as he understood the enormity of what he had witnessed. An assassination attempt on the highest-ranking member of a race under the Archangel's protection doesn't look good on your record.

I looked at Karsz and could see that despite the cool warrior demeanour, his eyes were wide and clearly shocked. That made me feel all the better, knowing that he almost certainly wasn't in on the Cabal's plans. Given what I had seen under the sea near Saindrescan, I had been concerned that the Vod had been secretly preparing for a new offensive, but I now suspected that this news would also come as a surprise.

The six Lords of Protocol, aged though they were, surrounded Karsz and created a defensive circle and wanted to hurry him away. However, the Vod was clearly in no mood to leave so soon, and he fixed me with a questioning stare as I warned Varael and his men to stay away from the exsanguinated blood.

"Ambassador?" he intoned, his voice rumbling like far away thunder.

"Yes, Vod of the Succae. It is time for answers," I replied, as Cam suddenly muscled in, shoving Varael unceremoniously out of the way to tower behind me protectively.

Chapter Nineteen

It took a while for the marquee to be cleared but when we did sit down, the Vod and his Lords sat on one side of the now incongruously decorated table and Cam, Sariel, Varael, and myself sat opposite. We also kept a space for Darophon in the hope he might return once the answer as to why the Horn had been sounded had been resolved. Anael would no doubt sit on the carved white chair on the plinth above us, but we all agreed the Arch's return was unlikely.

The Black Guardsmen stood behind their Lords, and Varael's Angels of the Keep stood behind us. Ironically, it felt very much like the day of the original Accord itself when mistrust was rife and writ large on the scowls of all the senior attendees.

When we got to talking, my first concern was Lytta's whereabouts, but she had apparently not joined the Vod's entourage and none of the Succae here knew where she was. I had to assume she had got caught up with Dursc, and I could tell I was testing Karsz's patience by dwelling on the matter, although I instinctively knew something had gone wrong.

So, I started telling pretty much everything I knew and what Lytta and I had uncovered. I talked about the Cabal that had found unlikely allies on both sides of the Tether and how and why Naschinne, Saaya the Siren and probably Ischae herself had died. I talked of Hostmann, of how he was probably recruited by Benazzarr and then silenced when he had learnt of his blend's true purpose. I named Jasniz and his pagan followers as the key operators within the Succae, their abduction and torture of Yggael and Kael and his Halokim as Benazzar's doers of dirty deeds. I left out much of Dursc's involvement, as I knew it would probably vex Karsz, and didn't mention events at Saindrescan, partly because it wasn't immediately relevant but also for fear of what Karsz might decide to do with that knowledge. I had to admit that even though I thought of the Vod as a friend, he was still the leader of a declared enemy nation with whom a tenuous peace had been established, and that deep down, he frightened me.

Karsz listened quietly as I let my story spill out as efficiently and cogently as possible, ignoring his excited Lords, whom he silenced with the occasional raising of his left hand. When I had finished, silence filled the hall and it felt like the space around Karsz grew darker, shadows bending and folding in on the Succae's leader. I could feel Sariel shift uncomfortably on her seat, but like me, she was diplomatically savvy enough to know when to keep quiet. Cam, on the other hand, does not like empty spaces and was indeed born for the purpose of filling them.

"So, what will you do now?" Cam said, surprising the Vod. His Lords stood up and waved angry fists at Cam for speaking out of turn, but he just kept asking the same question again and again as Varael buried his head in his hands, and I tried to get him to sit down and shut up.

Karsz stood up and signalled those around him to calm themselves. He rested his fists lightly on the table in front of him and leaned forward.

"You say Jasniz is dead at your hands, and this Angel, Kael, is defeated?"

I nodded and looked at Cam for reassurance. His eyes darted in my direction, and I saw in his face that Kael had somehow managed to evade him.

"Yes, to the first, but no to the second. Sariel and I managed to hurt him, but he escaped before we could capture him. Not without trying as you can see," I said, my bloodstained and tattered jerkin testament to a battle.

"So, there is no-one I can question myself? I must take your word for all this?"

"Your Serrate can support much of what I have said, but as I believe Benazzarr was the leader of the cabal on our side, we can't prove anything until he is apprehended." I felt Varael flinch slightly at the mention of the Watcher and knew he had been another of Benazzarr's dupes.

Karsz interrupted me, "A Herald of the Flight."

"Yes, he is. However, I do not think Jasniz would have worked for him. I think there is still a leader on your side to be unmasked."

"Jasniz was a Low-Nin," Vachs said dismissively. "They work for anyone willing to pay them. Even if he were still extant, his testimony would be worth little. I think the Ambassador deludes himself, albeit for understandable reasons, and that the architect of this assassination is really an Angel, and an Angel alone."

"If that is so," I said, anger no doubt burning in my eyes, "then why did one of the Vod's own honour guard just try to kill him? Karsz, they were planning to replace you. That's the reason Dursc was also attacked, so that whoever came next would have a clear path."

"Why?" Vachs said angrily. "Why would they wish Karsz to be deposed?"

At that moment, white light filled the marquee, leaving only the Vod in darkness. Archangel Anael surprised us all.

"I think the answer to that is obvious, and the same reason my Watcher Benazzarr the Elder did what he did," he said. We all stood as he took his seat.

"And what's that?" Karsz said.

"We are both wartime leaders of warrior nations that chose peace. I suggest you look around you now, Vod Karsz. Who is not here who should be? Perhaps the same one who has quietly advised a different course of action to the one you have taken?"

It did not take long for Karsz to reach the same conclusion as I had done.

"Sarzh," he said, in a tone that was edged with thunder.

Sarzh's guilt suddenly seemed obvious once someone else, and importantly, someone Succae, had voiced it. The scale of the plot and the profile of the participants spoke volumes and possibly I felt a little foolish for not having seen it earlier.

The truth was that Sarzh had always seemed a mere bumptious factotum rather than anyone dangerous, and his talent for covert warfare now seemed to follow an alarmingly familiar line more in keeping with the Heralds than with the more straightforward Succae. I guessed he couldn't be certain of the outcome, but he had tried to stack the deck so positively in his favour, with a plan that would have removed both the present and surviving Vods. With them out of the way plus the activation of an army of newly animate Ashai and Angels, it would have been a very brave Succae Lord who would have stood against him.

After some minutes spent in consultation with the Vod, Vachs turned to Anael and bowed.

"The Vod thanks you all on behalf of the Succae peoples. We must now return to our lands and make enquiries on this new enlightenment."

Anael smiled briefly and nodded his ascent, adding diplomatically, "Yes, Lord Vachs. We, too, have some enlightenments of our own to come to terms with. Perhaps we can try meeting again at an agreed time and place, so that the business we came here to conduct can be brought to a suitable conclusion?"

Vachs nodded smartly but said nothing. Karsz was clearly already gathered and eager to leave.

"I would like to come with you," I said suddenly, and the Vod turned and looked at me.

"I cannot guarantee the Ambassador's safety," he said to no-one in particular, and I could see the anger in his clenched fists and hunched body language. Anael looked at me, perfect white eyebrows raised in enquiry.

"That is acceptable to me," I said in return. Much as I wanted to track Benazzarr down, I was worried about Lytta, and knew I couldn't rest until I was sure she was safe. I could see the Lords of Protocol didn't like the idea at all, but Karsz just shrugged and turned swiftly on his heel, ending any further debate.

Much as I would have liked to have left with Karsz and his entourage straight away, Cam and Sariel convinced me otherwise.

"You need armour," Sariel said, looking at the tattered remains of my dress uniform. "Indeed," Cam rumbled. "You have no idea of what you're walking into down there. The Succae could be on the brink of civil war." It was a fair point, and before long, Varael had me supplied with full battle armour from the Keep's armoury. It was not as elegant or tailored as my own, but it still felt good to be back in harness. Varael said nothing by way of apology, and I still had questions about his level of complicity, but I was certain that Benazzarr had used his prejudice as a tool of manipulation whilst Inias was his real inside man.

In the time it took to armour myself, I discovered that it was Pell I had to thank for saving both myself and Sariel from Kael's murderous intentions. Her response to my request for her to 'improvise' had left her in some degree of hot water, but I was confident that as a Power, she could weather the storm. When

I returned, I would be sure to see Anael and take my share of the responsibility. I had a feeling, though, that Pell's days as the Keeper of Sky Gate were over.

Nimrod in hand and suitably armoured, I was ready to head back down the Tether. I knew I owed Lytta my life and that a strange wyrd now bonded us. We had started this together and I was resolved we'd finish it together or die trying.

Chapter Twenty

Lord Vachs was waiting for me with a retinue of black armoured Ashai. Like me, he had taken the opportunity to don armour, but whereas mine was purely functional, his had a sophistication and intricacy that spoke of rank and superiority.

It began with the *Jhat*, a thick layer of martial undercoat made of brushed purple velvet studded with pearls. Dark swirling script had been sewn into the design, a visible reminder of Vachs's deeds and service to the Succae. Above the *Jhat*, the *Chet*, splints of solid dull metal that were either fixed or bound in place to protect the lower part of the limbs. His upper body was encased in a *Kiras,* a tightly bound cuirass, and underneath his arm, he carried an open-faced helm known as a *Shel.* Both had been beautifully crafted with scalloped grooves, silver fixings, and decorative engravings.

"Come," he said, donning the helm. "We must move quickly." The Ashai led the way at a trot, down winding black steps and on into a labyrinth of bleak, stone-walled tunnels that closed in like the confines of a tomb. My natural luminescence cast the Succae's advancing shadows on the walls ahead as we went, jagged angular shapes with sharp, pointed edges.

Before long, we emerged back on to the surface, and in the centre of Scarpe, there was a discernible tension in the air. I could see hundreds, maybe thousands of Low-Nin gathered in the marketplace by the Citadel. It was like an army of grey ghosts, standing silent and sullen in the pale light.

"What's all that about?" I asked Vachs, who hurried me along to the steps of the fortress where ranks of Ashai stood watching the gathered masses. Vachs responded with a shake of his head and the muttered word *"Jerzay"*, which loosely translated as "hopefuls".

"They think the Vod is soon to change, and they want the chance to prove themselves worthy of blood ink to his successor." It sounded like Cam had been right about the chance of civil war, no doubt stirred up by Jasniz and his collaborators. I paused on the steps and looked behind me, only to see a number of the watchers point at me, and a murmur spread through the crowd. I couldn't tell whether their reaction to me was negative or positive before Vachs chivvied me on up the steps and through the great vaulted doors of the Citadel's entry gates.

Inside, the halls were strangely quiet—or at least it felt that way to me. Previously, my visits to the Succae seat of power had been strictly monitored and managed. No hallway or chamber had ever been empty, staterooms bustled with functionaries. Now, fewer Ashai stood on guard and the place was silent, seemingly stalled of purpose.

On my previous visits, it had usually been a top-down affair, arriving on the wing to land on the upper battlements, and descending into the grand halls at the heart of the structure. Yet this time, whilst the direction of travel was still downwards, the starting point was the ground floor. Vachs was allowing me a peek behind the curtain and into the Citadel's dark under vaults, a place I had only heard of and never seen.

Vachs and the Ashai guards walked ahead of me, their vampire sight perfect in the pitch black. I maintained my pace behind them, my luminescence revealing each vault we passed through in tantalising snatches of revealed treasures. The vaults of the Citadel were the repository of Succae history and the plunder of the many worlds they had invaded. Here were the relics and artefacts Karsz had deemed worth saving when the retreat from Cerule to her moon had been decided. Art, sculpture, and historical documents, as well as inventions, antique garments, and much more were all literally hidden in the darkness here, awaiting their restoration and metaphorical day in the sun.

We walked a long crescent before arriving at a triangular-shaped arch guarded by the Vod's own Loyals in their distinctive red-stained armour. They parted ways for Vachs, but quickly closed rank to bar the way to the other Ashai and myself. "Wait here," Vachs said. He strode off into the gloom as the two groups of warriors glared at each other through the wide eye slits of their war masks. Vachs reappeared after a short while and beckoned us on. His Ashai escort seemed to gain a certain swagger as they brushed past the Loyals, but if they thought they had won some symbolic victory, it was soon to prove perhaps pyrrhic at best.

Chapter Twenty-One

Ischae once told me there had been just forty-six Vods before Karsz in over seven thousand years of recorded Succae history. I guessed that accounted for the same number of steps in the stairway I descended into Karsz's inner sanctum.

Green light cut through the gloom, and there was a pervasive scent of burnt incense that hung heavy in the air. Despite its width, the chamber felt claustrophobic and oppressive, and I sensed it was more ovoid than square.

Vachs hurried to join the three other Lords of Protocol positioned around Karsz whilst his personal guards joined those of the other Lords to form a precise outer circle. The Vod was seated in a basalt chair that was intricately decorated with bas reliefs of martial scenes. Directly in front of him, a copper bowl sat atop a pedestal of blackened stone. Here, a flame burned brightly, illuminating Karsz in a pool of emerald green light. I knew this for what it was, and it made me hold my breath; it was pure Necrenic power, the vampiric life spark of the Succae.

Shrouded Sirens appeared from the gloom, voices ululating and wailing in unison. Each one bore a piece of armour, and Karsz stood, as in turn, they dressed him for battle. The Vod's armour was stained dark green and patterned with etchings of flowing dragons that looked both voracious and deadly. The last piece was a dragon maw helm with a black and white braided mane. Three more Sirens approached, their faces painted red, and laid the Vod's weapons in front of him; a long-hafted great axe, a pair of long swords and a bow made of white bone. Karsz sheathed the blades at his side and hefted the axe, spinning it in his hands before leaning it against the seat and turning his attention back to the green flame.

The Sirens fell silent. Karsz plunged his hands into the conflagration, and it flared in intensity and size. Motes of sparkling emerald light floated upward like sparks from a fire. Soon, the flame in Karsz's hands had been totally transformed into a glittering swarm that radiated malevolence. It moved without warning, suddenly and silently, to engulf the Ashai.

The first few crumpled instantly. A handful tried to run whilst the rest kneeled before their Lords. Each mote of Necrene energy drew a freed vampire spirit back to Karsz, and the Vod grasped hold of their spectral forms, appearing to bind them into his weapons and armour. I could hear a guttural chant begin around me that soon became louder and louder. It was a phrase that Ischae had often spoken, and a well-known Succae saying that I could see now was meant literally:

The Vod is One
The Vod is All
The Vod is Us
We are the Vod

Karsz retook his seat, and the remaining motes of light fell back into the bowl and reformed as a glittering flame. The chants died down, and I saw the Sirens retreat into the deeper dark and disappear, followed by Vachs and the other Lords to leave Karsz and me alone.

I cannot say exactly what happened next. All I do know is that the room seemed to spin on its axis and I stumbled slightly forward. In the immediate moments before that event, Karsz had spent some time just staring at me through the flame.

Perhaps he managed to exert a form of mind control over me. I don't like to think that is true, but I must accept it as a possibility. Whatever, the world spun, I stumbled, and suddenly we were elsewhere.

It was another cavern, although this one was colder, darker, and bleaker than that from whence we had come. A swirling opaque grey mist obscured everything below knee height, and I felt the chill of icy water encase my lower legs and feet. There was a discernible taste in the air that was recognisable—the taste of Necrene energy. It had been present in the caverns near Tzir's hold, where Lytta and I had dealt with the Necrenic beast, and I suspected that this was a distant but connected part of a greater vast network where the essence of the Necrene well flowed freely.

Karsz waded forward swiftly and silently, and I followed in his wake. Shadows cast by the little ambient light that came from the crystalline walls shrouded him and seemingly repelled any brightness. He did not speak or turn to look back at me at all.

Soon, the passage turned downwards and narrowed, water churning and rushing faster as a result. The Vod strode down an ever-steepening incline without breaking stride. I chose to fly and follow, as I was pretty certain Karsz wouldn't thank me if I fell and gave away any surprise we might otherwise have had over Sarzh and whatever other Citadel forces he had taken with him. As things turned out, though, I was worrying unnecessarily. They knew we were coming.

We emerged into a vast cavern where great crystalline stalactites hung like blue icicles from the roof whilst sharp-fanged red-veined stalagmites grew up from the cave floor. It was like entering the maw of some monster whose symmetry was beyond ready understanding.

Ashai awaited us, clad in the shiny black carapace armour of the Citadel. They bristled with weaponry but none of it was pointed at the Vod. I looked around but could not see Sarzh or Lytta. I could, however, feel the Necrene well. Its power pulled and tugged at my spirit like the winds of a tempest, and I steadied myself for a moment before feeling confident enough to walk on into the storm.

Karsz approached the first line of the Ashai, and they did not move an inch. He kept walking, and not one soldier moved until he was within a breath of their position. Then, with the martial crash of salute which suddenly filled the cavern with noise, they separated, creating a narrow passageway. I followed in the Vod's wake, doing my best to maintain a calm and fearless demeanour. As we passed by, so the Ashai closed ranks and retook their guard, only this time, the line faced towards where we were headed, and I had the sense of a trap about to be sprung. The only question was to whom it belonged.

Chapter Twenty-Two

The Well Chamber was circular with a gradual slope that led down to the well-head itself. Sigils and other sacred markings were scored into the stone and a great brass cover-plate, secured by hefty chains, covered it. Lytta's body was slumped at its edge in a kneeling position. Her head drooped, chin resting on her chest. I wanted to reach for her, but the draining effect of being this close to the well was debilitating, and I briefly lent against Nimrod for support as the room spun around me, the masked faces of the watching Ashai, a solemn blur.

As my equilibrium returned, I saw Sarzh standing behind the well. He was stripped to the waist, revealing the extensive tattoos that told his life story. They snaked across his chest and arms like the shadowy tentacles of some vast monster. I had always thought of the Succae Marshal as a factotum, a politician who had worked hard to achieve his rank but was in all ways lesser than Karsz and so not much of a threat. However, here and now, I saw him anew with more cynical eyes and realised how those that shrouded their ambition the most effectively were often the most dangerous. I had no doubt now that Sarzh fell into this category, and he smirked at me knowingly before turning and kneeling before Karsz.

"Great Vod," he intoned in a certain, steady voice that seemed to reverberate around the chamber.

"Stand up Sarzh," Karsz replied in a tone that could not be mistaken for anything other than what it was—angry. The

Marshal rose slowly, and the two men made eye contact.

"Explain yourself, and do so quickly," Karsz said slowly, ensuring every word was clear and understood.

Sarzh looked momentarily confused, and I hoped the Vod could see through a man so clearly about to lie as I could.

"I have done something to displease you?"

"Treachery has that effect, yes."

"Treachery," Sarzh said, rolling the word around his mouth so that each syllable sounded like a single word. "How have I betrayed you, my Vod?"

"Do not play games with me, Sarzh," Karsz yelled, inches away from his face, his aura darkening in the process. Sarzh did not move a single muscle.

"With the greatest respect, great Vod," Sarzh said quietly, but loud enough so that his gathered guards could hear him, "I do not understand what I am accused of doing that would make me guilty of treachery." It was a careful choice of words, and with his back to Karsz, he smiled at me as he said it.

"Then let me make it clear," Karsz said through clenched teeth. "You have conspired with a cabal of others, both Angel and Succae, to break a treaty which I formally agreed, without my agreement or knowledge. You have sought to undermine my authority and develop plans to succeed me. You have inspired insurrection and rebellion among the Citadel Ashai to the point that one felt empowered to attempt my assassination! Do you dare deny it, Sarzh?"

There was a murmur among the gathered Ashai as clearly, some of this was news to them too. Sarzh would be on thin ice if all that Karsz had accused him of was, indeed, true. However, the Marshal of the Black Citadel had not got to his level of power without being a master of statecraft, and I had an uneasy feeling as he seemed vastly untroubled by the Vod's accusations.

"I see," he said, bringing his hands together as if in prayer.

"Yes, that would be treachery indeed. If it were true. I wonder, though, who has told you such a tale and what evidence they have provided of the truth? I presume there are witnesses. Articles of evidence perhaps?"

Karsz remained silent, which I took to be a very bad sign indeed. It was true that I had brought little in the way of physical evidence and surviving witnesses would be hard to produce. Lytta and Dursc would be my only allies in all this, and Sarzh had seemingly taken care of one whilst she had hidden the other.

The Marshal turned to look at me. "This Angel is my accuser, I presume?"

I stood firm. "I know what I have seen and heard, Sarzh. It is only a matter of time until Benazzarr is captured on our side of the Tether, and as he was the architect of rebellion among our kind, so it will be revealed to all that you were his Succae counterpart."

"I see," Sarzh said. "So, you seek to blame an insurrection among the Angels on us? Expert deflection, Ambassador."

"It is not I who has built an army in the sea of Saindrescan. Or sought to poison both Succae and Angel alike with the drug Rain."

Sarzh grimaced theatrically. "No? Well, it was not me either."

"Then who?" Karsz growled quietly.

"Dursc, of course," Sarzh said with an exaggerated sad sigh. "I have been waiting for the chance to tell you that Dursc sought to rebel against your wise rule but was suppressed. I suppose the loss of the trappings of power ultimately proved too much for him to bear."

"That's a lie!" I shouted, but I could feel the walls of Sarzh's trap closing in. Karsz looked at me sharply.

"I have to say I was surprised to hear reports from my commanders that an Angel was fighting alongside the usurper. I presume that was you, Ambassador?"

I stared back at Sarzh silently, white knuckles gripping Nimrod's haft.

"No denial, Angel? No problem, I can provide several of my trusted Ashai who can identify you from the battlefield."

"Where is Dursc now?" Karsz said.

"Hidden by the Serrate who, by the way, also supported Dursc. I had just received her confession when you arrived."

"You silenced her you mean," I said angrily. "Murdered her before she could tell the Vod the truth about you."

"And what so-called truth would that be?"

"Karsz, Sarzh brought the Serrate into play as he knew she would eventually lead him to Dursc. He planned to not only depose you but to take care of the only surviving Succae that others might rally to." I hoped I was getting through to Karsz, but he remained implacable, enigmatic and impossible to read.

"Ha! A superb fantasy, Ambassador. It is a given that you Angels lie extremely well. However, as all here know, Dursc's time is done and past. No Vod has ever returned to power because the decision to pass the mantle on to another proves weakness, and only the strong can rule the Succae." Sarzh smirked at me in a condescending manner.

"Return the Serrate," Karsz said, suddenly breaking a silence in which, I could feel fire running through my veins. Sarzh acknowledged the Vod's command before turning to Lytta. He chanted arcane words in guttural tones, and the temperature in the chamber grew notably warmer. He pulled back the cover plate on the well-head, and the room darkened as the light warped back towards the well. I could feel that pull on my lifeforce again, but this time it was a literal tug that needed to be physically resisted. I boosted my radiance and saw dark vampire spirits wrap around me, bodies entwined in black, shadowy tendrils that recoiled as the light around me grew brighter and more intense. There was an explosion of colour as the Serrate's spirit, in its full majestic glory, became manifest before pouncing on Lytta's inanimate flesh and repossessing her body. She lurched forward, her eyes and mouth wide open. I moved towards her, but Sarzh placed himself between us and I heard a hostile murmur of approval ripple through the watching Ashai.

Karsz strode forward and pushed his Marshal out of the way. Sarzh took it all in his stride, and even managed a smile for his Ashai. The Vod bade Lytta to stand, which she did slowly.

"Serrate," he said quietly, "I ask you to answer me in the matter of accusations of treason that the Marshal levels against you and this Angel here."

Lytta looked odd to me. She would not look at me straight or look directly at Karsz either. I knew then that Sarzh had anticipated this moment and had done something to secure her silence. I couldn't imagine her willingly co-operating, so for a moment, I was lost and confused. Then I looked at her again and saw not the Serrate but rather, her host. I remembered what Lytta had said about the debt that the spirit owes to her sacred vessel: "First honour the flesh, then let your honourable soul be your guide." Lytta had withdrawn inside her host to protect her, and now I understood that fact, I knew I would have to intervene before Karsz lost his patience. I remembered what Dursc had possibly presciently reminded me of – that all Succae can be challenged.

"Enough!" I said, my voice echoing round the chamber. "If it's a fight you want, Sarzh, then it's a fight you'll get. I challenge you to prove my words are truthful and right."

I could see the Vod turn and look at me, his face as solemn as a grey sky.

"Are you certain, Ambassador? A Succae duel is a sacred rite and once you step into the square to fight, not even your Prince and all his brothers will be able to save you." I appreciate he wasn't just speaking to me, but I had to suppress a hysterical laugh. An Archangel would intervene to save someone like me? Yeah, right.

Sarzh accepted the challenge with an odd look on his face. I think he was trying to work out why I would take this potentially fatal gamble. I must admit that at that moment, I didn't really know myself. I was following the advice of some inner voice that had a great deal more confidence in me than I did. The subconscious fanatic can be one hell of an idiot sometimes.

Ashai stepped back, and around us, a duelling square was drawn with Karsz overseeing the proceedings. I had saved the Vod from the bother of having to make a difficult, divisive, and potentially fatal ruling, although his enigmatic demeanour showed little in the way of appreciation. Sarzh stalked around the perimeter of the square, beating his breast, and roaring at his supportive Ashai, who were keen to cheer on their champion.

It was a suitably partisan crowd, and with the Vod's aloofness and Lytta's deeply concerned scowl, I knew there was no help to call on. This was it. I was on my own.

Chapter Twenty-Three

Osi.

Sarzh marched to the centre of the square and sat down cross legged. He said nothing. Just fixed me with an impassive stare which was no doubt meant to be intimidating. The smoke from the incense which burned at each corner of the square drifted lazily between us, and it had an unwelcome effect on me.

Up to that moment, I had been too angry to think about what I was doing or the potential danger involved. I'm no pushover, but in the time *Osi* allowed me to think, I began to wonder what Sarzh had gone through to become the Marshal of the Succae, and whether I was really in his league or not. Doubt is a harsh mistress, and she populates her fields of mental uncertainty in a hurry. As I watched that incense trail drift past me, I began to think it might be a visual warning of an impending fate, the final link in a chain of consequences that led to a disastrous end.

Yes, I did doubt myself, and I also knew fear at that moment. I felt momentarily weak, sick to the core of my being, and part of me wanted to throw Nimrod down and walk away.

Then something happened. I saw Lytta stand, and her frown became a thin smile of the kind Ischae would give me when I was trying to make her laugh at some crass joke or poorly thought-through observation. At the same time, a masked Siren appeared beside Karsz and sat at his side. That's when the fire reignited the anger that had got me this far in the first place. I felt righteous anger for the innocent victims in all this—Saaya, Naschinne and Ischae. They deserved satisfaction, and it seemed at that moment, I was their instrument of vengeance.

Gata.

I stepped forward into the battle square and spun Nimrod around me. It was unnecessary, but it made me feel a little better. Sarzh rose slowly to his feet, and in the centre of the square, he knelt and drew a line in the sand. I walked right up to it and stood there. Sarzh stood up and looked me straight in the eye. Up close and personal, I realised how big a man he really was. I was taller, but he was twice my width at the very least. Veins stood out across his neck and chest as his blood mastery enhanced muscle. Soon he was bulging, his body hard and toned. I stood passively, waiting for the real fight to begin, my face an enigmatic mask—or at least that's what I hoped I was doing. We stood face to face like that, silent and unmoving for some time. I wasn't sure whether I had gained or lost anything by speaking or offering him a way out. I decided it didn't matter, as I was not part of their society or their honour system.

Sarzh whispered to me, breaking the spell, and ending *Gata*. He said, "One heart left, Angel, and I know which one." I wasted a valuable second understanding the full implications of what he had said. It cost me, as at that moment the fight had begun, and I had given Sarzh the initiative.

Tambo.

For a large man, Sarzh moved surprisingly quickly, and I was swiftly grappled, pinned in the grip of his massive muscular arms. The momentum of his attack sent us both crashing to the ground with me below him. Dust exploded around me on impact, and I felt Nimrod crushing into me as Sarzh tightened his grip. I felt excruciating pain as my wings fractured, and then a terrible crack as their mainframe structure also broke under the pressure. I screamed, and Sarzh laughed and released me. He pulled me to my feet, headbutted me in the face and threw me away to land in a broken and bloody heap.

I could taste blood, and my left eye had closed, but otherwise I was curiously conscious and aware of my situation. My sluggish constitution was taking action, and whilst I could feel broken wings beginning to heal, I knew Sarzh had acted quickly to even the field. Taking flight and wearing him down bit by bit, which had been my hastily conceived plan, was now off the table. I would need to think up a Plan B and do so quickly.

Sarzh charged again and I rolled out of his path, narrowly avoiding a hefty kick. I scrabbled to my feet and called Nimrod to me, but my opponent intercepted the weapon in mid-flight and proceeded to use the haft as a rod to beat me with. Multiple blows hammered into my midriff, pushing metal armour into flesh. I could feel muscles caving and ribs breaking. Things began to blur in a haze of pain, and I could feel my body beginning to submit to the beckoning darkness. Sarzh set about my lower legs so that I fell to my knees before him. He stood back for a moment and admired his handiwork. Then he walked forward and spun Nimrod so that the tip of the spear scraped against the metal of my breastplate.

I wish I could say that, in the face of my final demise, I had an epiphany or revealed insight into my place in history. Mostly, I felt nothing except a deep sadness and self-pity. I tried to feel the fire that had once come so easily from within, but there was nothing there. Maybe that's why they called it Rain—it effectively extinguished our flame. I looked up at Sarzh as he raised Nimrod, my own treacherous weapon, and plunged it straight through my heart. Or rather, the space where a heart had once been.

I doubt Sarzh knew much about what happened to him in the last few seconds of his existence, but it went something like this. He let go of Nimrod as it passed through the cavity where my first heart had once beaten in perfect syncopation with the one that remained. He turned his back on me and looked at his adoring Ashai, who were premature in their cheers and congratulations. I rose to my feet and, in one swift and admittedly painful moment, converted Nimrod into a slim sword and pulled it free. In a second fluid movement, my weapon transformed again into a sharp-edged sword as it struck the treacherous Marshal's head from his shoulders. It rolled along the floor, still grinning, as scarlet blood gushed from the body that stood still and upright for a moment before collapsing forward.

I felt the rush of Sarzh's vampire spirit move past me, a black-winged spectre with multiple heads and talons. It fled swiftly for the well, only for the cover to be moved back into place before its arrival by the Vod himself. I saw the Serrate's spirit rise before it, and within seconds it was devoured, gone in a swirl of light.

Epilogue

By the time I returned to the Horta Magna, Benazzarr was dead. Word had it he had been slain by Anael in the main hall of Trinity Palace. That seemed more than a little convenient from my perspective. I had no real reason to suspect my Archangel, but I couldn't help but remember Saaya's warning that this went to the highest levels on both sides of the Tether. I was certain of Karsz's surprise at the turn of events being genuine, but could I really say the same of Anael? The lack of opportunity to ask questions of the main architect of the plot left a sour taste in my mouth.

There were life-changing consequences for us all that meant things could never be quite the same again. The Red Roof and its occupants seemed sad and quiet. Sylvenell had rooted in the Inn's foundations and was now a permanent fixture and fitting. I would sometimes find Cam alone in the leaf-strewn basement, staring at her simulacra in the tree's bark, golden eyes brimming with tears. At least they had all survived Kael's assassins, but for Cam, that was cold comfort; he knew that when the Flight finally departed, there was a good chance his former love would die. It put a strain on our relationship and would take valuable time to heal.

Pellandriel came off worst in the inevitable enquiry that followed. As I had expected, she was stripped of her position as Guardian of the Dawn Gate and was widely condemned by the Heralds for not having followed their protocols. Sariel and I appealed to Prince Anael directly on her behalf; she was later pardoned, but she would forever be regarded as a Power who had failed.

The enquiry and subsequent report was a classic piece of Herald manoeuvring which bore little relevance to actual events. I could have got upset about it all, but I knew there was no point. The sad truth was that no-one in power wanted to confront the stalemate that we were caught in.

Benazzarr, the dead watcher, became the scapegoat—a madman whose wild schemes had been easily seen and stopped well ahead of any real danger to the peace. No mention was made of the Succae conspirators. Varael kept his captaincy of Vigil Keep. The Vod and Prince eventually renewed the Accord, and the truce continued.

I knew my presence would be unwelcome in the enquiry. Darophon was at least honest enough to say as much when we met. He took written statements from me and said that they would eventually be filed in Narinel's archives. To this day, I have never found them.

As for Lytta, she and I would soon be reunited on an altogether different mission, but that, as they say, is another story. Oh, and I eventually confessed to Sariel about how her Sunpup ended up on the wrong end of the Tether, and I was immediately forgiven—by Sariel anyway. The Sunpup and I are wisely avoiding each other.

THE END

Printed in Great Britain
by Amazon